CRIMEUCOPIA

The Not So Frail
Detective Agency

A Murderous Ink Press Anthology

****

Murderous Ink Press

CRIMEUCOPIA

The Not So Frail Detective Agency

First published by Murderous Ink Press
Crowland
LINCOLNSHIRE
England
www.murderousinkpress.co.uk

Acknowledgements

To those writers and artists who helped make this anthology what it is, I can only say a heartfelt Thank You!

And to Den, as always.

Contents

The puzzling murder of a beloved teacher leaves Detroit Homicide Detective, Sam Roma, searching for answers. To her chagrin, not only does she have a murder to solve, she's also been assigned a new Homicide Investigator, Tom Green—who comes with his own set of problems and challenges.

As Tom makes a series of rookie mistakes, Sam wonders if she's up to mentoring a partner with personal struggles—especially one she suspects is involved in departmental politics.

To top it off, Sam's personal guilt over her own history intersects with the conflicts faced by the middle school students close to the murder. She needs to navigate complicated relationships and memories which have haunted her for years, all the time keeping family secrets safe.

As Sam delves into the case, she uncovers a web of deceit and lies surrounding the school staff, students, and a former gang leader, revealing a complex game of luck, betrayal, jealousy, and unexpected twists.

But is she strong enough to see it through to the bitter end?

With a strong female detective, A Game of Luck is the mystery/suspense novel you've been searching for and will enjoy reading.

Available from all good outlets April 2026
Pre-Order available from February 2026

Compact, Lipstick, Snub-Nosed .38...
(An Editorial of Sorts)

Historically, it would be tricky to define exactly when the concept of the Female Private Investigator first appeared in fiction. But *The Female Detective** and *Revelations of a Lady Detective*** —both published in 1864, independent of each other—proves that it was a genre whose time had come. And while *Miss Gladden* may be the first by all of 5 months, it is *Mrs. Paschal* who is more the not-so-frail ground breaker —and it should be noted that Conan Doyle was only 5 when these ladies hit the streets.

So what better way to present the modern female investigator than by gathering 15 top class authors and let them tell you all about their creations?

Candace Cane—from new Crimeucopian, *Debra H. Goldstein*—opens with *Candy Cane on the Case*—followed by *John B. Elliott*'s Paula, in *Beggar*, who adds an additional character twist as well.

Another new Crimeucopian is *Steve Liskow*, who gives us Tatiana 'Tats' Kova and a case that turns out to be anything but a *Slam Dunk*.

Meanwhile, back at the *High School Reunion, Sandra J. Cady* makes her Crimeucopia debut by introducing us to Bonnie Rutkowski, before the fourth—*Debra Bliss Saenger*—gives us Reddy, and the thriller-chiller, *The Case of the Fractured Mirror*.

From there, a trio of familiar names— *Kathleen Marple Kalb, Wil A. Emerson,* and *Karen Odden*—give us Diana Czednik, Laura Holms, and Kit Jimeson, in *Danno and the Shadyside Butcher, Right as Rain,* and *A Story of Unusual Interest*, respectively.

Then we have new Crimeucopian, *John W. Salvage*, who presents Jessica Dupris, in the nice little three-hander he calls, *Lies of Omission,* followed by *Michael J. Ciaraldi* who brings Summer Cum Laude to us once more in the form of *Hunted.*

Another returnee is *Shannon Lawrence* who, along with Mariska, explains in no uncertain terms why it's *None of Your Farbin' Business,* before our sixth new name, *Elle Higgins,* lets Emma Grant recount why she has the *Backyard Blues.*

After their outing in our *What The Butler Didn't See, Bonnar Spring* allows both Mamie and Alice to explain away the damage in *Shattered Melody.* Then, a change of perspective as *N.M. Cedeño* gives us Maya Laster—of Laster Genetic Genealogy and Investigations—who recounts all about the *Disappearance of an Easy Lover.*

And to close out this gathering of The Not So Frail Detective Agency anthology party, *Adam Meyer* takes us—and Rosie Perkins—back to April 1932, and Albany, NY, and the details of *The Roosevelt Affair.*

And so, as we turn out the light and lock the office door behind us, we hope you'll find something that you immediately like, as well as something that takes you from your regular comfort zone—and slips you, gently or otherwise, into a completely new one.

Because, in the investigative spirit of our *Murderous Ink Press* motto:
You never know what you like
until you turn over the page and read it.

*(J. Redding Ware, writing as Andrew Forrester)
** (William Stephens Hayward)

Candy Cane on the Case
Debra H. Goldstein

Candace Cane — Private Investigator, looks good on the door to my office and my business card, but when the Lowell Chief of Police or my on-or-more-often-off boyfriend, Detective Todd Burns, calls me "Candy," I cringe. I've asked Dad why, considering he used to be a cop and surely would have made fun of someone by using the nickname, Candy Cane, he stuck me with the moniker. His response is to bluster something about Candace being a perfectly lovely name to go with Cane unlike those Hogg sisters whose parents tagged them with Ima and Ura.

Let's face it, I'm never going to win this one with Dad. Nor will he ever bless the fact that after a year at the academy, unlike fair haired Todd, I dropped out and did what it takes to become a licensed P.I. To him, private investigators are a hindrance to the police force. That's why, when he retired, he refused to follow that path like so many of his fellow early retirees. But just maybe, he's beginning to see the light.

Last week, he sent one of his former partners, Eddie Norville, to my office. Eddie had to leave the force because of a gambling problem, which he apparently still has. "I got fleeced," he said.

"How?"

"Ever since I got a settlement from when that drunk plowed into my car, I've played a lot of poker at the Palm Lounge over in Huntington. That's a few towns west of here."

"I'm familiar with it. That place has a legal license for that type of gambling," I observed.

"Right. I play there because it's always been a clean operation. Win some, lose some." Eddie chuckled. "Okay, the house wins more, but at least I have runs where I do come out ahead. Enough runs that a year or so ago I moved into the back high rollers room."

"From what I understand," I interjected, "that back room is completely legal."

"Until recently, I'd have agreed with you. There are two tables in the room. I played at Table One with guys like me for about nine months. Three months ago, I ended up seated at Table Two with a few hotshots like that former quarterback Robbie Worth. Things were the same as at the other table except that Robbie did seem to bet high and win a lot of hands. We all kidded him about wanting to rub his thick hair for luck, but being afraid the only thing that would happen was that we'd get the black shoe dye he used on it on our hands. Anyway, about six days ago, he took me for six figures."

"That can happen when you gamble with the same people over long periods of time. They hit a streak of luck while you don't."

"No, this was more than that. I'm telling you that he somehow cheated. Based upon the exposed cards, he and everyone else should have folded at the level we were at."

"The others folded."

"Yeah, but he stayed in and raised me again. When he put down his cards, he had the only hand that could have beaten mine. I swore he cheated and well, I made a scene. The result was that Trent Mitchell, whose run the place since his uncle retired, came over and asked me to leave. He kept my IOU, but banned me from playing for six months at the Palm Lounge."

As Eddie leaned over my desk, I instinctively sat further back in my chair. "What is it you want me to do?"

"Prove that I'm not crazy. That the room is rigged. I talked to Detective Burns at the station. He basically dismissed me as being a broken-down old grunt."

"He acted like you were a snorting pig?"

Eddie threw his hands up in the air. "Gather you were never in the military. It's a low infantry position. I served honorably and I want justice now. When I told all this to your father, he suggested that I contact you. Said you were creative, but safe, with your investigations. Will you help me prove that there's more to the game than is meeting the eye? I'll pay you."

It wasn't like I had a lot of other investigations going on. Especially ones that were offering me a paycheck. I accepted.

Eddie pulled a roll of bills from his pocket and peeled off five one-hundred-dollar bills. "Enough for a retainer?"

I swallowed hard and said, "Yes."

He threw them on my desk and stood. As he started out of my office, I found my voice, "Wait. Let me give you a receipt."

"Not necessary. If you're your father's daughter, like he says you are, you're as honest as they come. Just get to the bottom of this for me."

I mumbled something like, "Yes, sir." After Eddie left, I called Dad.

When Dad answered, I didn't mince words. "What's going on? You actually sent Eddie Norville and his problem to me?"

"Yes," Dad said. "Eddie may be a gambler, but he's nobody's fool. If he thinks something crooked is going on, I'm inclined to believe his gut feeling. Your Detective Burns didn't take him seriously, but I do. That's why I thought you might have the ability to help me run a little con."

"A con? You, Dad?"

"Look, even when I was on the force, I knew Trent Mitchell and his uncle sometimes cut corners, but we never could prove the Palm Lounge was anything but an up and up operation. For me or any of my other cop buddies to go in and play a few rounds wouldn't accomplish anything. Plus, not being sanctioned with department funds, we wouldn't have the time or money to earn our way into the high rollers room."

"And you think I can?"

"You and a friend of mine."

"Sounds like you've already worked this out in your head."

"Not entirely. I need to introduce you to my friend, Cassie Smith, and let the two of you take it from there."

"Her name sounds familiar, but I can't place her."

"She's a P.I. like you. Does acting and other odd jobs since she got fired from the agency she was working with, but Cassie is a good egg."

"If she's such a good egg, why did she get fired?"

"She was hired to find out 'Who Shot J.R.?' Through some clever and hard gum-shoe work, she succeeded, but then, because of circumstances she felt were right, she refused to turn over the information to her boss. He and his agency lost a big fee, and she lost her job. I've already talked to her and she's willing to come on board as an independent contractor to your agency, Candace."

Me, myself, and I, I thought. Some agency. I fingered the five hundred dollars Eddie had left on my desk, maybe Candace and Cassie would have a nice ring to it. I listened to the rest of my father's idea, hung up, and called Cassie. She answered on the first ring.

"This is Candace Cane," I said.

"Oh, yes. I've been waiting for your call. Walt said he was sure you'd call."

Walt? Dad had said Cassie and he were friends, but other than my late mother, I didn't know anyone who didn't call him Walter.

"Well, here I am. Did he fill you in on the details of his plan?"

"Yes. He thought, based upon my age and grey hair, I would take on the role of being your mother, and we should present ourselves to Trent Mitchell or whoever his hiring person is as a mother and daughter cleaning team. Your Dad didn't think anyone would believe we were dealers, but we could easily slip into the background if we were hired as cleaners. Nobody pays attention to servers or cleaners. I'm game to work for you, including doing the paperwork and most of the cleaning, if you're willing."

"Why not? Let's meet for coffee and work out the details. Rock Around the Clock Café at two?"

"See you there. You'll recognize me by the bird pin in my hair."

Great I thought when I hung up. Dad has either paired me with a new girlfriend he's never mentioned or with a bird brain. When I met

Cassie at the café, I realized she was neither of these two things. Rather, while she might have a touch of ADHD, she was a bright woman willing to get her hands dirty while seeking justice.

Cassie told me how, in one case, where the firm she worked for represented the husband in a custody dispute, she discovered, by posing as a survey taker, that the mom was keeping the child out of school and planning a move to a different state. In that instance, to seem believable, she spent most of a day going from the furthest point in a trailer park to her goal trailer, knocking on doors while carrying a clipboard and asking questions. It had worked. By the time she reached the trailer in question, the information she gained from the child who answered the door, was sufficient for the father to win custody and the firm she worked for to get a big fee.

Maybe, by combining our talents, not to mention our cleaning skills, we could achieve the same success. I hoped we were as successful as another cleaner I'd read about. She and her husband had been the loyal house people for a multi-millionaire who was getting on in age. The woman was used to being ignored when she did her tasks throughout the house. One day, from the next room, she overheard her employer complain to his finance man that he'd been surprised that neither she nor her husband had thanked him for the sizable gift he'd recently told the finance person to bestow upon them for their years of service. Knowing she hadn't seen this money, she discussed the situation with her husband.

After much thought, they approached the millionaire, explained what she'd overheard, and swore they had never received such a gift. The millionaire made some calls about other things he'd asked the finance person to do and when the answers he received were all unsatisfactory, he contacted his lawyer. The lawyer, not a lover of the finance person, brought the matter to the local police. An investigation, based upon what the woman overheard, resulted in it being discovered that the finance man had swindled the millionaire out of most of his fortune.

For Cassie and me, the first step of dressing for the part was a cinch. We both had things in our wardrobes that worked. The second step, getting hired, proved easier than we anticipated. When we presented ourselves at the Palm Lounge, ostensibly to offer our services as cleaners, we discovered that the personnel manager was desperate as the regular cleaning crew had had a family emergency that necessitated them being gone for a week or two. We were hired on the spot. Before we left the manager's office, we were told where to obtain uniforms and to report back to work at four p.m.

Cassie and I did as we were ordered. For that night and the next one, we made ourselves useful cleaning ashtrays, wiping up drink rings, and of course keeping the floor and anything else that needed cleaning in the facility spotless. On the third night, as I was addressing the mess made by a spilled drink in the main room, Mr. Mitchell, himself, waved me over to him. I responded like a summoned cab, quickly and directly.

"We're running two tables tonight in the next room. The folks in there are high rollers. The room must always appear perfect. You also need to understand that some of the players may get confused and ask you to get them a drink from the bar in that room."

"No problem. I clean, serve drinks, and do windows as necessary. So does my mom."

Mr. Mitchell laughed. "I like your attitude." He handed me a ten-dollar bill. "For giving me a good chuckle."

For the next three nights, Cassie and I blended in and out of the big roller room. Robbie Worth was at Table Two, with his back to the bar and mirrored wall, each night. In the beginning of the night, he played alone, but most nights, a little after ten, some patsy would be ushered into the high roller room. The patsy would fawn over Robbie and be thrilled when he invited the guy to take the table's empty seat across from him. Cassie and I kept an eye on everything and compared notes each night, or should I say morning, when we went back to my office to debrief each other.

"It's the same M.O.," Cassie said. "Most of the players at Table Two win or lose in the normal course of action of a poker game. The patsy seat works differently."

"Right," I said. "The patsy wins three or four of the first hands and for the next hour or so, he's in the mix like the other men at the table. During that time, Robbie wins a couple and from what I can see, throws in some other hands that he could probably have won."

"No question about that. I saw him fold with a straight in his hand."

"That's about the time things get more interesting. The patsy starts being on a winning streak and Robbie begins raising the bidding stakes. When they hit a crescendo hand about midnight, Robbie or the house wipes out the patsy. I looked, but I couldn't see any sleight of hand tricks with the cards or indication of microphones or cameras."

"But I have noticed one possible tell," Cassie said. "Robbie puts his glasses on and off all night. About eleven-forty-five, when the lights are dimmed, he clutches and rubs his eyes with his fingers, then puts on his glasses. He never takes them off again."

"Were you able to see a microphone in the glasses?"

"No. But they were lying on the table earlier tonight when I bent to give the man on his right his drink, so I glanced through them." Cassie mimicked how she had bent over. "They seem like magnifiers, but I had the feeling they had night vision capabilities. What if the decks are marked and he's reading the backs somehow with his glasses? It might seem wild but with today's advances in AI and other things, maybe he's getting some blue tooth messages through the glasses or something being flashed on the wall behind the patsy that only he can see."

"Sounds plausible," I agreed. "Here's what I think we should do to try out our theory tonight. I'm going to ask a friend to be in the Palm Lounge in case we need some backup. Somehow, I have a feeling our days as cleaners will be coming to an end soon. I don't think the family emergency for the regular cleaning crew will be extending too much more as the money keeping them away is running out."

When we got to work a few hours later, we made sure Mr. Mitchell saw us cleaning both rooms. About eleven-thirty, we assumed our positions in the second room. Right after Robbie put on his glasses for what we thought would be the final time, I stood in front of the wall on which we thought messages might be being flashed. I acted as if I was cleaning a large concave mirror that I held up. Cassie positioned herself nearer the table cleaning ashtrays and refreshing drinks as the big hand was dealt.

Robbie looked up and suddenly said, "What are you doing?"

When no one answered, he pointed at me. "You. What are you doing?"

"Cleaning this mirror."

"Well, put it down. It's reflecting in my eyes."

"Yes, sir." I kept the mirror where it was.

In the meantime, Cassie, with a loud exclamation of "I'm so sorry," poured a drink on the patsy's chair, making sure some caught his sleeve. Grabbing napkins, she dabbed at his arm, then yanked him from his chair. She grabbed the chair and started pulling it away from the table.

The surprised patsy went along with her while Robbie started yelling something at them.

"Relax sir," Cassie said. "I'm just getting him settled in a dry chair." She positioned the chair back at the table, but slightly off from where the first one had been.

"You're crowding the man next to him," Robbie said. "Move his chair over to where it should be."

With an apology to the man he was crowding, the patsy repositioned his chair while Cassie, talking over Robbie, said, "I'm so sorry. I'll be back in a moment with a fresh drink for you." Rather than going to the bar in the high rollers room, she opened the door and obtained a drink for him from the bar in the other room. Bringing it to him, she left the door cracked.

As the game resumed, Robbie glared at me again. I lowered my mirror and moved nearer to Cassie to watch the big play. The cards were dealt. The patsy's bet was called and raised by Robbie. Second cards were drawn by those who wanted them. Another round of betting ensued resulting in only the patsy and Robbie being left. As they lay down their cards and Robbie pulled his winnings toward him, Todd entered the room. Several men in blue followed swiftly. The lounge was being raided.

"What, the…

Todd flashed a piece of paper at Robbie. "We have a search warrant. I'll take those glasses, sir."

I'm not sure what happened next because Cassie and I slipped out of the room. We made our way to the ladies' restroom, shed our uniforms, and, wearing the shorts and t-shirt we had under our uniforms, helped each other through the ladies' room window. We jumped into the car we'd parked nearby. While others were being detained in the two gambling rooms, we drove away.

It took two days before the local paper announced the arrests of Trent Mitchell, Robbie Worth, and others for running an illicit gambling operation at the Palm Lounge. I may not have understood all the technical aspects of why the mirror deflected the light's reflection like Cassie did from a stint when she'd taught science, but I'd comprehended enough to do what I needed to do—including bringing Todd in for the kill.

As for our fee, we'll probably never see it. Eddie is going to be a witness against the men who were arrested, but it's doubtful he'll ever recover the amount he was fleeced. Cassie and I talked about the situation with Dad. Afterwards, even though I was angry at putting the work in without a paycheck, Cassie was the one who made me see that maybe I've earned something of greater value than the lost money—an element of respect from my father. I'm thinking that in the future, Cassie and I might be a good team. We might even call ourselves Candace, alright, Candy and Cassie.

Beggar
John B. Elliott

"What are you, deaf?" McGreggor shouted gleefully as if he was making a joke which everyone would appreciate and smile at or even laugh.

"As a matter of fact, I am," Paula answered.

McGreggor's face filled with doubt. "Bullshit! Now you're pulling a joke on me!"

"I doubt it. Do you need me to?" Paula walked away.

When at dinner that night Paula told Gabriella about McGreggor making a joke of her deafness, Gabriella said: "I'd have kicked him in the Never-Neverland."

"Well, you're a quick thinker. I'm merely a pleb."

Gabriella straightened, arched her eyebrows in her best teacher-disapproves face and replied: "You're not a pleb and you're certainly not common. Can you name any other deaf private eye who successfully runs her business?"

"Not in Santa Barbara, at least."

"Not anywhere."

"Largely with your help."

Gabriella scoffed. "I think you would have succeeded by yourself. You're young, smart, attractive—"

"And totally deaf."

"And totally great at reading lips. Speaking of lips, if you dislike my rigatoni alla Norma, we can skip to desert."

"Oh, no. That's all right. It's passable."

"Passable!"

"I'm joking, Gabriella."

"Like your friend McGreggor?"

"Yes, I suppose so—never make fun of the cook. And the stupid oaf who insulted me is not my friend. He's on temporary assignment from Los Angeles. At least I think he is. He's working with Detective Donelan, who, by the way, corrected him about my hearing."

"Good of him, though J. Jim is slightly prejudiced in your favor. I assume he still loves you."

"Yes, but he loves his wife more." Paula looked out toward the Pacific and the Channel Islands. "Santa Rosa is obscured by fog tonight, and I feel the same way about McGreggor. There's something about him that's murky but I can't put it into words."

"Well, finish up your dinner and we'll digest him some other time. We have a recital to go to and we don't have much time unless you want to eat dessert when we return."

Paula frowned and Gabriella replied: "Tarta de Sevilla. It might be passable."

"I'm sure it is! You really take care of me."

Gabriella smiled and said nothing. Paula knew Gabriella did not like mushy talk. A retired high school math teacher, she took Paula under her wing shortly after Paula graduated from high school. They both enjoyed their found family relationship, but Gabriella was averse to dwelling on emotions.

They drove Gabriella's aging Mercedes downtown and Gabriella enjoyed the exquisite violin playing of Anne-Sophie Mutter at the Arlington. Though Paula couldn't hear the music, she knew Gabriella liked having her along. She did what she usually did in a theater, observed people, but this time not only the audience. She was surprised she found pleasure in the physical actions and body language of Anne-Sophie Mutter as she played one selection after another.

Like everyone else in the theater, Gabriella couldn't get enough encores after Anne-Sophie finished the published program, but eventually the performance had to end. As Gabriella and Paula stood to leave, waiting patiently for the crowd to file out, a man, husky in build and with a broad grin on his face, made his way to them.

"If I had known you were coming tonight, I would have made arrangements to sit with you!"

"Perhaps that's why I didn't let you know."

"Oh, come on. Don't tell me you're still mad about my little gaffe."

Gabriella raised her eyebrows in disapproval, but Paula only shrugged.

"I'll walk out with you," he said. He waved them forward.

As they slowly made their way toward the exit and the street, McGreggor kept up his chatter. Because her back was to him, Paula didn't know what he talked about but she knew Gabriella would fill her in later if McGreggor said anything significant. Outside, they walked with the crowd toward parking. In an alcove of a bookshop entrance, a man was sound asleep. McGreggor tapped Paula on the shoulder to draw attention to him as he spoke about the homeless man.

"This is really disgusting. He should get a job and pay for a decent place to sleep. All these homeless people are a drain on society. He should be contributing like everyone else."

"I don't know," Paula replied. "I think he contributed something to me. I could never go to sleep while an army of people walked by. He has a talent I don't have and I have to admire it."

"Oh, come on! You don't think that."

"How would you know what I think?"

"Okay, I don't, but now that I have your attention, will you have dinner with me tomorrow night?"

"I'm busy. And the next night and the next. Gabriella is trying out new recipes and I'm her trusted taster."

"I could take some of that!"

"No, I don't think so."

Paula and Gabriella walked on.

"Thank God, you turned him down," Gabriella told Paula after they were in her Mercedes and driving home. "And a self-invite to my dinners—ugh!"

"Did he say anything worth mentioning as we walked out?"

"Probably not. His father died recently. He lived here in Santa

Barbara, which is why he is glad for his temporary assignment. He has a lot to do to settle the estate and the will."

"Maybe I should be nicer to him."

"Maybe not. Death isn't a free pass to act like an idiot."

The next day Paula had lunch with Detective Donelan, or rather, she hoped to. He called ten minutes before they were to meet.

~Paula? She read on her caption phone.

"The same."

~I'm going to mess you up, the captions continued.

"Same old, same old. When have you ever not?"

~Don't be like that.

"I'll be whatever you want with the exception—"

~Knock it off

They met after three o'clock and Paula, considering that Gabriella was hard at work on dinner, only ordered a salad.

"Two of them in one night. Do you believe that? Both homeless. The first one was shot and the other stabbed to death."

"So, you're thinking two assailants and they aren't connected?"

"Maybe. The Medical Examiner believes the gunshot victim was killed first, but the stabbing happened soon afterward. They might be connected."

"What time?"

"After eleven. Eleven-thirty, twelve or so."

Paula snorted. "Then it could have been McGreggor. We were out of the theater by ten-thirty."

"Oh, come on, you don't think—"

"He was pretty antagonistic about the homeless."

"A lot of people are. Doesn't mean they go out killing them."

"The one with a dog, it wasn't—"

"Your friend Sam? No. A guy named Festus. He's new here, I believe."

"His father died recently."

"Festus'?"

"No, I meant McGreggor."

"What do you have against McGreggor, for God's sake!"

"Just a bad feeling."

"Because he insulted you. You should know better than to let feelings get in the way."

McGreggor came into the café, saw them and quickly made his way to the table. "Caught you goofing off," he said with a big grin as he sat down.

"I'm eating my lunch. You know I was working the homeless homicides."

"Any leads?"

"Not yet. No one heard or saw, as usual."

"No one heard a gunshot? Great group of people. But then look at what they are. Homeless people aren't reliable."

"About like anyone else is the way I see it. As soon as I finish lunch, I'll be back out there talking to them."

Paula interrupted. "When did your dad die? Had he been ill?"

McGreggor looked happy Paula was interested. "The 14th. Just days before I was scheduled to be up here."

"Makes it convenient."

"That's not the word I would use," McGreggor replied.

"Yeah, Paula," Donelan added, "don't be mean spirited."

"I don't mind," McGreggor smiled. "I like someone with zap. Zip, zap, kaboom!" He let that sink in and added: "I'm waiting for that invitation."

Paula raised her eyebrows.

"To what?" Donelan inquired.

"To a dinner cooked by Paula's friend, Gabriella. Do you live with her?"

"I have for a while."

"I admit my dad's death was convenient. It was also convenient he had seen his doctor the week before—I didn't have to wait on the coroner before burying him. His doc wrote it was global decline, so that was that. He had COPD, you know."

Paula stood up. "Well, I have things to do. Don't overwork yourself, J. Jim."

"I won't," Detective J. Jim Donelan assured her.

As she walked away, McGreggor said: "Pretty girl, too bad she's deaf."

Pretty or not, Paula had something she wanted to do. That a homeless man with a dog was murdered made her think of her friend. She drove to where he usually stayed behind the Ralphs grocery store and he wasn't there. As she walked around to the front of the store, a poorly shaven man in unkempt, mismatched clothes was sitting on the ground with his back to the building.

"Enjoying the sun?"

"You bet."

"Have you seen Sam and Baby Girl?"

"He died."

"What? When?"

"Just happened."

Paula felt a grip in her chest. "How?"

"He was murdered. Shot. Bang, bang!"

"That was Festus."

"Oh. The new guy. I didn't know him."

After talking to several other homeless, Paula realized Sam had left the area. As she knew she would get more information from him than anyone else, she made the two-hour drive to Pasadena where she suspected he was. There she found him under the Colorado Street bridge, also known as suicide bridge. There were several homeless in the encampment. Baby Girl, a pit bull, was as she usually was: under a blanket. She came out to greet her, and Paula gave her a chew bone she purchased before leaving Santa Barbara. Sam was dressed in all black, including his flat-crown bolero hat.

"Yeah, I heard about Festus and that's why I'm here. Too much shit going on up there. Made myself scarce."

"What shit is going on?"

"Oh, you know, rumors. One was that a guy was going around wanting to pay good money for murdering someone. He wasn't that blunt, of course."

"What did he look like?"

"Never saw him, but guys told me he was a tall, skinny guy, but who knows? Didn't see him."

Damn, Paula thought to herself, doesn't fit the stocky McGreggor. "I was hoping too much," she said out loud.

"What?"

"Oh, I miscalculated, thinking the tall, skinny guy was someone I knew, but it's not. Went down the wrong path, I guess."

"Are you investigating the murders? Have there been more?"

"I only know of two."

"The scuttlebutt is the tall, skinny man found a homeless guy who acted as a go-between between him and another homeless, a guy with a dog. There would be no contact with the skinny and the guy who did the murder. Payment went the same route. Then the guy who hired the two killed them both. Used a knife on one to throw off the police." Sam snorted. "And who cares about a homeless man anyway? After a while, it will go cold."

"Not if I can help it."

"I'll be here until it blows over. That shit who killed the dude with a dog might not know for sure he had the right guy. That's one of the rumors. The first guy who arranged it never told him who the murderer was except that he had a dog. The crazy might kill all of us with a dog, including me. Then where would Baby Girl be?"

"How many guys up there have dogs?"

"Five or so."

"Can you give me their names and where they camp?"

"Yeah. You'll do something?"

"Of course."

"Let me know?"

"Yeah, but you stay here, will you?"

"Until I hear from you. Do you know what happened to Festus' dog?"

"Haven't heard."

"Damn Humane Society. They probably pulled Sparky and put him to death."

When Paula returned to Santa Barbara, she went down the list Sam had given her of homeless men with dogs, but as it was late in the afternoon, she only managed to speak to three of them. For each one she brought a treat for their dog and gave them money for dog food. Not one of them gave any indication they had been a participant in a murder or was approached and asked to participate. "Know nothin' 'bout it," was the often heard mumble.

She slept restlessly that night and the next morning searched for the remainder of homeless men on Sam's list. She found them, and like those the afternoon before, they knew nothing that was helpful. She again treated their dogs and gave money for dog food. Two of them had heard the rumor that a tall, thin man was asking for someone who would commit murder for hire. Each time she heard the story, the jackpot grew astronomically. It began to sound like being homeless and hired out as a murderer was a high paying occupation. She did get one useful tip. The source of the information about the tall, thin man looking to hire someone to commit a murder was pointed out by two of the men she interviewed. The origin was a homeless man called Moses, though she learned his given name was Loki Moros.

She found him begging at a downtown freeway off-ramp, and for the price of an extra large pizza and a soft drink, he told her what he knew.

Paula went home for a sandwich after interviewing Moses, who wasn't inclined to share his Meat Madness pizza with her. Gabriella was busy preparing that night's dinner: lamb tagine with dates and honey.

"I don't know how reliable Moses is," she told Gabriella as she fixed herself a sandwich. "He insists the man who wanted to hire a murderer was tall and thin. That doesn't fit McGreggor at all."

"Perhaps you should give up on McGreggor for the obvious reason he's not tall and thin."

"No. I still feel it might be him." She sighed. "I admit I don't like him, but I also think he's involved. Moses told me a lot of details no one else knows."

"A talker? Proud to know-it-all?"

"That's right. He claimed Lamar Johnston was the one who found a willing murderer for the tall, thin man, and though Johnston didn't give the tall man the name of the prospective murderer, he mentioned he had a dog. Festus, after he did the murder, told Lamar the details so he could claim the money. Then, either because of the relief of talking about it or the need to boast, Festus also told Moses. Moses doubled checked everything with Lamar, so he got all the details of how it was set up and how the murder was done."

"Which you now know."

"Yes."

"Told Donelan?"

"No, not yet. I'm not telling him because he doesn't believe it might have been McGreggor."

"Which you still do."

"Absolutely. This is how it happened. The tall, thin man hired Lamar to recruit someone unknown whom he would never have direct contact with or be able to identify him. That person was Festus, and he carried out the murder of someone who has yet to be identified as being murdered. The victim had COPD, and Festus entered his house late at night after the victim had already taken a sleeping pill and was groggy. In the dark Festus pretended to be his son giving him medicine, and he gave him several more pills from a bottle at the victim's bedside. Then he increased the man's oxygen. He left, but came back before dawn and returned the oxygen to the normal setting. His victim, of course, was dead from excess CO_2."

"Hypercapnia. I know about that. My husband suffered from it. Did Moses say where or when this happened?"

Paula laughed. "Not where. I asked him when but all he said was: What day was Columbus Day? I told him the 13th and he smiled, saying: The day after."

"Well, if Moses is telling the truth, it's not McGreggor."

"And if he's lying? He could be misleading about the tall, thin man and about Festus."

"Well, I hate to suggest what I'm going to suggest." Gabriella smiled wryly. "But it might be the solution you're looking for."

That afternoon, Paula returned to talk with Moses. She asked for his help in doing something fairly easy to do. When he was hesitant, she told him he would have a five-hundred-dollar reward. She then called McGreggor for a brief chat. When she hung up, she realized it was the first time she felt good after talking with him. She returned home early to help Gabriella with dinner, but the only help needed was to go to the liquor store and get an Italian Barolo and a hazy craft beer. At five-thirty McGreggor arrived. He wanted a beer to go with dinner, so only Paula and Gabriella drank the Barolo.

"I really appreciate the invite. Though Santa Barbara has a thousand restaurants, a home-cooked meal is the best. This is delicious!"

"Thank-you," replied Gabriella. "I know after your recent loss, you need a little care."

"My dad was old. It wasn't unexpected, but like in his early days, he was stubborn and hanging on. I thought he would live forever."

"So many deaths recently."

"When did your dad die?" Paula asked.

"Not that long ago. The 14th of this month."

"Sad," continued Gabriella. "And those two homeless men murdered. Bad times."

"Well, they were living off others. Good riddance! Is that the right way to live? What they were doing? Not working but getting a handout?"

"Our nation being Christian, I don't think it's unimportant to help. When Christ was told there wasn't enough food, what did he do? He provided. He didn't say waste and fraud!"

"You can't save everybody, and I don't see why we should try."

"Well, those two homeless who were killed hadn't done anything wrong," Paula said. "At least that's what Detective Donelan told me."

"Preposterous! I'm sure they did something to deserve what they got."

"Maybe the guy that was killed with a gun, the first one," she continued, "he might have, but they know the stabbing victim, the one with a dog, was innocent. He only arrived from up north the day he was killed."

McGreggor looked uncertain. "Okay, you two weeping hearts. Maybe I'm a little bit wrong about the homeless. As they say, walk a mile in another man's shoes, but I still think they are nothing but a drag on society. Beggars have been known from time immemorial. That doesn't give them legitimacy."

After McGreggor left, Paula and Gabriella looked at each other. "Maybe," Paula said.

"He didn't seem interested in where the homeless man who did the murder is camped out even though you told him about Moses."

"He heard, all right. He heard despite his poker face. He didn't want to give himself away."

Paula drove to Detective Donelan's house. Doris answered the door.

"Do you need to be alone?" Doris said as they walked to the living room where J. Jim was watching the news.

"No," Paula said. "I need to borrow him, and I don't want you to think there's something going on."

Doris chuckled. "Oh, I think a little fling would do him good. He is getting a bit flabby."

"Are you two talking about me? Please do it behind my back!"

Paula explained herself briefly, and she and J. Jim set off for one of the homeless hideouts.

"So, why are you dragging me out in the cold?" Donelan said as they hid in the bushes close to a homeless man with a dog.

"That's Moses, also known as Loki Moros. I told him I would give him five hundred dollars if he acted as a decoy. He was very enthusiastic."

"I bet! A decoy for what?"

"If I told you, you'd get up and leave. I will say that I found out today while I was interviewing the homeless men who have dogs, that most think Festus was innocent and the rumor is that another homeless man with a dog will be killed."

"Why did you bring me here? There are camps and places to sleep all over town. Could be at any of them."

"The bet's on Moses. I borrowed the dog, by the way. Cost me fifty dollars."

"Don't ask for reimbursement."

"I won't."

The wait was long. A light fog rolled in, making the sensation of how cold it was lower than the air temperature. They talked about his two kids, a boy and a girl, Doris' wealthy sister living in Morro Bay whose husband makes more money as a software engineer than the payroll of the police department, and about some of the cases Paula and J. Jim worked together.

"By the way," Paula asked. "Do you need a warrant to search a homeless man's belongings?"

"Unless there's probable cause."

"There will be."

Close to midnight, they heard someone approaching. Whoever it was, he was bundled warmly in a hooded jacket. He approached Moses cautiously, stopping at times for a minute before proceeding. Moses had his back to him, and when the man was near, he pulled a knife from his pocket. J. Jim jumped up and ran toward the man, grabbed the back of his jacket and flung him to the ground. Paula picked up the knife by the blade tip to keep her prints off the handle.

"Doesn't look tall and thin to me," Paula said.

"No, it doesn't look that way to me, either. Looks like a hefty Scot ready to knife a homeless man with a dog. Get up McGreggor."

"This is all a mistake."

"On your part, I agree. We have you for attempted murder of this gentleman, Moses by name, and I believe forensics can tell us if this knife was used to kill Festus. The gun is in your lodgings."

"You won't find it," McGreggor smirked.

"You want to tell us your motive?"

"For what? I've done nothing."

"Except to hire a homeless man to murder you father. I think the coroner will have to examine him even though his doctor claimed natural causes. Was he taking too long to die?"

McGreggor shrugged, then he turned to Paula and said: "Bitch!"

"Absolutely!" Paula laughed.

Patrolmen arrived, responding to Detective Donelan's call. After they took McGreggor away, Moses burst into talk.

"You sure nabbed him, didn't you? Glad I didn't see him coming. I knew he was there since the dog whimpered, but I wasn't going to turn around since I didn't want to scare him off. I'm not frightened by guys like him. I've seen a lot of fights, people killed. It happens in the camp sometimes, mostly a fist fight but sometimes worse. I've never backed down and never will. But now that you've caught the guy everyone will... Hey, what are you doing?"

J. Jim was at Moses' grocery cart and was opening bags and boxes and unrolling blankets, giving Moses' belongings a thorough search.

"Don't you need a warrant?"

"There's probable cause that you've committed murder of an old man who was already dying of COPD." Detective Donelan held up a bundle of money. "How much? A thousand?"

"A little less," Moses responded. "I had to celebrate my good fortune. That's how I kept warm tonight."

"Giving me all that info about the murder," Paula said, "made me realize you had done it yourself. McGreggor didn't know who you were, since the man he gunned down wouldn't tell him anything except that the hired murderer was a homeless man with a dog. Of course, you don't have a dog. That's a minor detail."

"It looks like the state will be giving you room and board for a while," J. Jim added. "I doubt much of this stuff will travel with you."

Moses looked crestfallen. He turned to Paula and asked: "Does this mean I won't get the five hundred dollars?"

Slam Dunk
Steve Liskow

AmyLee Nzangi's brown face had no lines, her hair fell across her chest in pink, blue, gold, red, and silver cornrows, and her fingernails might have escaped from a Swiss Army knife. Tatiana Kova sat across from her and wondered how much the woman's extensions cost.

AmyLee stared at Tatiana's left arm.

"Nice ink."

"Thank you." Thick ivy leaves covered Tatiana's scars from wiping out on her boyfriend's motorcycle mere days before graduation. He broke his leg, and she fractured her left arm in two places. That ink was the other reason people called her "Tats."

"But enough about me. What can I do for you?"

"I'm pretty sure my husband is cheating on me."

"What makes you think so?" Tats took notes on a legal pad in her lap. Old school.

"Well, I was one of his girlfriends until we got married. That was four years ago, and I'm not sure he ever dumped any of the others."

"You've been married four years?"

"Right after he graduated and got drafted."

Stanley Dunkaniewicz, now the starting center for the Hartford Colonials, was a former All-American, number three draft pick, and seven feet tall. Tats only followed the UConn Huskies, especially the women, but everybody knew Dunkaniewicz by his Instagram handle, "Slam Dunk."

"I wrote half his papers for him in college." AmyLee's pleated slacks looked custom-tailored, too. She wore heels that might make her tall enough to kiss her husband without a stepladder.

"Like a good girlfriend," Tat wrote it down.

"If you knew about his other relationships and you still married him, it could be hard to get a decent settlement in a divorce, couldn't it?"

AmyLee shook her head and the cornrows moved enough to reveal creamy brown skin between the open halves of her blouse.

"I signed a pre-nup, so I'm screwed on the divorce anyway. Damn, that's the wrong way to say that, isn't it?" The woman took a deep breath and started again.

"I'm supposed to love, honor, and obey him, so I want some of that for myself, too. I'm not some cheap ho he picked up after a game."

Whatever else AmyLee was, Tatiana was sure she wasn't cheap.

"If you think he's been seeing other women for as long as you've been together, why are you only upset about it now?"

"I've always been upset." AmyLee's face melted from angry to sad. It made her ten years younger. "But now I'm pregnant. I want the baby, but if I get fat, he'll be trying to ride any chick with a pulse."

She sighed. "Any time, any place, any woman. Shee-it, I don't think he'd kick a walrus out of bed."

"If he's cheating on you in other cities, I can't help you," Tats said. "I'm not going to fly all over the country to do bed checks. And I'd charge you for the travel expenses."

"He broke his ankle in San Diego two weeks ago," AmyLee said. "The season's over for him now. He's had surgery, but he's in a walking boot for at least another six weeks. He's in town, so you can follow him easier."

Tats nodded. "Okay, but is he really going to be in the mood for sex, especially with strangers?"

"A stranger is only a friend he hasn't laid yet." AmyLee's eyes narrowed. "He's on painkillers that would put me around the rings of Saturn, and he doesn't even seem to notice them."

Tats looked at her nearly blank legal pad.

"You only need solid proof of one one-night stand, is that right?"

"He's got a regular side piece across the river. She posts pictures on Tik Tok, her and him. They're almost funny. He's seven-two, she comes up to his belt buckle. Well, makes some things easier, you get what I mean."

Tats was five-six, and AmyLee looked about the same height.

"Suppose I *do* get pictures," Tats said. "What happens then? Will you try to break the pre-nup and divorce him anyway?"

"I love the SOB. Yes, I'm pathetic, shoot me. I just want to make sure he takes care of me and the baby."

When AmyLee fumbled in her purse for a tissue, Tats gave in. She hated to see a woman cry.

"Do you have a name or address for his side piece?"

Twenty minutes later, Tats had a signed contract on file and a check in her desk drawer. After her client left, she went online to find the other woman's Tik Tok posts.

"Anastasia Lungstadt" was an influencer and posted dozens of pictures of herself with clothing, jewelry, kitchen appliances, furniture, and—yes—sex toys. Tats wondered if she got them as samples. Happily, her posts didn't include video demonstrations.

The easiest way to find where she lived would be to follow her seven-foot-two lover, who would be hard to lose in a crowd. According to AmyLee, her husband usually left in the early evening, so Tats had six hours of down time. She plugged her camera's batteries into a charger and went back online to read up on Stanley Dunkaniewicz.

She found hundreds of links, which was no surprise. The guy led his team to the NCAA championship five years earlier, averaging 26 points and 15 rebounds per game. He signed with the Hartford Colonials for a reported 40 million dollars over three years and renewed that contract for another five years and 80 million dollars. He was twenty-six years old, seven feet, two inches tall, and weighed 300 pounds. Tats caught herself wondering about the mechanics of intimacy with a man that big.

Dunkaniewicz had even more endorsements than his girlfriend: shoes, shirts, software, an airline, a credit card, energy drinks, analgesic ointment, and an SUV, possibly the only car he could fit into. His current worth was estimated at 200 million dollars. Not bad for a twenty-six-year old.

Four women had accused him of harassment or sexual assault—one of them when he was in college—but none of them went to court. Tats studied pictures, all showing a man with shaggy brown hair and large ears towering over everyone else in sight.

For the next two nights, Tats parked her car half a block down from the Dunkaniewicz home, a tasteful Georgian in West Hartford, but Slam never stepped outside. Tats exchanged texts with his wife, who reported he was asleep in bed at eleven.

Thursday, the third night, Tats slid into a Black Watch flannel and tossed a windbreaker and a blue hoodie on the seat beside her. She had a Yankees cap, a Red Sox cap, a battered fedora, and two sets of sunglasses, too. She liked to change her look if she followed someone for a long time, and she always wore long sleeves because of her tattooed arm. She drove a four-year-old silver Nissan that looked like half the other cars in Hartford County.

A car pulled to the curb outside the couple's house and a giant emerged from the front door. He descended the three steps with the help of a cane and climbed into the limo, which headed toward Capitol Avenue in Hartford. Tats stayed four cars behind until Dunkaniewicz unfolded from his ride in front of a five-star restaurant and disappeared through the door. Tats didn't want to risk going into the bar alone, so she waited on the sidewalk until she saw the man take a table in the dining room. Then she parked in the garage a block away and walked back.

She returned in time to watch the maître d' escort a brunette to Dunkaniewicz's table. Even in stilettos, she was only about half his height, with a dress cut down to *here* and a skirt slit up to *there*. Her dark waves fell below her shoulder blades. The server materialized, took their drink order, and vanished.

Slam Dunk and Anastasia—if that was her real name—would be at least an hour even without dessert. Tats left the garage and drove Hartford streets for forty-five minutes, then grabbed a parking space that providentially appeared half a block from the restaurant.

Twenty-five minutes later, the brunette came out of the restaurant and walked by Tats, who debated following her instead of the basketball player. When the woman disappeared into the same parking garage, Tats crossed her fingers. Minutes later, Anastasia cruised to a stop in front of the restaurant and Slam Dunk joined her.

Tats followed the couple through Hartford and across the Connecticut River into Manchester. The car eased into a parking space in a condominium complex, and Anastasia got out first, going around the hood to help her boyfriend fight his way out of the passenger seat.

The woman unlocked the door of a townhouse and they disappeared. Tats knew she was out of luck. The bedrooms were certainly upstairs, and the one where the main event was taking place might even be on the other side of the building. No way could she take a photograph AmyLee could use in court. She waited half an hour until the lights downstairs went off and noted the address so she could find the woman's real name in the morning, then returned to her own apartment.

According to the white pages and the bureau of records, Anastasia's real name was Brianna Adair. She was twenty-two, graduated from Central Connecticut State University with a degree in marketing, and had five hundred thousand followers. Tats dug deeper and found that Brianna occasionally modeled for art classes. No photos were available, but she understood why the woman would have been in demand.

She texted AmyLee to say she'd followed hubby to his girlfriend's home the previous night and asked when he returned home.

About 6. He went to take a shower and I could smell another woman on him. U get pix?

Not yet, Tats replied. The implication was that she'd grow tall enough to peek in the girl's window. Fat chance. She wondered if Slam and Brianna had another love nest, but her crib was only ten miles away, so they didn't need alternatives.

Tats remembered how she felt about her own divorce, several years before. She left the Hartford PD and had only seen her ex a handful of times since then. The closest she had come to a new relationship was occasional dinner with her former best man, and those always ended with a chaste kiss before going home in separate cars.

When you were an ex-cop with more ink than the *New York Times*, good men were hard to come by. It would be easier for AmyLee, attractive, intelligent, and younger, except that she was still in love with her cheating husband.

Tats opened her computer and looked at Brianna Adair's information again. Maybe she should follow the woman to learn how the other half lived. She'd watch Slam again that night, and if the two didn't hook up, she'd switch her attention to the woman instead.

That day was Friday, and Tats realized that Slam would have to spend date night with his wife. He took her out to a long leisurely dinner and Tats almost drooled over the food she saw through her telephoto lens. Both selected some kind of fish and followed with what looked like cheesecake.

They returned home, and Tats hovered outside until midnight before deciding that hubby wasn't taking a late field trip.

Saturday afternoon, Tats and Mitch Hunter sat across from each other on the terrace of an outdoor restaurant in Old Wethersfield. The sun was warm on her back and two dogs lapped from water dishes beneath nearby tables. Mitch, a full professor of psychology at the West Hartford branch of UConn, was her own thirty-one with a sense of humor she suspected he polished in his lectures. He worked his way through a gyro while she nibbled a Greek salad.

"You need to get out more, Tats." Mitch sipped his wine. "You clean up well, and there are lots of guys out there waiting for someone like you."

"Yeah, a chick with ink and a concealed carry permit. Every biker's dream."

"Oh, come on, guys all secretly yearn for a bad girl. You should know that by now."

"Then how come we've never hooked up?"

"We've known each other for years and we're good friends. Sex would screw things up."

"Nicely put."

Mitch shook his head. He wore a Grateful Dead T-shirt under a safari shirt, and it made him look like a cleaned-up hippie hunter. Well,

Hemingway and Jerry Garcia both had beards.

Tats slid the pit of a kalamata olive under her tongue while she chewed, then spit it discreetly into her napkin.

"How come you've never married, Mitch?"

"Short attention span, I guess. Or maybe I know too much about how people mess up relationships. That's the danger of being a psych guy. You over-analyze things."

"What would you say about a woman who knows her husband is cheating, but won't divorce him?"

Mitch watched a beagle lapping from a water dish two tables away.

"I'd need more info."

"They're both in their mid-twenties. The guy's filthy rich and white. His wife is black and probably the smarter one."

"She knows he's cheating?"

"Absolutely." Tats remembered when she caught her own husband cheating. She kicked him out and filed for divorce within days. Mitch turned away from the beagle.

"Um, maybe scandal, maybe she loves him in spite of himself."

"That's what she says. Could it be true? It sounds to me like Stockholm syndrome, being in love with an abuser."

"Hmm. If he's rich, was there a pre-nup?"

"Actually, there was."

Mitch nodded. "Well, at the risk of sounding glib, maybe that's it."

"Which?"

"All of them. Or there's something else you haven't mentioned."

Tats decided AmyLee's pregnancy was too personal to share. She told herself this was as close as she got to a date, so she should enjoy it and stop dragging her work along as a chaperone. The beagle looked at her like it agreed, then watched a server bring the humans' meals.

Mitch grabbed the check.

"You want to do something else? Maybe a mall crawl?"

"Why? Do you have something in mind?"

Mitch gave her a look somewhere between an older brother and a lecherous uncle.

"Let's find you some serious dating duds."

Four hours later, Tats stood in her bedroom looking at a party dress, two funky tops, a skirt, and pleated slacks she wasn't sure she would ever really wear. She told herself it could have been worse. Mitch didn't suggest lingerie, too.

Sunday morning found her outside Brianna Adair's Manchester condo at seven, wide awake after a night of resisting the urge to try out the new dress under real-life conditions. Now she wore her usual follow-the-cheater uniform with the alternate hats and tops in the back seat.

Fortunately, she also brought a book because Brianna didn't open her blinds until after ten o'clock. She appeared at her door an hour later, dressed in jeans and heels with a top that strained to cover her weapons. Now that Tats could see her in an untouched photo and natural light, she looked even younger, like precocious jailbait that might hang out along the Berlin Turnpike during working hours.

Brianna drove to the same mall Mitch and Tats visited the day before and spent two hours meandering from store to store, buying nothing but checking her phone every five minutes. Finally, she returned to her car and retraced her route, stopping at a supermarket long enough to pick up a few items. Tats decided to break all the rules of an investigation. She stepped out of her own car and approached the woman climbing her front steps.

"Excuse me. Ms. Adair."

The woman turned, her eyes narrowed. She was even smaller than Tats thought before, maybe not even five feet tall, but her eyes held a firmness that didn't match the rest of her young face.

Tats stopped at the bottom of the steps.

"How long have you been having an affair with Stanley Dunkaniewicz?"

"Who?" The woman's voice felt as if she had a million other things to worry about.

"Slam Dunk. You do know he's married, don't you?"

"Who are you?"

Tats held up her PI license without moving closer.

"I'm a private investigator. I've been watching you for several days, and I know the man spent the night with you a few days ago. And he's done it before."

"And your point is…?"

"His wife could divorce him for adultery. And your face and name would be dragged through the scandal."

"Scandal, my ass. Me and a star athlete who makes more in a year than most people make in their entire lives. I'd get a million more followers the first day."

"What about his wife? She loves him, and you're hurting her."

"If she really loved him, she'd give him what he needs."

Tats lowered her license. "So *you're* giving him what he needs? You love him, too?"

"Wow, nothing gets past you, does it? If he didn't love me, he wouldn't be with me, would he?"

"He's a guy," Tats pointed out. "And you're willing to sleep with him with no obligations. Does he pay for your condo? Buy you clothes? Jewelry?"

"We love each other."

"Then why doesn't he divorce his wife and marry you instead?"

"It's complicated. You wouldn't understand and it's none of your business anyway."

Brianna picked up her groceries again. Tats cleared her throat.

"I'm going to keep watching you, Ms. Adair. Brianna."

"Good. I love attention. So does Stan. Too bad his wife doesn't understand that. A man like him, he needs a lot of loving, and she's not in his league."

"Meaning you think you are." Tats almost smiled. "But if you know he's married, and he's buying you stuff and sleeping with you, you're just a whore. An expensive one, but still a whore."

The other woman's eyes became even older. She slid her key into the door.

"Get out of here before I call the cops."

Tats returned to her car. She knew that tipping her hand meant she'd never get a photo op, but AmyLee already knew of her husband's affair and was unwilling to divorce him. Tats knew from bitter experience that if someone didn't want to solve a problem, nobody else could solve it for them.

She drove to her office and pulled up AmyLee's contract. When she dialed the cell number, the woman answered on the second ring.

"Ms. Dunkaniewicz, this is Tats Kova. I've decided to drop your case."

"But you've made such progress. Why are you…?"

"Your husband and his lover are carrying on at her townhouse, and there's no way I can get a vantage point to get the photographs you want. You know he's cheating, so I'd suggest you contact an attorney and go from there."

"But I signed a pre-nup. I can't divorce him."

"Then I'd suggest a separation. Or counseling."

"He'll never agree to that."

Tats remembered saying the same thing several years before, and it was true.

"Then move out. Eventually, he'll do something about that. But until you take action, nothing's going to change. I'm sorry, but that's the reality of this situation. I wish I could do more, but I can't."

"Um…let me think about it for a day or two."

"I'm cancelling your contract as of today. I'll send you an invoice. I'm sorry I can't be more help."

Tats ended the call and felt like she'd failed. She knew it wasn't true, but she became an investigator to give her clients a happy ending. Why couldn't Brianna and Stanley hook up at a motel like normal adulterers?

Four days later, Tats didn't even have her computer booted up before her cell chirped.

"Ms. Kova." AmyLee Dunkaniewicz's voice shook like she was riding a roller coaster. "I need you. It's an emergency."

"What's wrong?"

The voice in her ear shook even more. "Stan is dead. He killed himself."

Tats was glad she was already sitting down. "What happened? Are you all right?" *What a stupid question.*

"I'm…the police are at that woman's house. I'm here, too. They called me."

"Ms. Dunk—AmyLee, what's happening? Slow down."

"He hit her. Then he killed himself. Can you come? It's so crazy."

Tats reached the townhouse, where an ambulance and a Manchester police SUV sat in the parking lot, in thirty-two minutes. She strode to the door, digging in her purse for her PI license before she recognized one of the cops.

"Benjy, what's going on?"

Benjy's frown turned to surprise when he saw her. "Whoa, Tats. What brings you here?"

"I was doing a job for the guy's wife. She called me a while ago and told me her husband is dead. What happened?"

"Well, you'll hafta talk to Sturgis, he's in charge, but it looks like the guy and his chick had an argument and he hit her. She went to the ER, and they called us to check on him. The door was locked and nobody answered, so we broke in. Found the guy dead in bed."

"How'd he die?"

Benjy looked over his shoulder and up the stairs. "It looks like he cut his wrists. They're still checking it out."

Before Tats could enter, the EMTs came through the door with a covered body that reached well beyond the end of the stretcher. Benjy did a double-take.

"Christ, how tall was the guy?"

"Seven-foot-two."

Tats rushed through the tastefully furnished living room and followed voices upstairs to the bedroom on the right. Sure enough, it was on the rear side of the townhouse so she couldn't see it from the parking lot the night she followed Slam Dunk and Brianna. When she stepped inside, four men turned to her, their faces serious.

"What the hell?" Detective Sturgis, resplendent in a cheap gray suit, stepped toward her, but AmyLee spoke first.

"I called her. She's the investigator I told you about."

Tats produced her license and looked around the room while the detective studied it. The carpet was faint lavender, and the curtains, walls and bedclothes were soft pink. A computer desk sat near the window, the chair overturned. A crime scene technician was bagging the sheets from the bed, and Tats saw rusty red splashed across their normal pink. She looked at the walls, where dark red letters appeared against the pink background. Leaning closer, she recognized the faint copper smell.

"He wrote a note?" She turned to the detective and took back her license.

"Looks like it. We found painkillers, too. The guy had a broken ankle, must've been taking stuff for it."

"I told you that," AmyLee interjected.

"Yeah. The squeeze—um, the woman who lives here—says they had a fight. The lady here says pills made him touchy as hell." Sturgis glanced toward AmyLee, who nodded. Even dressed in jeans and an old T-shirt, she was gorgeous, her cornrows the most color in the room.

"What was the fight about?" Tats asked.

"The girl didn't say. She was kind of woozy. They're keeping her overnight to check for a concussion."

Tats turned back to the blood on the wall. The red letters became fainter as they went, as if Dunkaniewicz ran out of blood and had to dip his fingers in it several times.

Screw it I blew it all goodbye.

Tats looked at the man in the polo shirt with a doctor's bag.

"What did he do, cut his wrists?"

"Yeah, and he did it the right way, up the arms from wrist to elbow. Well, you see the blood on the bed. He would've bled out in minutes. Obviously, I'm just guessing until the autopsy, but it looks pretty clear."

Tats turned back to AmyLee. "When did they call you?"

"About…two hours ago. I got here and they showed me the body. Stan."

"How long has he been dead?" Tats asked the doctor.

"About six hours. Rigor was just starting to set in."

"I assume you're going to check to be sure the blood is his."

"Well, yeah." A technician stared at her. "Duh."

Sturgis looked at Tats, then the doctor and technicians.

"Ms. D, why don't we go downstairs where there's more room."

Tats drove to the hospital and found Brianna Adair's room. She sported a huge purple bruise on the left side of her face, even more dramatic because of her pallor, and Tats thought it would go well with the pink in her bedroom.

"How do you feel?"

"They gave me Tylenol." The woman's voice was soft but steady. "What did they do? Is he under arrest? I should let him go back to his wife. She deserves him."

"What happened, do you remember?"

"We were going to sleep after…well, you know. Then he got up, said his ankle was hurting. I told him he'd already taken two of the pills and I was worried, 'cause he's only supposed to take one every twelve hours. He took one anyway and came back. I told him he should stay awake for a while to be sure he was all right, and he got pissed. I said something else, I don't even remember what, and he hit me."

She gestured toward the bruise. "Knocked me out of bed. The next thing I knew, I was looking up at him, he looked tall as a steeple and he was blurry. I felt dizzy, but I managed to get up. I hurt and I wanted to call an ambulance, but he grabbed my phone. I put on a bathrobe and grabbed my car keys. Drove here…"

"What time was that?"

"I don't remember. Late."

It was nearly noon. Tats remembered the doctor's guess that Slam Dunk had been dead about six hours. That sounded close enough.

"Are you going to charge him?"

"I don't know. We'll talk. If he apologizes…"

"He's dead, Brianna. After you left, he killed himself."

Brianna's eyes widened around her dilated pupils.

"No."

"Yes," Tats said. "And I only have one more question."

She leaned in close to the woman and stared into her eyes.

"Did you slice his arms, or did his wife? I'm guessing it was his wife."

Brianna bit her lip. Then she lay back on the pillow and closed her eyes. Tats waited until she saw the first tear escape and run down the woman's cheek, then she left the hospital and called Sturgis.

He called her back before the end of the day.

"You were right," he said. "They've both confessed. They were in it together, and the Adair woman got fifty grand to help. The wife cut hubby's wrists and wrote on the wall, then she hit Adair with a bar of soap wrapped in a sock so it would look like a fist. But she did that an hour after the guy was dead. They wanted to make sure before Adair went to the hospital and they called us."

"She couldn't divorce him," Tats said. "So they did it for the insurance, right?"

"Yeah. And the guy's will leaves her a truckload."

Tats shook her head. "If she'd left well enough alone, just let you guys build the narrative, they might have gotten away with it, but she had to write that fake suicide note to rub it in."

"Yeah," Sturgis agreed. "Guess she needed the last word."

Tats couldn't blame her.

"But she forgot that Slam was a foot and a half taller than she was. The writing was too low, at my eye level."

When they ended the call, Tats looked out her window in the direction of the XL Center, where the Hartford Colonials played their home games. The cops had closed Dunkaniewicz's case in mere hours, thanks to two confessions and the writing on the wall.

They had a slam dunk.

High School Reunion
Sandra J. Cady

Throwing open the door with a loud bang against the doorstop, Lorraine made her grand entry into my small office located in the Greektown district of Detroit. I couldn't afford a receptionist so I was the only audience. Dressed in designer clothes and ridiculously high Louboutin heels, she looked me in the eye, adjusted her elaborate hat, and fluffed her shoulder length blond hairdo, "Bonnie, you haven't changed a bit since high school, and it's been thirty-two years."

Since I was a nerdy dork in high school, this was not a compliment. I last saw Lorraine in 1965 when we graduated. We were never friends. Back then, she was a conniving manipulator and gossip. Taking a casual sip of my coffee, I remarked "You're still sporting a Farrah Fawcett look. Didn't that go out of style in the early eighties?"

"You've developed a sense of humor over the years. I need an investigator and someone at the Grosse Pointe Junior League highly recommended you and I recognized your name." Not waiting for an invitation to sit down, she plumped herself into one of the two chairs across the desk from me. "I need help. My husband, Harvey Harris, died in an accident a few weeks ago while driving on Mack Avenue in Detroit. The Seventh Precinct police are taking their sweet time closing the investigation, and I need access to Harvey's funds immediately."

Harvey had been the acne faced irritating jock Lorraine hooked me up with for the senior prom. She was dating Harvey's friend, Fred, the captain of the football team. Fred wanted Harvey to have a date to the prom but Harvey was turned down several times. Lorraine extorted me into saying yes to him by threatening to reveal to everyone in the class of 1965 that she caught me kissing Betsy McKinnon, a cute cheerleader.

Wanting to preserve Betsy's reputation, I caved to the pressure. Lorraine must have ended up marrying Harvey and I bet it wasn't for his personality.

"Sorry, I'm fully booked for the next few months. I can give you the name of another private investigator." There's no way Lorraine would become my client. Comfortable and confident in my own skin now, I've been in a great relationship for the last several years with my life partner, Lucy, and nothing was going to intrude on that.

"The Wayne County Chief Prosecutor is a very dear friend of mine. We're extremely close if you know what I mean. Isn't he the one that signs approval on your private investigation license every two years?"

Damn. Lorraine hadn't changed a bit. This was no empty threat. A confident smirk on Lorraine's face metamorphed into a thin-lipped fait accompli look.

Narrowing my eyes at her, I said, "If you need money, surely you had accounts that you shared with Harvey."

"Guess again. Harvey tied everything up tight with him holding the strings. I've started a dating website called *FindYours* and need a large cash infusion. I know it's going to be a success. Doesn't everyone want to find their happily ever after?"

Absurd. Who would use a computer for matchmaking? If Lorraine had a close relationship with Chief Prosecutor Arnold Van Antwerp, why wasn't she utilizing him to speed up the investigation by putting pressure on the police?

Watching me closely, Lorraine read my thoughts. "I can't use Arnold. I have plans for him soon and must remain honest and above board until then. Arnold will be our next State Attorney General."

"I'm not working on this without you signing a contract with a down payment of one thousand cash. Maybe you'll need to hock a few things to produce the money."

Opening her purse, Lorraine let out a low throaty laugh and laid out the thousand bucks on my desk. "Harvey did let me have a few dollars on hand for spending money."

Shit. She just played me. I flipped out a contract from a drawer onto the desk, and she signed it without examination. Lorraine regally gathered herself up from the chair and made one last remark before exiting. "Here's my card with my contact information. I expect results within a week. There will be another two thousand for you upon completion." A wafting of Chanel Number Five hit my nostrils as she slammed the door on the way out.

Typical Lorraine. She gave me no details, which meant she only wanted me to discover a minimum of facts and not dig any further than pushing the investigation to a close to obtain Harvey's money. This whole thing smelled to high heaven and I doubted Harvey's accidental death was a simple one.

Leaving my second-floor office, I nimbly hit the stairs and emerged on the first floor next to Pegasus, one of Detroit's premier Greek restaurants. I did my best thinking over good food.

Arnold Van Antwerp, a leftover from former Mayor Coleman Young's democratic machine, was still a formidable elected political player. Pay to play and embezzling funds marked the past era and our current Mayor was doing his best to clean out the remaining old guard. I'd heard about Arnold's ambition to run for State Attorney General and to get out of Wayne County while the getting was still good. His buddy, former Detroit Chief of Police William Carter, sat in prison after being convicted of embezzling $2.4 million. Rumor had it Arnold received a half million from him in kickbacks but the feds couldn't make the case and former Chief Carter wasn't talking.

Contemplating my situation over stuffed meat grape leaves with lemon sauce, I downed a glass of Retsina. Normally, I stayed as far away from Detroit politics as I could. However, I believed Lorraine's association with Arnold to be real.

I called my contact at the Seventh Precinct detective division on my new portable Motorola flip phone while finishing some baklava. "Hey, Dwight, it's Bonnie. I need some help."

"Hell no. Last time I assisted you on a case I ended up shot in the leg."

"That wasn't my fault. How I was I to know he was armed? It's been six months. Laura will bake you a batch of her oatmeal chocolate chip cookies if you give me a bit of information." My niece, Laura, a former Detroit cop, mentored Dwight Broadnax when he was a rookie. She remained close friends with Dwight even after being shot and paralyzed in a robbery attempt. He knew me from his attendance at dinners and barbeques at Laura's home.

"As long as I don't have to leave my desk and because your Laura's aunt, it's a deal."

"I need info on Harvey Harris's accidental death which occurred in your precinct recently."

"Accidental? He got himself murdered while trolling in his vehicle at 2:00 a.m. for prostitutes on Mack Avenue. He was found dead next to his car with his wallet intact and 38-caliber bullets to the chest and head. It's a red-light district but the odd part is the killer didn't take his money."

"Sorry, I had some sketchy details from my client. So, is the investigation done?"

"We're still looking for witnesses and interviewed several females who work that location without any luck. Next, we're going to have Vice Division do a crackdown in that area and hit them where it hurts. Someone will trade info for making a deal to get off."

"Your cookies will be delivered tomorrow. Please keep me informed. My client is a pain in the ass and I'd like to wrap this up as soon as possible."

"Let me guess. Your client is Lorraine Harris. She's hounded me daily. Evidently, the insurance company and banks aren't releasing any money until they're assured she had nothing to do with her husband's murder."

"Sorry, P.I rules say I can't divulge the name of my client. Do you have anything that points to Harvey's wife being at the scene or hiring someone to murder him?"

"Nope, but I wouldn't put anything past that woman. There's been no tears just greed emanating from her. If she's your client, get your money up front."

"Thanks, Dwight," I said, ending the call.

Damn that Lorraine. I tried thinking of next steps as I went back to my office. First thing I did was call Laura.

"Laura, I need you to bake a dozen chocolate chip oatmeal cookies for Dwight by tomorrow."

"Well, hello to you too, Bonnie. I'm wrapping up a physician background check and kind of busy. What's the payoff for?" After being shot and having to use a wheelchair, Laura found employment in the Credentialing Office of Medical Staff Services at Ascension Hospital. She loved her work and was good at spotting doctors who inflated their resumes.

"I've got a crappy client I need to scrape off my shoes. Dwight gave me some information and will keep me updated in exchange for your cookies. I'll pick them up tomorrow morning before you go to work and fill you in more."

"Great. I haven't seen you for a while and I'm glad Dwight is talking to you again. He's a good man and friend of the family."

"See you tomorrow then, bye."

Laura is my confidential sounding board. She helped do research for me on past investigations. Our family's secret weapon is we're all a bit fey along the maternal line. My specialty was the "educated hunch" which frequently turned out to be true. Laura experienced infrequent bouts of prescient viewing which turned out to be accurate but never with a set time period in which they would occur.

Getting a cup of murky coffee from my reliable, old Mr. Coffee pot, I sat down, took a sip of the strong, thick brew which had been warming all day, and pondered my situation. I needed to satisfy Lorraine as soon as possible and get her permanently out of my life again. Picking up my desk phone, I called her.

"So, when were you going to tell me Harvey was murdered. It was no accident."

"He could have jumped out of his car for some reason and caught a few stray bullets. That's an accident. They told me his wallet was still on him, and all his money and charge cards were still there."

"He got out of his car in one of the most notorious pick-up areas for prostitutes in the city and riskily exposed himself to a possible slew of criminals accidentally?" I said, trying to keep the sarcasm out of my voice.

"You've no idea of what Harvey was like. He taught me so many things. Did you make any progress yet? Is the investigation closed?"

"The police are still looking for witnesses. There's no way I can hurry them through the process. You're just going to have to be patient."

"I'm not paying you for patience. Find how to move things along and earn your money. I'm meeting Arnold later for dinner at Carl's Chop House. I won't bring you up tonight but don't keep me waiting too long before I need to have a talk with him about you."

She clicked off without a goodbye. Maybe the rumors were true about Arnold on the take for a half million.

I called my acquaintance, Pete Walden, a long-time reporter at the Detroit News. I'd done investigative work for him in the past and used his direct number. Pete had his ear to the ground on what was happening in Detroit politics.

Lucky for me, he picked up. "Hey Pete, it's Bonnie. Hope you're doing okay after our last episode. I need some help."

"Bonnie, I was nearly killed last time I collaborated with you. My broken arm took months to heal."

"There's nothing involved like that this time. I need the 411 on Arnold VanAntwerp."

"Our glorious Wayne County Chief Prosecutor is currently digging for democratic support to run for state attorney general. However, the dems cash bucket is rather empty right now and they're saving for a more viable candidate with deep pockets. Word is Arnold's having trouble raising any money for his campaign from private funds. He might have to reach into that rumored half million stash. Maybe he stuck the cash up in his ceiling just like our corrupt former police chief and he's waiting for a way to spend his money without leaving any financial tracks for the Feds."

"Are the Feds still pursuing any investigations against him?"

"The FBI dropped any active investigation as far as I know. However, the IRS is supposed to be closely observing him."

"Is there something I need to watch out for while checking him out?"

"I've never been able to get a story from him. He's single, gruff, and rules his office with an iron hand. Plus, he's vindictive. Take extreme care in any interactions you may have with him."

"Do you know if he was friends with Harvey Harris who just died?"

"You mean Detroit's financial and real estate whiz killed on Mack Avenue at a suspicious time of night?"

"That's him. I didn't realize Harvey was well known. I don't read the financial news much."

"There's been rumors he assisted certain vendors in obtaining favorable contracts from the Detroit City Council. He ran in some of the same social groups as Arnold but they weren't friends as far as I'm aware. Ok, I've got to go. Got a hot story and I'm under deadline. At least this was a safe contact with you for a change."

Time for action. Well, sort of. I opened my computer and did internet searches on Arnold, Lorraine, and Harvey. Harvey's net worth was considerable. Lorraine married upward and belonged to several social groups in the Grosse Pointes. I couldn't find anything negative. Perhaps they had the clout and money to squash anything derogatory on the worldwide web. However, I had an idea.

I called Lucy, "Sorry I won't be home until late tonight. I'm working on a new case and I'll fill you in when I get home."

"There'll be leftover Irish stew in the frig and soda bread that you can warm up if you're hungry," she sighed. "Just be careful and come home in one piece."

"Love you and see you later," I said, signing off. Since I worked alone for the most part, Lucy had become used to my odd hours. Not only was she beautiful inside and out, but a hell of a cook having learned from her Irish mother. Currently, she was head chef at McShane's Irish Pub in the Corktown district of Detroit.

I did my second-best thinking while driving. Thoughts circled around in my brain; and, as I concentrated on the road on my way to Carl's Chop House, subconscious ideas popped to the forefront. Arnold seemed like a person to follow up with further. I might catch a break in the case by tracking him and Lorraine when they left the restaurant.

Sitting in my car with a great surveillance view of the front of Carl's Chop House, I consumed my own version of gourmet cooking. A full sack of White Castle burgers disappeared as I waited for them to leave. I heard there were no White Castle's west of the Mississippi. Too bad for those people, and it reinforced my preference to never travel far from Detroit.

Not knowing which car they drove, I kept a close watch on the valets while the smell of oniony burps filled my vehicle. Arnold was about twenty years older than Lorraine and he probably wouldn't make a late night of it. They emerged around 7:30 p.m. and the valets brought out two cars. They had traveled separately to the restaurant.

Arnold gave Lorraine a quick kiss that didn't look very romantic. She turned away to get into her car with a slight frown on her face. Maybe things weren't as lovey-dovey with Arnold as Lorraine projected.

Following Arnold's black luxury Lincoln, he didn't appear to be headed for his Lafeyette condominium address which I discovered earlier. He pulled into the driveway of a fancy mansion in the Boston-Edison district. He rang the doorbell and got immediately admitted, but I couldn't see who answered the door. I gave up on the idea of prowling around the home since it was fenced in with a large sign warning of Dobermans on the premises.

The front porch light came on an hour and a half later and a striking brunette stepped out on the porch and gave Arnold a hell of a goodbye kiss while he grabbed her buttocks. She appeared to be about ten years younger than Lorraine. Suppressing a yuck, I got great pictures of it all with my compact camera.

After that, Arnold walked to his car with a rather jaunty step and drove off. Following him again, he turned into his condominium building driveway, put a key card in the gate, and parked in the private lot. Yawning, I decided to call it a night now that I had leverage on Arnold and could check the address of the Boston-Edison home in the morning on my computer.

By the time I got home, I found Lucy fast asleep since she gets up by 5:00 a.m. to shop for fresh ingredients at the Eastern Market before going to work. I silently slipped under the covers and fell into dreamland hard.

I woke at 7:00 a.m. and Lucy was gone. She left me a note: "You didn't eat any of the dinner I made. Let me know if you're not feeling well. Or is it my cooking?" Oops, I might have to confess my culinary indiscretion of last night.

I grabbed a coffee and heated up the Irish stew and a piece of soda bread for breakfast. At least Lucy would know I enjoyed the meal she prepared. Quickly getting ready, I jumped in my car to drive over to Laura's house nearby. I'd have to check the Boston-Edison address from last night later.

Laura opened the front door before I could ring the doorbell. "Come on in. I've got time for a coffee and I baked you some extra cookies."

Hoo, boy. I couldn't get two members of my family circle irritated by showing a lack of appreciation for their cooking. So, even though I had a full breakfast already, I sat down at Laura's dining table for more. Baking was not my forte and my family loved to relate the tale of the cream cheese brownies I made one time long ago. How was I to know that the cream cheese had chives. Despite the oniony taste, my brothers ate them.

"These are great cookies as usual," I said. "Too bad I didn't have you come with me on surveillance last night. I can always use an extra set of eyes." I then filled Laura in on my case and what I had observed.

"I don't mind doing research for you, Bonnie. However, I draw the line at actively participating in an investigation with you. I need to be around for Samantha." Samantha was Laura's daughter and my grandniece.

Widening my eyes in surprise, I asked, "What do you mean?"

"Haven't you noticed those who actively help you end up getting injured? It's like you have a lucky charm hanging over your head but it doesn't offer protection to others."

Laura was right. "Thanks for pointing it out." I did tend to follow my hunches full steam ahead without fully considering consequences.

"Be careful with Arnold. I recall a few incidents when I worked in the Seventh Precinct in which he inserted himself into cases that were never brought forward. Supposedly, he took payoffs."

"Thanks for the warning. I'm on my way to drop off your cookies to Dwight and see if there's anything new about Harvey's murder." I bent over Laura's wheelchair and gave her a warm hug. "I'll see myself out. I know you've got to go to work."

Turning into the Seventh Precinct, I could see Dwight's car parked next to the building. I waved to the Sergeant at the desk and he told me Dwight was free and expecting me as he buzzed me inside the detective section. This might not be good. Usually, Dwight didn't bother clearing his schedule for me.

Sitting in his glass enclosed office, he motioned me in. "I've got good news and bad news. First, let me take possession of my well-earned cookies," he said reaching out for the bag.

As he took the cookies from me, I decided to start on a positive note, "Laura says 'Hi' and she's going to be contacting you for a get together."

"She's a fine woman. Now, down to business." No chitchat this morning from the Lieutenant. "After Vice did their targeted arrests last night, we do have a witness who gave us a good description of someone who parked behind Harvey's vehicle. Both men got out of their cars and proceeded to have a yelling match. The witness didn't stick around but took time to note the make and model on the car which was parked behind Harvey's vehicle. She's helped us do a sketch of the man shouting at Harvey. We recognized him."

"Who was it? Does the car he used match him to his vehicle registration?"

"Before we get into that, what were you doing following Arnold Van Antwerp last night?"

Yikes, busted. "I had information he was a close associate of my client and not entirely trustworthy. I thought he might be involved in the case."

"And you didn't think to tell me this yesterday?" A vein pulsed in Dwight's forehead.

"I didn't realize it would be pertinent to the investigation until later in the day. How did you know I followed Arnold?"

Opening his desk drawer, Dwight laid out several pictures clearly showing my Pontiac Bonneville and me sitting outside Carl's and then later at the Boston-Edison home. They even had pics of me driving away from Arnold's condominium.

"Don't feel bad you didn't notice being followed. The IRS has some of the best investigators around plus the latest tech equipment, and they have the backing of the FBI in this case since an arrest is imminent. The IRS is like the Pinkertons—they always get their man no matter how long it takes. Since Arnold lives in the Seventh Precinct, we received courtesy notification from the FBI and IRS yesterday they would be in the area closely surveilling him and his acquaintances for the next twenty-four hours. They came to me early this morning and showed me the pictures to see if I knew who was spoiling their investigation."

"Did you know Lorraine was involved with Arnold and didn't say anything to me?" I asked.

"Not until this morning when I saw the pictures of Lorraine and Arnold exiting Carl's Chop House. Stay away from Arnold. The IRS made their case and now he's the chief suspect in Harvey's' murder. We'll be bringing him in this morning. We also have another witness in custody who might take a deal and promised crucial information."

"Got it. Have a nice day, Dwight," I hustled out of the precinct and called Lorraine on my mobile phone.

She picked up after one ring. "Tell me the police closed the investigation."

"We need to meet now. I'd rather not talk by phone." The IRS or FBI probably had a tap on her phone. "Meet me at the International House of Pancakes on Jefferson. The one Anita Baker and her husband own after they tore down Little Harry's restaurant."

"Geez, what's the rush?"

"Just do it, the faster the better." The feds couldn't set anything up quickly enough to monitor our conversation.

"Okay, meet you in ten minutes."

I arrived at IHOP in five minutes, grabbed a table, and ordered two coffees. Facing the door, I observed Lorraine enter the restaurant. We were alone except for the staff. The customer parking lot contained only our two cars.

I didn't wait until she sat completely down. "It's over. There's a chief suspect in the investigation and an arrest is about to be made."

"Wow, fast work Bonnie. Who did it?"

"Arnold and let me tell you he is not the man you thought he was."

Moving suddenly forward in her seat and looking at me fiercely, Lorraine said, "This is all wrong. Did you do something to mess up all my planning?" Strange, she didn't seem to appreciate her husband's suspected murderer had been found and now the insurance company and banks would release Harvey's funds.

"I found out he needed money for his campaign for attorney general and thought you might be getting taken for a ride or worse so I followed him last night and saw him in the loving embrace of a young woman. He's cheating on you."

"So, did Harvey. I selected Arnold for my future and looked forward to being a political wife and Arnold's connections would have been good for my new business. I could have dealt with his indiscretions. Men will be men, after all."

So much for true love and matchmaking. This was about two greedy individuals on the take from each other and others for financial and political gain.

"Wait a minute, Bonnie. How did this get from Arnold with another woman to Arnold being arrested for murder?"

"The Seventh Precinct found a witness who placed him at the scene having an argument with Harvey shortly before he was shot. They also have another witness who may have seen more. Did Arnold tell you anything about this?"

"Sounds like a poor case and probably with dubious witnesses. No, Arnold never said anything to me about an argument with Harvey," she said looking away from me and down at her purse.

I wasn't going to tell her about the FBI and IRS monitoring Arnold. She'd know soon enough and Dwight would expect me to keep this piece of information confidential. Time to end my association with Lorraine for good. My sixth sense tingled down my back plus Lorraine's statements and behavior didn't add up.

"I've completed my part of our agreement. You can hand over that two-thousand-dollar bonus."

"Not on your life. You didn't do anything to deserve it. The police did the work," she said as she stood up ready to leave.

I jumped out of my seat as she tried to brush past me. Grabbing her arm and yanking her back, her purse fell to the floor and the contents spilled out with a metallic clunk. Eyeing several rolls of bills but more importantly a Smith and Wesson 38 Chief Special, I pounced on the gun as Lorraine fell on top of me struggling to get it out of my hand. I quickly overcame her and wrestled her to the floor while twisting her arms behind her back. I yelled at the gaping server staff to call 911 for a murder suspect.

I secured Lorraine with the cuffs I always carry in my purse and sat her back in a chair as we waited for the cops. I left the money rolls and purse on the floor as evidence and kept the gun on her.

My cellphone rang the entire fight. Keeping a close eye on Lorraine while making a dial back, the call went to Dwight.

"In case you are going to meet with Lorraine, I wanted to warn you. The second witness says a woman matching Lorraine's description got out of the car during the argument and shot Harvey twice. Both then quickly took off in Arnold's car. Keep away from her."

"You're a little late. I'm at the IHOP waiting for the police with Lorraine secured and a 38 special I'm sure is going to match the bullets found in Harvey. You might want to send your detectives on the call also."

"God damn it, Bonnie. You end up in the middle of everything. Stay safe until we get there."

Smiling, I put down the phone. "Looks like they have you identified as the shooter. Why would you extort me into investigating the case if you killed him?"

"You think you're so smart, figure it out," Lorraine answered. Which was almost a confession but not quite. Murderers don't tell you everything once they're caught like on my favorite show, *Murder She Wrote*.

The police and Dwight arrived in no time and took my statement and led Lorraine away. Dwight told me the Boston-Edison woman had been identified as the wife of a notorious mobster who had ties to Arnold for fixing cases.

The most likely scenario was that Arnold pressured Lorraine for money for his campaign and Lorraine wanted Harvey dead so she could have access to his substantial funds to give to Arnold, develop her business, and become a future political wife. They followed Harvey, knowing his late-night predilections, and took the opportunity to shoot him in a high crime area and let the blame fall on prostitutes and pimps. Once the investigation bogged down, Lorraine tried to use me to get the investigation closed quickly thinking I'd be under her control and still the nerdy, malleable person from high school. Guess again, Lorraine.

The Case of the Fractured Mirror
Debra Bliss Saenger

The owner of a less-than-thriving private investigation business had headed out the office door feet first. After twenty years of hunting down errant husbands and wives, lost dogs, and other assorted oddball jobs, his ticker gave out. His less-than-exciting cases couldn't have caused the last heart attack. But it might have been the bottles of gin and snack wrappers stashed in his drawer.

Soon afterward, his children put the business up for sale. The owner, a former cop who had covered a downtown beat in a North Carolina city, then retired and shifted to private investigative work. He operated out of a small office in a town off the Blue Ridge Parkway. It was his last stint, and my first foray into the world of being a PI.

As his offshoots cleared out the trash, that's where I came in—literally. I was running down the street, squeezing in my morning four-miler, and saw the "Private Investigative Services" sign for sale. It might have been lit up and in neon because it sure caught my attention.

I paused and peered through the front window of the street-front building. It was difficult to see anything because pollen and dirt had crusted on the front window. Two young adults, who turned out to be the dead owner's kids, unlocked the door so I could look inside. I stepped over the threshold.

By the end of the week, I had plunked down a sizable chunk of my savings to buy the business. The office lease and the client list were mine, including, apparently, the front desk administrative assistant. She came with a year-long contract and an attitude.

The office walls reeked of tobacco smoke, and the rank smell assaulted my nose at first. But after sitting immersed between the resin-leached walls for the past week, I must have become immune to it. I stacked the chipped ceramic ashtrays and overdue bills into a pile in the room's corner, and put an "Open" sign in the window. I was ready for business.

Okay, I didn't want to be a private investigator. I wanted to be a hotshot detective, not a PI, spending my days and nights hunting for trace evidence and chasing down leads. Yeah, wearing the side holster with a badge tucked in my pocket—the real deal.

But there were no detective positions in the backwater town where my mother lived, in the Appalachian Mountains. The same place where she reared me after my father passed, swatting my bottom when I misbehaved. Getting by in an old house with a fridge ready to gasp its last breath every time you opened it.

Yeah, kind of like my mother's condition now.

I retired from the Army's investigative service last year, after reaching my 20-year milestone. I didn't expect to retire so soon, but there wasn't a choice. My mother was in the last mile of a marathon, trying to beat cancer. In her third round of chemo, there was the possibility that the finish line for her wasn't too far away. But if she had a chance, I wanted to be there.

My first two and a half months as a private investigator had me spitting out cases that helped cover my bills. I didn't even have to lift a finger or leave my desk for the first case. A law office hired me to work on an issue they couldn't resolve.

While administering the will of an 83-year-old deceased woman, the lawyer could not locate her beneficiary. Her daughter inherited over seven acres of decent tobacco-growing land, along with a drying barn. Who wouldn't want to kick back and live off the land?

The lawyer employed me to locate her daughter, whose relationship with the deceased mother was more than strained. According to him, the daughter had taken off on the back of her boyfriend's motorcycle. This was ten years earlier, and no one had seen her since.

After searching the internet, social media sites, and public databases, I found her hunkered down in Columbus, Ohio. She was using a different last name. For that quick search, the lawyer's office paid me a fat fee for her address.

The following case proved to be another breeze. The client even insisted on paying me in advance. An eccentric older man wanted me on the hook because I looked downright reluctant to take the case. He was a decent judge of character because he wanted to engage me to find his lost dog. Yawn. Not my dream case. Playing the role of an animal control officer did not excite me. I must say, though, that the cash deposited in my account excited me.

The hound had taken off the week before and not returned. I captured the scallywag as she gulped down the last bit of dog food I left as bait in a cage near her old haunts. But that was only after I had released a raccoon, a skunk, and a feral cat that the food had tempted. Another creature made off with the dog chow without triggering the door catch, but that theft case remained unsolved. Case closed.

These cases discouraged me. They were less exciting than a sleeping pill. My hours chasing down a daughter and a dog barely paid the rent but offered little else. With minimal investigative work, there was one small bonus. I had plenty of time to take my mother to the clinic for her treatments.

Over the next few months, the stress of keeping a new business afloat grew. The cases barely covered my bills, and I even considered retrieving the ashtrays from the back bin and taking up smoking. I needed a break and an interesting case. Pronto.

Then a woman stepped through the door, peering around the front of the office. She looked to be in her early forties, with auburn-red hair slicked back into a scarf. Her light blue eyes, pale skin, and hair color made her look otherworldly, almost like a zombie from the movies. She intrigued me.

Even the woman's blue eyes seemed ghostly, sunken into her face, which gave her a haunted look. Every limb on her body seemed to twitch, and I wondered if she was part of the drug crowd every community harbors, even here in the mountains. A thought crossed my mind. Maybe I'm her next victim. After all, it looked like a druggie might have found her way to my doorstep. I patted my jacket to be sure my holster held a gun tucked nearby.

It turned out that looks could be deceiving, and first impressions were not always right on the nose. Carla displayed every tic in the book, but she was understandably just plain nervous. I saw her approach my office administrator.

Standing before Lee, the client shifted from one foot to the other. Like I said, she was a nervous Nelly.

"I need your help," the woman told Lee. "My name is Carla Reilly, and I want to find someone."

Lee was my go-to assistant. She was part of the business purchase, along with the office furnishings. She had worked for my predecessor, and there was never any talk of her leaving when I took over the company.

Nothing flustered her. Even when her former boss fell to the floor, dead, she calmly picked up the phone to call 911. She handled the front office like a speed bump, barring anyone who wasn't a paying customer. Beware, her body language told everyone. I listened and kept her on. She was a gem.

Lee ushered Carla to a seat and had her fill out new client forms. With the build of a linebacker, my administrative assistant barely fit behind the desk. Besides fielding phone calls, she directed lost citizens who mistook our office for the post office next door. I relied on her experience and formidable presence.

With her help, I could finally focus on getting a foothold in the community so my PI work could grow. Maybe even expand beyond cases involving dogs and daughters. Lee had many talents, and she could juggle the bills without having enough resources to pay them like a pro.

Lee was a valuable asset because she knew everyone in this town, including the surrounding counties. Heck, she seemed to know everybody—except the person signing in. Carla was a stranger to her. She waved the woman back to my office.

"My mother is missing."

Carla's voice was so soft, it sounded like a whisper in a confessional.

I leaned in to hear her better. Meanwhile, her heel tapped on the floor like a drum as she sat across from me. In her clenched hand, the completed forms rustled. With a burst of emotion, she gulped as she held a tissue to her nose. She finally continued.

"We live in Bradford County, and she's been missing for over a week. The sheriff's office put out a notice, but that's all."

I reached for her forms and scanned the paperwork.

"It looks like your mother lived here for sixteen years?" I asked. Carla nodded. "And you recently came to live with her?" Carla nodded, and I continued. "Do you think she may be with other family members without you knowing?"

Carla folded her arms and spoke louder.

"She would let me know. We are close, especially since my father died during his military service."

I leaned back to consider this. Taking a gander at the woman sitting across the desk from me, I observed Carla's appearance. Despite her worn clothing, she appeared clean-cut, with manicured fingernails. She was nervous as a caged dog, but seemed earnest. And Lee had given me the nod that it appeared the woman's down payment check for services would clear the bank. This client might be legit after all.

Scanning the paperwork, I dove in to flesh out some details. And I thought back to when I first encountered a military uniform and a funeral. Even though it was long ago, the memories stayed vivid.

My Pops' Army uniform remained in my mother's hall closet, wrapped in a dry cleaner's plastic. He had died during the Iraq War, supporting the troops as a supply clerk. And he was one of the first casualties when a cargo load slipped and hit him on the head. I was seven years old and determined he could do no wrong.

Okay, maybe he wished I were a boy instead of a girl, but that did not deter him from taking me hunting and fishing. Together, we even took a battered drill to build a lemonade stand for me. But then he left for a deployment and never returned.

I stood at his funeral in a dark dress, wearing fancy shoes that pinched my toes. The minister droned on, and then three loud rounds from a military salute completed the brief ceremony. Pops was now a name on a headstone for me.

The day of his funeral was bitterly cold, and I could not stop shivering. Goosebumps covered my arms and back, and I had to shake my limbs to keep warm. But I never could shake off the cold, because his death dug a hole in my life as deep as his grave.

Joining the Army was a simple decision when I turned eighteen. Working at the local dollar store didn't appeal to me, and I wanted to get out of town. I intended to enlist in my father's division of the military, but I ended up in another branch. After taking a series of tests, the U.S. Army Military Police School admitted me, and I graduated with the skills to conduct thorough investigations and maintain law and order on base.

My five tours ranged from Georgia to Texas, and I arrested drunk soldiers, carted off abusive spouses, and kept occupants in housing from running the on-base stop signs. In one case, I worked with others to investigate a warehouse theft. We pulled in five enlisted bad boys who were selling merchandise to locals on the side. It turned out they were also tagging those same sources to distribute meth for a gang based in the next-largest city. Now that was excitement, and the perps ended up busted on all counts.

My nickname was "Reddy." It came from my hair, which was ginger-colored and cut to chin length per military regulations. The name also spoke to my desire for action. But less than twenty years later, I ended up back here, in my small hometown. Yes, my hair was longer, but my desire for action still went beyond what the county offered. I hoped my private investigative work would spice up my caregiving role, while still earning me a living wage.

So far, that had not been the case. But little did I know that Carla, sitting before me, would help push my private investigative business in a different direction. Still, her twitches made me nervous, and I attempted to calm her down to get the facts.

What was her mother's name? Where was she last seen? What was her last known address? What was her height? Weight? Photo? What were the places she frequented?

Carla pulled out her cellphone and texted me a photo of the two of them against a mountain backdrop. Both the people and the location looked familiar, but I could not immediately place them. The area wasn't far from this town, and I recognized the lookout spot where tourists took selfies. It wasn't far from my mother's more-than-modest home either.

I had worked with less information. And Carla looked like her mother, with longer hair and a lighter complexion. The mother was wearing a green sweatshirt in the photo boasting "Asheville" on the front, the same hometown as my mother. It was a start.

I spelled out my advance costs to Carla, and she didn't blink. It looked like I might cover this month's rent after all. I took a deep breath. That would lessen the stress of opening an office and keeping the business going.

"Please," she said in a pleading voice as she stood up. "I need to find my mother soon. I am so worried about her—if she is safe." She wrote her cellphone number and email address on one of my business cards and pushed it toward me.

I pocketed the card and reassured her.

"I'll email you each day to let you know my progress. Don't worry, we'll get on this right away."

Three days later, I found Carla's mother. It took me two extra days because the county clerk's office was closed for the weekend. By that Monday, I had the information I needed. In setting up a meeting with Carla, I picked a specific site on the outskirts of town.

Carla stood waiting for me at the designated spot. She had tied her hair back, but the mountain winds whipped strands of her reddish hair across her face. She stood ramrod-straight next to the iron gate.

By her side, my assistant, Lee, held her arm. I was glad that she comforted Carla, although surprised to see her out of the office. I didn't complain. After all, referrals and repeat business would keep us going.

"I'm glad you found this place," I said, greeting Carla. "It's a little far from my office."

Carla nodded as she reached into her pocket and pulled out a tissue. She dabbed it over her eyes as she silently wept. Lee moved to edge her through the gate. I followed them as we made our way up the stone path, stopping at a freshly dug grave.

"It's my mother, isn't it?" Carla choked out the words as sobs shook her body.

I nodded. After all, seeing is believing, and apparently Carla was here last week to witness this burial. That was according to the minister I interviewed on the phone this morning. The county clerk's office verified that Carla's mother had passed recently. The cause of death was cancer.

I rooted through my handbag for an extra tissue to give to Carla. Instead, I drew out a small hand mirror with a crack formed down the middle from years of use. In its reflection, I stared at my face.

Startled, I almost dropped the mirror. The tissue floated onto the cemetery grounds. The image staring back at me was Carla. I was seeing the world through her blue eyes. My body shivered and twitched with nervousness as I realized she was me, and her body was my body.

The trauma of returning home to a sick parent, opening a business, and tending to my mother had taken its toll. Reluctantly, I had to accept the demise of my last remaining parent within the past week. Although the hope was to keep my mother going for many more months, my mother unexpectedly died during her second-to-last chemo treatment.

Lee reached down to leave a small bouquet at the gravesite, took my arm, and tucked it gently under hers. "Time to say goodbye?"

I nodded. As my body collapsed, I braced my weight against her. We headed toward the parking lot, leaving the cemetery behind us. This case was closed, and Carla was gone, but the mirror said otherwise. It was time for me to do my own reflecting. I had to stand on my own two feet. But I sure was going to miss depositing Carla's payment.

Danno and the Shadyside Butcher
Kathleen Marple Kalb

Nine days out of ten, P.I.'s spend their days researching and making phone calls. And then there's the tenth.

That fall day in 1987, the ink was barely dry on my license and gun permit when a slim gentleman walked into the Golden Triangle Investigations office. His three-piece charcoal wool suit was immaculately tailored, as was his pale pink oxford and deeper rose silk jacquard tie, both harmonizing with the pinstripes. Of course, this was decades before we talked about LGBTQIA+ and pronouns, and in steely, scruffy Pittsburgh, the outfit might as well have been a float in the Pride Parade.

"May I help you?" I asked. My boss, Mr. K, mostly treated me as an equal, but since I was the one with secretarial training, I handled the receptionist duties, sitting at the front desk and greeting our few visitors.

Mr. K kept the books and always made the first pot of coffee, so it was fairer than it sounds.

"Are you Diana Czednik?" the visitor asked, pulling out one of my brand-new business cards, emblazoned with my name and title of Junior Investigator.

"Dany," I said, holding out my hand to shake. True, I'd been born with the same name as the Princess, but no one would confuse me as anything regal: half-Irish, half-Polish, all hardscrabble ambition to do better than the limited life offered girls in Big Run, a hundred miles and a world away from the Steel City. If not for the recession and missing out on a scholarship, I'd have a law degree instead of two-thirds of one and be an assistant DA or associate at a big firm right now.

But the universe has a way of putting us where we belong.

"Mark McKinnon." He took my hand with a firm but not crushing shake and gave me a warm smile. "We have a mutual friend—Gary Bigelow?"

One of my two roommates, my brother from another mother, and as closeted as this man was out.

"Yes." I nodded, indicating the guest chair. "Do you work at Industrial Bank, too?"

"Honey, do I look like a banker?" He laughed as he sat, a down-to-earth guffaw in sharp contrast to his fabulous outfit.

"I guess not." I couldn't help laughing too, even as I wondered what he was thinking of me in my olive polyester Dress Barn sale suit, which didn't do much for either my pale skin or my tall but chunky frame. Not to mention my latest mishap with home hair color.

To his credit, he gave no sign of judging. "Banking is definitely not my thing. I'm the artistic director at the Versailles Arts Center."

He pronounced it Ver-SALES, the way people do around here, but with a little cringe that told me he wasn't a local. Probably came here for the job, which likely let him live within a relatively safe and accepting bubble.

Well, it *was* safe and accepting until bad things started happening in Shadyside.

"Would you like some coffee?" I asked.

"Best not. I'm having enough trouble sleeping as it is."

"Fair enough. How can I help you?"

"Are you following the Shadyside Butcher case?"

"Um, yes, of course." The murder series had only received its lurid moniker after the third man was found scattered among several dumpsters across the city several days after he was last seen at a gay hangout in Shadyside.

It had taken until that third death for the less-than-enlightened Pittsburgh PD to get interested, too. In Shadyside, though, the closest the city had to a gay-friendly neighborhood, the first killing had cast a chill that had only deepened in the following months. Six months now…but three days since the latest victim was found.

Gary, whose partner was even more on the down-low than he, only went out in large groups now, when he went out at all. And I worried about him.

Damn right I was following the case.

"Good," said my visitor. "That makes it a lot easier. Your friend and I—and a few others—were talking and decided it was time to bring in some help."

"I can't argue."

"I suspect if it were steelworkers, or more to the point, police sergeants, being butchered and sprinkled across the city, they would not have waited for a third body before starting a task force."

"Probably true," I admitted. "But they have, now, and they're everywhere." While my friends and I could not afford to live in Shadyside, the closest bus stop to our rundown Oakland rental was there—and the area was now crawling with cops.

"And you really think they'll solve it?" he asked.

"You think I will?" I asked, wondering the hell what Gary had told him. As much as I'd love to stop the guy, I know my limits. I watch *Spenser: for Hire*, I don't live it. I'm very good at the precise, dogged work of researching financials, records, and such—two years of law school comes in handy—and charming people into telling me things, but that's as far as it goes. Even if I have a gun and know how to use it.

"I think you actually care, which puts you ahead of the cops."

"Well, that much is true." I tried to sound confident. "Did Gary tell you how this works?"

"Seventy-five a day plus expenses, two-day minimum." He sounded like he'd memorized the agency rate card.

"And final approval from the agency founder, Danno."

Mr. K stood in the doorway, back from checking out an accident scene in an insurance case, an edge in his usually friendly voice. His sharp green eyes flicked over Mark McKinnon with something that could have been concern, annoyance…or worse.

More than six months ago, Mr. K had hired me on the spot because I was the first person TempStar sent over who could pronounce his name: Koziekiewicz. It's Koz-a-KEV-ich, easy for someone with a Polish grandma. Once he found out I had most of a law degree, an immigrant-daughter work ethic, and a country girl's comfort with guns, he urged me to consider training to become a PI. And I turned out to be good at it.

Mr. K calls me Danno, a joking reference to *Hawaii Five-O*. He is kind of the McGarrett—the craggy and experienced older statesman. But he actually has a pretty good sense of humor. Most of the time.

"Hi, Mr. K," I said. "Mr. McKinnon wants to hire me to look into the Shadyside Butcher case."

"Oh, he does?" His dubious expression sharpened as he held out a hand to our visitor. "Last name's Koziekiewicz. Miss Czdenik is a newly-licensed junior investigator. I'm not entirely certain I want her involved in a murder inquiry yet."

"I completely understand." McKinnon shook Mr. K's hand. "We're just looking for some leads to take to the police. And I believe an open-minded young woman is more likely to be successful than the judgmental types we've seen investigating."

"You may be right there," Mr. K said, his tone still a bit harsher than necessary. "But I don't want a new investigator on the front lines."

"I understand."

"No crime scene work. No bodyguarding," Mr. K said. "And you pay the retainer up front."

"Fair enough."

"All right, then. She'll start by doing a records check on the victims…"

Ten minutes later, the paperwork was done, McKinnon had gone on his way, and Mr. K and I were re-upping on coffee.

"You sure you want to do this?" he asked.

Something in his tone bothered me. While he was an old-school standup guy like my grandfather and uncle, even to the same dapper dress style of tweed blazers and wing tips, he had never seemed remotely prejudiced. His best friend is a Black police lieutenant, and I'd never heard so much as a mild slur of any kind from him. He'd even met Gary. But older guys are sometimes kind of weird about openly gay men, especially considering AIDS and everything right now. I really hoped he wasn't.

"Do you have a problem with gay people?" I asked. Might as well know.

"No, Danno." Mr. K topped up my cup. "I have a problem with my young investigator taking on a multiple murder case."

"You sure didn't like McKinnon," I said.

"Because he's dragging you into something very dangerous." Mr. K held my gaze. Took a breath. "Look, Danno. I don't have a problem with gays. I do have a problem with the way the world looks at them. My brother volunteered to go to Korea and got himself killed because my father was more comfortable with a dead hero than a live sissy. That's what we called it then."

"I'm sorry," I said. "I didn't know…"

"Why would you? The point is, it's been a longish life and I've buried more than a few people. And I'm not going to bury you because you're trying to play Sherlock. Got it?"

"Got it."

"Good. Now, get on the horn and start checking records on those poor guys. This kind of thing doesn't just happen. They have something in common…and when you find it, you can point the cops to the killer."

I would have felt a lot more confident of that if my contact at the PD hadn't responded to my request for info with: "So you want the book on the queens of Shadyside, huh?"

* * *

The evening found me in the worn-down Victorian parlor of my shared apartment, going through the records, with the "help" of our rescue kitty Lambert, a giant fluffy gray tabby named, of course, for the legendary Steelers linebacker. I'd laid three piles out on the footlocker that served as a coffee table, one for each victim: Dave Coyne, 26, associate at Smith, Lanyard, last seen alive at Cinnabunz Bakery early on a Sunday morning; Tony Wisnewski, 25, sous chef at La Baronne, last seen at the Dance Furnace on a Saturday night; and Allen Maitland, 27, a legislative assistant to a state senator, who disappeared after midnight pancakes at Garofalo's Diner, also in the middle of a weekend.

What was left of them appeared a few days later, in several different dumpsters across the neighborhood. No apparent rhyme or reason to the dump sites, nothing special about the trash bags. The dismemberments were relatively clean, but not especially professional—something a hunter could do.

Not unique around here, where about three-quarters of the males over twelve have a rifle, orange camo vest and hunting knife.

"How's it going?" Gary asked, as he handed me a plate of pierogies.

We're both half-Polish, and while the frozen ones from the grocery store aren't as good as grandma's, they'll do for a fast, cheap weeknight meal. He'd cooked up a big box for us, and our roommate Berniece, a resident at East End Hospital, due home soon from a sixteen-hour shift.

"Thanks," I said, dipping my finger in the sour cream topping and giving Lambert first dibs, as expected. "And thanks for the case."

"Glad to." He sat down on the other end of the ancient, battered hobnail leather couch that had come with the apartment. "Some of the fellas were at Cinnabunz Sunday morning talking about this whole mess and decided it was time to bring in our own help. So of course, I thought of you."

"Thanks. I hope I can help. These guys deserved better."

"Roadkill got better," Gary said, an angry cast to his usually cheerful face. "If somebody'd been butchering the Steelers instead of the queens of Shadyside, the cops would have done a lot more."

"No argument." I took a bite of pierogie. "You're going to make someone a lovely wife one day."

"I can only hope."

We laughed together.

"Anyhow," I said, putting down the plate for a moment, "here's what I know. They all disappeared between Saturday night and Sunday morning, all last seen in a three-block area of Shadyside."

"That's interesting."

"A little. But serial killers usually stick to a particular area and a particular type of victim, so…"

"So it doesn't really get us much of anywhere."

"No. Maybe their jobs. Coyne was with a white shoe law firm, Maitland a pol on the way up…and Wisnewski cooked where the power people eat. The suspect might run in fancy circles."

"Plenty of guys on the down-low in the high end," Gary said. "Make all the right family-values noises during the day and pick up a rent boy at night."

"Which is true, but our victims were not rent boys," I reminded him.

Gary nodded. "These were men on the way up."

"True." I picked up the credit reports, almost forgiving my police contact his bias for his help in sending over copies of the paperwork. "And they lived like it. Bar charges from Dance Furnace, opera tickets, clothes from the high-end shops at Oxford Centre."

"Guy works at Smith, Lanyard isn't going to dress from Kaufman's basement," Gary said. Most of his—and mine and Berniece's—clothes came from there.

"Well, yeah."

I looked from report to report as Lambert moved on from me to Gary, who offered a taste from his plate.

As the cat licked sour cream from Gary's finger, making happy slurping noises, I noticed something.

"You realize Coyne and Lawrence both banked at Industrial?" I asked Gary, holding out the credit records.

He put his plate down and took the papers.

"Not just Industrial. That's the private banking code. They had to have at least a million dollars. What about Wisnewski?"

"No. He banked at Pittsburgh National."

"I guess it makes sense." Gary picked up his plate again, just in time to avoid a full-out cat attack. "The other two come from money, right?"

"Yeah. Maitland appears to be from the Gateway Steel Maitlands. And Coyne's family owns a bunch of grocery stores."

"So both have a fortune. Or maybe get an allowance from a trust."

"Is that how it works?" I asked.

"It can. Depends on the family, corporate structures, all kinds of things. What about Wisnewski?"

"He bought his clothes at the same places, and he's almost maxed. He doesn't have the bar or entertainment charges."

"Hmm." Gary thought for a moment. "He's the one who was gorgeous, right?"

"Tough to tell from the license photos, but I think you're right."

"Okay, so that makes sense. He didn't need money."

"What's up?" Berniece asked, walking in the door, looking tired and miserable, no glow to her coffee-colored skin, far from her usual bright-eyed ambitious self. She was on her oncology rotation, so no surprise there.

"Pierogies," I said.

"With a side of the Shadyside Butcher," Gary added. "Our PI is pitching in."

"About time somebody did," Berniece went straight to the kitchenette. "Potatoes in pasta. White people are weird."

"If it weren't so good," Gary replied, continuing our usual joking wrangle.

"Well, there's that." She loaded a plate, including a separate dab of sour cream to offer Lambert. "So somebody hired you to look for the Butcher? Scary."

"His friend," I nodded to Gary. "And Mr. K's only letting me do research and funnel leads to the cops."

"You really think that's going to help?" Berniece asked.

"Better than leaving it to the old straight boys," Gary said.

"And you never know what you might find in records," I added, picking up the page of overexposed copies of the licenses, studying them as I chewed on a pierogie. Yes, white people are weird, but if there's anything more comforting than the little pockets of pasta filled with mashed potato, topped with sour cream and fried onions, I don't know what it is. Maybe it was the thought of family comfort that made me notice it.

"Oh, hell," I said. "Gary, look at this."

"Coyne's middle name was Maitland," he read.

"Coincidence?"

"Cops—and PI's—hate 'em." It's one of the first lessons Mr. K taught me.

"Maitland?" Berniece asked, walking in from the kitchen, looking a bit less ragged with a plate of pierogies in hand. "Speaking of coincidences…there's a Mr. Maitland on the ward right now. Must be a big muckety-muck—he's got a private room, security, the whole deal."

"What's his name?" I asked.

"Laird Maitland."

"Our guy was Allen Laird Maitland." I looked at the records. "So we've got two victims with similar names who have a lot of money."

"Unless white people are weirder than I think, it's not a common name, either." Berniece settled into her chair, and Lambert swaggered over, purring in anticipation of his treat.

"It's not," Gary said. "As far as I know, the only Maitlands around here all have some connection to the steel clan."

"Well, he doesn't seem to have a lot of people holding his hand. I've only seen a guy who looks like a lawyer…and a grandson who's a real jerk."

"Know his name?" I asked.

"Johnny, I think. Rude to everyone—especially anyone darker than beige." Berniece gave the cat an ear scratch. "Only seen him a couple times. Got the sense he can't wait to see the old man go. It's sad."

"Ugh." Gary shook his head. "When my granddad died, we filled the house for a week, making sure he was surrounded by people who loved him."

"That's the way," Berniece said. "Rotten family."

"Well, if the patriarch is dying," I said, returning to PI business because I didn't want to talk about my own losses, "there's going to be more money flowing through the family tree."

"But where does the middle guy, Wisnewski, fit in?" Gary asked.

I had a theory about that, but I didn't want to ruin everyone's appetite.

* * *

Next morning, Saturday, I started the day at the big Beaux-Arts Carnegie Library, appropriately on the border of Shadyside. It took a couple of hours of searching the *Who's Who* volumes and microfilms of old *Pittsburgh Post-Gazette* social pages, but I managed to cobble together a pretty good Maitland family tree—and print up a picture of my potential suspect.

Before I took off for Cinnabunz and Garofalo's Diner, a few streets away, I called home and caught Berniece on her way out the door for another shift, asking her to let me know if the jerk grandson showed up.

I got the answers I was hoping for at Cinnabunz and Garafalo's, as well as a couple of overpriced cups of coffee on Mark McKinnon's dime. But I knew, based on that comment from my police contact, it was going to take a good bit more than a theoretical motive and a couple of tentative ID's.

First of all, it would take a nighttime visit to the Dance Furnace.

Gary was more than happy to come out with me, though he flatly refused to let me try out my Madonna wannabee outfit: "You're fabulous, but you don't want to attract attention. Just butch up a little."

Which is how I ended up showing the newspaper photo of Johnny Maitland to the bartender and shouting over high-volume Depeche Mode at the obscenely early hour of ten p-m, wearing my baggy jeans and a *F*ck the Patriarchy* t-shirt.

Nobody was looking at me anyhow.

While the Furnace wasn't at peak yet, it was already the most fabulous—and diverse—crowd in the city, with people of every race, gender, and sexual persuasion showing off their moves to the hottest music.

Even a serial killer couldn't stop this party.

"Guy was around a lot in the fall and winter," the bartender told me, sending Gary a flirtatious smile. No need for him to know Gary was happily partnered.

"Did he give a name?"

"Nope. Paid cash. Not a great tipper," he said as he set up our IC Lights. Iron City Light beer tasted like diluted nail polish remover, but it was the safest and cheapest club drink. I really wanted a Brandy Alexander…but that would almost certainly out me as straight.

I dropped a five in the tip jar. The bartender actually turned his gaze to me.

"Saw him buying drinks for that poor cook, the one who ended up in pieces."

"Really."

"Can't swear it was that night…but can't swear it wasn't, either. Think that'll help with the cops?"

"It might," I said. "Mind if I give your name to the detectives?"

"Fine by me. Anything I can do, you know? It should matter. *We* should matter."

Gary and I nodded. A guy waved at the barkeep and he made a show of pocketing my card, then moved down to his new customer.

We'd been drinking and observing for about ten minutes, trying to work up the nerve to join the hot scene on the floor, when the bartender smacked my arm.

"You know somebody named Berniece?" he asked.

"Yeah."

"She called—told me to tell you 'He's here.'"

"Great. Thank you."

I turned to Gary. "Showtime."

"Just tell me you have your gun in your bag," he replied.

* * *

From the hospital lobby, I made a quick call to Mr. K, knowing he would have much better luck bringing in the cops than I would—even if he would yell at me later.

On the oncology floor, Berniece saw us coming and stifled a snort at our club outfits. She nodded to a private waiting room where two men were sitting. One was about Mr. K's age, plump, graying, and wearing a very plain and very expensive suit. Probably the lawyer.

The other, preppy in khakis and a navy blazer over a polo shirt, was about the same age as the three victims, with an unmistakable air of entitlement. High-end everything, logos and labels carefully visible—even the backpack at his feet, top-of-the line LL Bean. Dark hair moussed up in an expensive style that didn't quite draw attention away from his pudgy jaw.

Johnny Maitland.

Now, the sole surviving male in his generation of Maitlands.

Not by accident.

Gary opened the door and I walked in.

The reek of Johnny's Obsession for Men hit like a smack.

The lawyer looked up at me, more puzzled than bothered. Underrating me, as men so often did.

"Who the hell are you?" Johnny asked.

"My name is Dany Czednick. I'm a private investigator. I know what you did, and I've come to urge you to turn yourself in."

"Screw you, you fat bitch."

Gary, standup guy that he is, took a step toward Johnny to defend me.

Mistake.

Almost forty years later, I'm still not sure whether Johnny grabbed Gary or pulled the knife first. What I do know is, in one breath, we went from zero to life and death.

"Now, what was that about turning myself in?" Johnny Maitland asked, his forearm across Gary's neck, a giant hunting knife in his other hand.

Gary's eyes widened as he realized what that knife had probably been used for.

My job to stay cool. "I've got the financial records right here, Mr. Maitland. I know the first and third victims of the Shadyside Butcher would have shared the Gateway Steel trust with you. And I know staff at the three places the victims were last seen saw you with them. So…"

"You've got nothing!"

As he snapped back, the lawyer finally came to life. "Come along, Johnny…"

"No." He tightened his arm around Gary's neck. "You've got nothing."

Pick something and stick with it, anyway.

But it gave me an opportunity.

"Here," I said, pulling my messenger bag toward the front. "Let me show you. Maybe it's all a misunderstanding."

For the instant I needed, Johnny Maitland waited.

I reached in my bag, but I didn't pull out the documents.

I brought out my .38.

"Let him go." I aimed right between Johnny's eyes.

He blinked. But he didn't let go of Gary.

"Hell no, bitch. I know how this ends. And if I'm going, I'm taking one more of these Shadyside queens with me."

"No, you're not," I replied, amazed that my voice came out cool and steely. "I'm a country girl. I can drill a squirrel's eye at a hundred yards. The only thing stopping me is that I don't want to ruin Gary's good sweater with your brains."

Gary, quite rightly, looked like he was worried about a lot more than his Polo sweater.

Standoff.

Johnny Maitland stared at me, trying to decide just how serious I was. And just how dangerous. I glared back, knowing he was almost entirely sure I wouldn't pull the trigger.

Almost.

His three victims had been at least partly drunk, comfortable with him, had no idea what he was planning. Thought they were safe.

I knew we weren't.

New experience for young Mr. Maitland: a target who was prepared for the fight.

My heart was beating so loud he had to hear it, and the gun seemed to get heavier with every breath. How the hell was I going to get us out of this?

"Take the shot, Danno!"

Mr. K's shout startled Johnny and he turned frantically toward it.

Just enough.

I followed my boss's advice.

* * *

Three hours later, Johnny Maitland was a few floors down having my bullet extracted from his backside. The rest of us were at the police station at the end of the block, sorting it all out. Gary came through without a scratch. So did I, though being printed and paraffin tested didn't do much for my nail polish. (I'd forgotten to take it off for my disguise.)

The detectives on the case weren't thrilled to be shown up, or to have a Maitland as their killer…but they were grateful it was over.

When I finished giving my statement, Mr. K was waiting in the lobby, along with Gary, Berniece, and Mark McKinnon.

"Well, Danno, you got him."

"*We* got him," I said, waving an inky hand to Gary and Berniece.

"So this was all about the Maitland fortune," McKinnon shook his head.

"It was," I said. "Johnny figured if he made it look like something else, they'd be gone and no one the wiser."

"Pretty horrific way to get there," Berniece said.

"Not if you don't think of your victims as people," Gary reminded us. "And I'm pretty sure he didn't."

"Nope." Mr. K shook his head. "Every time I think I've seen the worst people can do, somebody manages to surprise me."

Coming from Mr. K, that was a stopper.

After a breath or two, Gary spoke: "So Tony Wisnewski was just…"

I winced. "He killed him as a misdirect. A man with a few loose connections to the others would throw off all the investigators' calculations."

"And since he was already planning to butcher two men," McKinnon started.

"What's one more?" Mr. K spat the words, disgust dripping from every syllable. "I'm glad we're still a death-penalty state."

No good reply to that.

"Well, thank you Miss Czednik," McKinnon said. "You did a lot of good tonight."

"I sure hope so."

"Oh, you did, Danno." Mr. K gave me a little punch on the arm. "But if you ever pull a scheme like this again…"

"Yeah?" I expected—and honestly deserved, the riot act.

"You'd better bring me along."

"I don't think you'd fit in too well at the Dance Furnace, sir." Gary gave him a shy smile.

"Then I'll smoke outside with the bouncer, son. The whole point of being part of a community is that we work together. No freelancing."

"Community?" Gary asked, giving him as hard a look as he could manage after this night.

"Community." Mr. K nodded. "I may not join you on the float at the parade, but I'm damn sure not going to let anybody prey on you."

"Charming the guests as always, Koz," Lieutenant Hill—also known as Mr. K's best pal—said, walking out from his office and giving us all an impressive glare, ending with special emphasis on me. "You know the department position on civilian investigators?"

"Yes, sir. I came to you as soon as I had verified information." I attempted to look harmless and demure. Not the easiest trick any day, considering my size, but probably a good bit harder in that *F*ck the Patriarchy* shirt.

"All right, get out of here." The lieutenant's tone was gruff, but respectful. "Don't do anything stupid. We're going to need you for the grand jury and probably the trial."

"I'll be there with bells on." McKinnon winked at Hill, who rolled his eyes and nodded at Mr. K, who motioned to the door.

"Book it, Danno," said my boss.

It might not have been a happy ending…but it would certainly do until one came along.

Right as Rain
Wil A. Emerson

The rain hadn't let up for six long days. Not unusual for Detroit. Spring, winter, Detroit sucked. Summer, fall? If you didn't have a place in Michigan's up north territory, you might as well be dead. The humidity and smog could kill you in the Motor City.

Yesterday, Laura Holms had been on the verge of cashing in her savings and buying a little cabin near a lake for a get-away. Now, she felt like shooting herself. Anger drove her hand to her cell phone. One call, a call a Private Investigator or any officer of the law, should never make, would settle this unnerving situation.

* * *

The agony began with the rattle of the entrance door several weeks before.

She checked her Fitbit. Too early for Karl. Her son never arrived before nine. To know he arrived at seven in the morning did not bring happy thoughts. Out all night, something wrong? Emotional or legal, Laura could place a bet on either and win. Then she chuckled. Karl, twenty-five and laid back, the light in her life, made her smile in the middle of a thunderstorm. She tilted her head; he'd open the door to her office any second. The mystery of his early arrival would be over soon.

She turned from the window, but couldn't shake off the eerie feeling about Karl's arrival. At her desk, she scanned the open large ledger. Better to focus on what routine bills were due. Not actually due but soon. Two weeks. Debts now were always paid two weeks ahead of schedule. A means of saying thank you to the few well-heeled clients. A long time coming but she also appreciated those owners of small businesses who needed background checks and employment histories on pending hires. As their businesses grew, she felt as if she'd helped them thrive, had done her part.

What drove her to keep the smaller clients was the fear of having her electricity cut off, collectors hounding her. No, background checks weren't the most satisfying aspect of investigative work, but her bills were paid. Spying on people contradicted the notion of privacy in the work force. But a reliable income was necessary for her survival. Staying on a tight budget, almost guaranteed a little comfort.

Far too long she'd gone without niceties so her one and only child who, no doubt, had come to the office extra early because of a minor inconvenience, would have the best education. First the private grade school, then four years at St. Paul's Catholic High School. By the grace of God or maybe pure luck, some relief came when Karl received a full scholarship to the University of Michigan. Smart kid. Expenses still high for a private investigator's income, though. The rite of passage. His need of a car, pocket money, the right clothes, why deny him spring breaks, had her credit at the limit. She guaranteed he had what she never enjoyed.

Karl did, however, broaden her smile with a double major in Computer Technology and Social Justice. Proud mother at graduation. His goal was to join a law enforcement organization, the FBI or CIA.

'What about the Police Academy,' Laura suggested.

'Don't see myself as a Detroit police officer. Not for me,' he'd said a little too quickly.

That was a wound that didn't heal well for Laura. It was what she had wanted but didn't make the cut.

Why not give him time to sort out his likes and dislikes. No need to rush into a dead-end job if the required work didn't fit the larger picture.

Well, his picture got smaller as each month went by and his rent went unpaid. And Laura went further in debt. A broke P.I. and a disappointed mother. Enough to make her want to drink but back then she couldn't afford good bourbon.

Three months, fall setting in, the dark, gloomy winter days ahead and she'd had enough.

"You have to get a job. A real job."

"Why don't I work for you," he'd said.

Lightbulb on. Why not?

Laura let her less than ambitious son use the small filing room in the building she rented for her detective agency. In no time Karl had set up a newer, better system for files, bought several computers at bargain prices, bought burner cell phones for clients who needed confidentiality. To her surprise, he'd turned the closet space into what now looked like a hacker's network.

The office layout and his computer savvy wasn't the contribution Laura anticipated, but Karl's technology skills soon aided her investigations and brought in more clients. Those who needed deeper background checks, benefit searches and a cadre of other detailed services that traditional Private Investigative Agencies didn't have time for. Those new clients paid Karl's salary. Good fortune, ongoing for five years. The other benefit, she didn't have to meddle in the trivial nature of his side of the business.

Laura's intention had always been to handle more meaty investigations, those unsolved murders or disappearance cases, the ones that fell through the cracks with the police. The cold cases where families of means paid big dollars for worthy information. And in doing so, she contributed to a noble cause. Justice for the victims.

But she wasn't one to shy away from reality. Equality rights or not, the traditional agencies, run by men, got the best jobs because of their alliance with police departments. Many of them former police officers. Department heads expected brawn and a moderate degree of brains. The fact *she* wasn't by any measure a hard-core *dick* seemed to stand between her and those heftier investigations. No need to argue, she wouldn't win the battle.

Even with four years of military service, three with the military police in Fort Bragg, North Carolina, where she wrestled with too many disorderly marines who were also in training to be killers, her efforts didn't count. Detroit Police Academy didn't want her. Thus, she wasn't a seasoned police officer turned private detective who took on wealthy clients.

For the previous ten years, what she had on her side were mostly heartbroken women who paid dearly to catch a cheating husband in the act. Short on cash they contracted any private investigator who'd take their paltry offering. She took those cases to pay half the rent. About a quarter of her clientele were gender neutral looking for lost relatives, run-aways. The rest were a mish mash of disputes, aggravations and those cherished cold cases. Those cases were a crap shoot as far as income.

Up until Karl joined forces with her, Laura never turned away the smallest case. Within a short span, with his skills as a cyber spy, the majority of her cases became worthy and lucrative. That was the *big time* in her book.

Sure, Karl coming in early meant he was probably spewing over an emotional flair up with his wife. He'd get over it. Laura wasn't rushing in to 'rescue' her adult son anymore.

She looked out the window again. A zig-zag of lightening, deafening thunderclap, the rain in torrents. It took her back to another life-changing day.

The phone rang as she was about to close the office and she hesitated before answering. The clouds were heavy, she had planned to work out at the gym in her apartment building and a combination of not getting soaked on her walk and a need to burn off a chicken quesadilla with sour cream and refried beans prompted her to ignore the ring. At the door, a thunder cloud rolled over and then cracked open. Seconds later lightning made the electricity sputter. The subsequent roar caused her to dart back to her desk. Fall storms in Michigan were as bad as spring's air conflicts when jet streams dipped low and brought the nasty cold air from the north. Trouble. Throw in the fact you could only afford a small canoe in the middle of the Great Lakes, you might as well call yourself *gone*. Tornadoes hit often enough to make a woman want to fight back, say 'fuck it' and hit the road. Laura's decision on that most eventful night to wait out the storm wasn't pure luck. It changed from coincidence to opportunity.

Karl, smartest son in the universe, reached genius status that evening, too. Since working with her, he had saved Laura's proverbial ass from only living on the edge of success to the point she, on occasion, bought several nice items for herself. Waterford glasses, steak and lobster at Dino's, the best tickets for concerts. Jim Beam on the new sideboard at the office for an occasional after work drink with a client.

She answered the phone and shook off her Nine West shoes. "Holms and Holms Agency."

"I'd like to make an appointment with your lead detective. Can you help me with that?" The caller's voice was soft, not Detroit, not Midwest.

"Certainly. We are investigators, if that makes a difference. What day are you thinking?"

"When is the earliest opening?"

Laura wanted to mess with the guy and say '*why not now, the fucking rain is keeping me here*' but she had more business sense than that.

"We open at nine tomorrow. I can work you in with our lead investigator."

A bolt of lightning cut through the clouds and it sounded to Laura's sensitive ear as if it had echoed through the phone. Was that possible?

"If that's the earliest, darlin', then I'll see you all at nine."

Thunder shook the building. The phone crackled and brought with it the echo.

"Sir, is a storm over your head, too?"

"It sure is. I'm close to your office. Was going to knock on your door, but decided it might be better to call." Again that tone, short of a whisper, and definitely a southern edge. Not hillbilly, not pure Georgia. Laura knew her accents. This needed to be a longer discussion to pinpoint the origin.

"Well, you're in luck, the office hasn't closed officially. If you want to tackle the rain, you could come now. How long will it take you?"

"Well, darlin', not long at all. If Detective Holmes is there, we'll get through the interview. Take my case or not."

Or not, Laura thought. She was tired, needed a hard workout to clear her head; needed a strong glass of Jim Beam on the rocks and a thriller book. She glanced at the stack of unpaid bills, the ledger open and her eye went to the balance sheet.

"The door's unlocked. You'll get the last appointment of the day."

"Thanks, darlin'."

"It's Laura Holms, Ms. Holms, if you please." And clicked off. Let him think what he wants about darlin', she muttered. Back on with the black heels, a quick comb through her hair and her blouse tucked in tight for that professional, no-nonsense look. On the late side of forty, she still cared about her image. A matter of business.

The outer door rattled in its usual manner. The hinges needed silicone. Tomorrow. She'd said that yesterday. *Note to self, tell Karl to do it.*

She went to the foyer and there stood her prospective client. A drenched version of modern day man. Tall, dark and handsome. His hand shaking rain off of the droplets on his head; then one hand raked across one shoulder, then another. Dressed in a grey suit, a mix of light and dark, Laura couldn't tell if it was wet or dry. What was the hurry? And then she took a full gaze of the middle-aged man before her.

"You're Afro-American."

Why did that comment fly from her mouth? What a guffaw.

"I am?" He chuckled. "And you're white or you all say Caucasian." He chuckled again. "Yes, I am black. Doesn't make a bit of difference to me. And you're the darlin' I talked to on the phone?"

Laura blushed. Well, at least he didn't sound angry or defensive.

"I'm so sorry. Yes, Laura Holms. Please, come into my office. I'll turn on the fireplace and you can let your jacket dry while we talk." Laura rushed over and flicked the switch Karl had installed to ignite the gas flames.

The fireplace, original to the building, had once been traditional red brick but Laura had changed it to a white facing. And the mantel, too. Now a sleek black, instead of mahogany. Why did it now stand out so boldly?

Yes, it served to hold her favorite keepsakes. A framed picture of Karl and a small trophy she won in a 10-K charity run. A few candles for atmosphere and one glass vase on the rare occasion someone sent flowers. Often, she pulled her desk chair in front of the fireplace, propped up her feet and took a nap while the flames danced between ceramic logs that mimicked birch cut to the exact size for the grate. It fooled her senses enough to make her feel she was in a cabin up north instead of the dreary city. At that moment, because of the vocal blunder, she felt uncomfortable to sit in front of it.

Laura pointed to the side chair. "I'll move it closer to the flames."

"No, I don't mind sitting by your desk. Gives that professional, client feel, don't you think?" He smiled and sat down. Had he taken in the stark nature of the setting?

"So, what can I do for you?" She pulled out a legal pad and poised her pen to write.

"First, I'd rather you not do that." He pointed to the pen and pad. "No records. Probably the only thing I'll ask of you that is out of bounds."

"It's not the way I do business, Mr...."

"There's times in life, Ms. Holms, when you've got to break from the herd."

Was he purposely being clever? "I detect an accent. Not sure of its origin."

"I'll let you discover it. That's your field. I was going to say darlin' but that would make it easier for you." The man laughed. Soft and low.

Sly and witty? For what reason? Laura didn't feel threatened, but she did leave her hand on her lap. In a flash, she could push a button, a drawer would slide out and provide the best recourse a woman could have: a nine-millimeter Beretta. Perfect for fending off thugs disguised in expensive suits and cowboy boots.

Cowboy boots? Were those really cowboy boots? Two inch heels and a black, gray mix of soft grained leather on his feet.

"Okay. Tell me, Sir, how do you think I can help you?" No reason to ease into the subject with chummy nuances. Straight to the facts and then she'd ask 'no name' to leave.

"I want you to find someone who stole my money."

"It might be wise for you to go to the police, Sir. Theft is a felony. Did this person assault you in the process of taking your money? If so, it's a stiffer penalty."

"I'm not interested in penalties. I'm only interested in finding the person who stole my money. If you find that person, I'll give you half of what was taken from me. A simple deal."

"You'll sign a contract to that effect? That is, if the returned funds match my retainer, expenses and dollar per hour rate."

"You don't need to worry about a retainer. This is a very lucrative deal."

"Then, Sir, I'll need details. A lot of details."

"You haven't figured it out, have you? The accent." His dark coffee eyes twinkled. It made her think of a mischievous boy who talked his way out of a lie.

She pondered for a moment. "Texas. Damned if I know why." Laura put both hands on the desk. "Let's get something straight, no poker. I won't waste my time on a bad horse deal. Work for pay requires a contract."

"You're as tough as they say you are." He leaned forward and spread his fingers on the edge of her glass desk. "I won't sign a contract. For your sake and mine. But to ease your mind, for starters, I'll give you that retainer."

"At least we're closer to a binding agreement. I want substantive details."

"A twenty-five grand retainer. Is that enough substance? You'll still get half when the SOB is found."

Laura rested back in her swivel chair, turned to the window and for those few seconds watched a cascade of rain barrel off the roof. "Looks like the gutter is plugged. There shouldn't be that much water on the windowpanes. Something to fix."

"Ownership blues. Charley Pride sang something like that." Mr. No Name rested back in his chair, too. "Okay, fifty k retainer."

"That's a lot to offer for a plugged up drain that I don't want to fix. Let's say, I go for it, though. What's your timeline?"

"As long as it takes. If the retainer runs out. I'll double it."

"Eating away my net profit?"

"Ms. Holms, you'll earn half of what is returned to me. It's a simple case. Find the person who stole my money. I don't go back on my word."

"Would you care for a drink, Mr. No Name? I've got Jim Beam. Sit by the fire and talk about how we're going to work together."

Thunder roared overhead as Laura poured three jiggers of cool amber liquid into the Waterford whiskey glasses she'd taken from the sleek, polished credenza. Her new client pulled his chair next to the fire and stretched out his legs. Yes, there were two-inch heels on his boots.

"Cozy setting. Almost like home," he said as he tipped the glass towards Laura. "To our partnership."

"A deal's a deal." Laura said. Intrigued by the reasons why he sought her out, she decided to let him weave his story. No questions asked.

They sat together as if they were old friends. He described the ranch he owned. Somewhere near Ft. Worth she calculated by the description of his drive to the airport. Almost missed his flight, dust storm, traffic, long lines. Could have hired a private jet but that had its innate problems, too, he told her. Others involved, explanations but there was a one daily non-stop flight between his city and Detroit, he told. On a personal note, he had a field stone fireplace in his office and one in his bedroom. It sounded almost as inviting as a cabin up north. The talk came to its conclusion after he gave Laura a thorough description of the person to be found. Name, distinctive features, birth date, habits, affiliations.

He included a private cell number for updates. Call anytime. Only Mr. No Name had access to it. She'd report her progress and if the subject were found, he would return immediately.

With a flight back to Texas the next day, he made a gentleman's departure near midnight. Laura sat in front of the fireplace for a few minutes, then locked the office door and walked to her apartment building.

Early the following morning, Laura went online to check her bank balance. As promised, fifty thousand dollars had been credited to her account.

What Mr. No Name didn't know was that with Karl's skills and Laura's contact with a flight attendant she'd helped out in the past, the new client's identity took all of three days. He'd flown commercial and there weren't many direct flights between Texas and Detroit. Livestock and oil had made him a wealthy rancher. He owned a home in North Dallas, Preston Wood subdivision, where the Bushes had taken up residence. A dream come true lifestyle it seemed.

Three days later they located the man who had stolen six million dollars from Mr. No Name's livestock business and had, also, run off with his wife. Which one stung the most? Why he waited so long to seek recovery was never asked. The events had taken place three years earlier. Things seemed to run in threes for Mr. No Name.

The last place the embezzler was spotted had been Ontario, Canada. Without the runaway wife. Those sources suspected his relocation to now be Detroit, but they couldn't cross the border legally. Thus, this Texan sought out Laura Holms, local private investigator, to catch the crook. Why her, remained a mystery. She had to let that part of his story rest.

Easy enough to locate the embezzler-on-the-run with Karl's techniques. Airports, train and bus stations, all had cameras. People acquiesced for a lot of reasons. Money, a major factor. The thief lived in a not so pristine apartment dwelling on Jefferson Avenue. Not the worst of Detroit but in the midst of enough look-a-likes to not draw suspicion. He routinely picked up dinner at a small diner that did carry-out, paid with a credit card under the same false name he used on an Amazon account. Laura promptly relayed the information to Mr. No Name who informed her it would be a matter of hours only to plot out the guy's apprehension.

Karl, anxious to take a role, played stake out and Laura stood in line for take-out the night the encounter took place. Mr. No Name, and an unknown associate wearing similar cowboy boots, entered the restaurant at the designated pick-up time.

The embezzler and Mr. No Name caught each other's eye. No overt surprise registered on either one's face. No attempt to run on the embezzler's part. With a nod of his head, Laura's client directed the white, middle-aged man to leave. With food in hand, the guy walked in front of the two Texans.

Mr. No Name suggested Karl wait on the street while the Texans, with Laura and their adversary close at hand, rode the elevator to the tenth floor. The apartment consisted of a large open area, updated kitchen and broad windows for an expansive view. The Detroit River could be seen between buildings and the crossroads on Jefferson Avenue, with several riverside restaurants, were notable features. A pair of binoculars sat on the ledge of one window.

"You had my loyalty for seven years, Henderson. We both could have increased our wealth. You can't justify your actions by any measure."

Henderson glared back at the Texan and smiled. "Worth the adventure."

"A short run," said Mr. No Name.

And with that, the man accompanying Mr. No Name drew out a weapon and shot Henderson in the face. Flesh exploded, bone fragments scattered across the room.

Laura's knees buckled as fast as the dead man's descent to the floor.

Mr. No Name helped her up, kissed her forehead and tucked his arm around her shoulder. The executor pulled out a plastic bag, ripped off his gloves and put the gun and gloves inside the plastic bag. Then he put one arm under Laura's and Mr. No Name did the same. They walked, carried her back to the elevator, and rode down in that fashion to the street.

Laura braced herself as the doors parted, waved for Karl to leave and she and the Texans walked back to her office.

They sat together, the three of them, in front of Laura's fireplace. Her client pulled her chair closest to the warm flames. Her hands shook as she took the Jim Beam he'd poured into her Waterford glass. It surprised Laura he had unlocked the credenza, knew where she kept her keys. His next action shocked her more. He pushed the button on her desk that opened the drawer to her concealed weapon and pocketed it.

"Tomorrow, you'll feel better. I'll return your belongings in good time." He patted the pocket with the Beretta. "You might read something in the Free Press tomorrow. Crime ridden Detroit, things happen. I'll go home and you'll work just like any other day. Check your bank account. A deal is a deal."

"I'll report this to the police." Laura eyed the man, his companion.

"That you won't do, darlin'." He looked at his partner. "No records, no names. What are you going to tell them? Humor me."

"I discovered all I needed to know about you by the time you arrived back in Dallas the next day. You're not as elusive as you'd like to think."

Had she risked her life to tell of the discovery?

"Well, darlin', let's take a look on that network of yours. Entertain me with your skills. Then we'll get on our way."

Laura thought about her options. Eyed the computer, stared at her hands. This wasn't just a matter of law. Murder was a grave moral issue, and she was tired, angry and afraid. However, knowledge gave her strength, so she booted up the laptop and let her fingers run over the keys. The private files, unshared passwords, what she knew about him.

The first page came up blank. The second, third the same. His name, the ranch name, address and flight records were all missing. She googled the name of the ranch he'd registered with the farm bureau. Nothing there.

"No records, Laura Holms. Darlin, you did a great job. Our contract has been consummated. You've earned my loyalty."

He left Laura sitting in front of her fireplace with a second glass of Jim Beam. She remained there throughout the night. When Karl arrived at nine, she asked him to pull up her bank account.

They stared at the numbers. Indeed, she'd been paid as promised.

* * *

Laura didn't think of that event very often. It flashed back the most when it rained. Damn she hated the rain, hated Detroit, and hated those memories. But on the other hand, her bills were never overdue. She had two very secure IRA's that would aid an early retirement. Not all the ill-gained money went into a protected investment plan but a large portion. The rest she kept in a secret bank account. Three years had been long enough to see what the clever Texan would do. She no longer worried that one day it would disappear. Mr. No Name could have reneged on the deal at any time but didn't.

Laura eased into the security and flexibility that had evolved. She could buy that cabin up north. On occasion, she treated herself to Jimmy Choo shoes and recently had upgraded her apartment. Karl was given a nice wedding even though she and his father weren't keen on the woman he'd chosen.

She remembered the wedding last year. Berta Channing, five years older than Karl, but looked like a blushing bride. Beautiful to be sure. Karl's father whispered, "She's just not as bright as Karl. Kind'a carefree."

"Definitely smitten by Karl's charm," Laura said.

"Wish I would've had more time to influence his choices, teach him more about a man's way of life, careful about love. Why did you wait so long to tell me he was my son?"

It wasn't the first time Trevor Grant had asked.

"When he turned fifteen, I knew he could handle the news. And you seemed mature enough to know then, too."

Laura loved Karl's father, but she didn't like the array of habits that kept him on the brink of bankruptcy. She'd bailed him out twice but also lived by the rule of threes. If she gave Trevor money again, who was the bigger fool? She had given thought to the idea that when she retired they might share the cabin up north. If by a lake, Trevor could fish and she'd lay on the beach and read books. They'd have a glass of Jim Beam after dinner. In front of the fire, they'd re-ignite those romantic evenings before Karl was born. Yes, she loved Trevor, but living separately proved to be the better arrangement.

Grandkids someday? When their daughter-in-law Breta settled down, got her act together. Thirty-five in the picture soon. How long would it take? Laura had to be patient, then her efforts would be well worth the agony.

Would her conscience ever recover? She'd developed a sad, hard edge to her heart after the brutal murder. Had suffered emotionally about not reporting the hideous crime. What if the man wasn't guilty? RIP: An accomplice to murder.

It haunted her even more that Mr. No Name at the time had access to all of her files, manipulated them so he couldn't be traced. It frightened her to know an elusive cyber world existed. People could delve into the most sacred details of your life. The Texan was still in the shadows, always would be. She contemplated his return; another deal she couldn't resist?

What generated the most misdoubts, though, was the intrigue. The man, his lifestyle, the hidden story. At times she imagined a discussion with him while they sat in front of the fire. While the rain pinged the rooftop, while lightning illuminated the sky.

Laura's thoughts circled back to the present. Karl had arrived too early but hadn't come into her office. Why? With Berta in the picture, her son had become unreliable. Late for appointments, missteps with clients. Minor breaches confirmed he wasn't working to his best. Berta was to blame. The young woman was a conniver, a sweet looking one who had Karl under her finger. He never squirmed. It rankled Laura's nerves. If she talked about it with Trevor, he'd say 'I told you so'. Birds of a feather, she replied.

"Don't be so hard on me. I've always been around."

Granted, Trevor didn't stray far. Berta, however, didn't either and, yet, she caused the most unsettling feeling when she entered the room.

Damn it, Laura didn't like the situation at all. Who would have thought she'd turn into a nagging mother-in-law.

She'd pushed the intercom, the one Karl added because he often worked with a Bose head-set on. A yellow light on his desk flashed. A warning, he said when he installed it, he'd done something wrong. She laughed then.

She pushed it twice. Something was up. He usually responded by text or appearance. A few minutes passed, she pushed the intercom again.

Laura stood. "What the hell."

She tapped on his door, "Karl, I heard you come in. Awfully early. What's up?" He didn't have his head set on, the computers were booted up. Karl had his head on his desk.

"She's gone."

"Who the hell is gone?"

She knew. Berta.

If it were true, she had to be careful. No reason to mess with a son's broken heart. No salt on the wound. He wore that big, soft heart on his sleeve. Had that boyish soft side like Trevor. Good people they were but lived each day as if it were another party. Blowing in the wind, two kites, carefree.

Well, she was the one who consistently cleaned up after them, and it was about time someone else paid the piper.

"Sometime yesterday she left," Karl said with a groan. "I couldn't believe it. Closets empty. Car gone. Even cleaned out the wine refrigerator. A short note."

"Oh, honey, I'm so sorry. Maybe it's just a retreat. Sometimes people have to be apart to realize how much they love someone. She's young, she'll come around."

"No, don't think so. No doubt about that."

"Want me to call your father? He'd have good advice." Not that he would, but Karl would appreciate his father's commiseration.

"I bet she's having an emotional tantrum. Not uncommon. Not enough attention from her husband. Is she staying with a girl friend?"

"With her mother."

"Certainly not her mother. You told me they don't get along."

"I was wrong. They are joined at the hip. No doubt about it."

"Not Berta. Her mother is wicked. In all this time, we would have caught on."

Laura didn't feel too bad about the white lie. But there was no reason to add to his dilemma. It was common knowledge that Berta's mother had been divorced and walked away with more than her fair share of mutual belongings. The ex had sued but the money had been spent long before a judge looked at the evidence.

Karl said, "I just did some tracking. Her mother's been divorced four times. Each time a big cash win. Records don't lie."

"Berta's not like her mother." Her son loved Berta beyond reason. Blind love was his problem. Laura sighed with relief, though. Karl never saved money even on the decent salary he netted at the agency, so Berta didn't walk away with too much. Berta, if she never came back, would lift a heavy load off Laura's shoulders.

Unknown to Karl, Laura had been religious about saving another twenty percent of what Karl could have earned and put it into a mutual fund. When the time was right, she planned to turn it over to him. Maybe after the birth of her first grandchild so Karl and Berta could buy a home in the suburbs. Right now, all she wanted to do was help Karl through this heartbreaker. He'd heal and move on. With Berta out of the picture, Karl could pursue that career he wanted with the FBI or CIA. He certainly had the knack for cyber technology and the added experience of private investigations. He'd turned Laura's business into a near goldmine. Add to it the illegal gains from Mr. No Name and Laura had all Karl, Trevor and she needed. That is if and when she decided to share.

"Listen, Karl, in a few days things will settle down. If Berta loves you like she always says, she'll come to her senses and be back in your apartment. You two can take a vacation. Rekindle. It's been a busy year. You've earned a few weeks away."

"Impossible." He almost whined.

"I can do without you for a while. Maybe I'll close up shop and go up north. Neither one of us has had time off. Your honeymoon only a week. I'll treat—a get-away, renew your marriage vows. A cruise, fly to Hawaii. It's time I spend some of those savings."

"Impossible. It's not going to happen."

"Karl, listen, girls throw tantrums all the time. Probably that's why you father and I never married."

"You don't understand. She's not coming back. Neither is her mother. We'll never take a lush vacation. Impossible."

"Okay…what's this about?" Laura sat on the edge of his desk. "She's got another guy. Spill it."

"Hell, no. That would be easy. She's got all the money."

"Your money?"

Karl paused so long, Laura wanted to slap him.

"The agency's money. Her money, my money, your money. Every single cent."

Laura leaned across his desk. Her eyes burned with doubt. "Impossible."

"Absolutely possible."

"All of it gone?"

"Your private accounts. IRA's, your cash flow account, the expense account. The stash you got from that case three years ago. Frigging all of it. Every fucking dime."

"Impossible. Laura folded to her knees, attempted to stand but felt too weak. Twice in her life shocked to the point of instability. "How could she have my money?"

"Because I trusted her. Taught her how to be self-sufficient."

"So she'll get a job now." Laura's words didn't match her thoughts.

"She loved that I worked as an investigator. She called me her favorite 'spy'. I thought if she learned enough, she would work with us. Our business could expand. Me out in the field more. You on the front line. It all made sense."

"It's ridiculous."

"She got into the accounts."

"That conniving little bitch. How could she?"

"Please don't blame her. I let her do it."

"Blame her. Yes, I blame her and right now, I hate you a little bit, too. Weak and reckless. All that time, trying to keep you from careless influences. Taught you the rewards of responsibility and you threw it away. Why couldn't you guard your feelings?"

Laura stood but her knees still shook. "Do you realize how hard I've worked? And you're telling me it's all gone?"

"I'm totally ashamed. I don't know what else to say."

Laura had to keep her hand on the wall for support as she walked back to her office.

And now she watched as the rain poured from the roof. The gutter clogged again, splashing hard against the pane. What good was it to reminisce? Thunder cracked overhead. She eyed the cabinet that held the Jim Beam. Would it make matters worse? She thought about calling Trevor, but would he really be concerned? He'd say some senseless thing like 'start over, you can do it, Babe'. Could she? She was on the hard side of forty. Still in shape, a younger woman's body but appearances were deceiving. The fact remained, she could reach the hard side of fifty and still wouldn't be able to regain all she had saved. And the savings didn't include the ill-gotten money from Mr. No Name.

If Berta took everything but that, Laura would have gladly 'started over'. Damn, Laura thought she'd hidden it so well.

What mistake had Karl made? She keyed in the difficult password for those secured bank records. A paltry forty-eight dollars in the account. An added insult? Berta commented on Laura's age the last time they were out to dinner. 'Forty-eight, long past your prime' she'd said. Laura still picked up the bill. She rechecked the office cash flow account. Another dig. Twenty-six dollars. The SOB had jabbed at Karl. A dollar for his age, too. With every click, Laura saw her son spoke the truth. All gone.

Laura did have a thousand dollars hidden in her Brighton purse. Money she'd tucked into the lining as an 'emergency' fund. Little good it would do her.

She gazed through the window. Wouldn't you know it? Always in the rain, the worse events of her life. The gods roared, thunder and lightning, added drama.

What were her options? She looked at the button she could push for her line of defense. The Berretta always ready for action. The nine-millimeter served as a reminder that the world was cruel, and she needed to look out for herself. Yet, she'd never been the kind who thought she could kill a human being. Did that conviction mean she couldn't take her own life? Hell, she'd just begun to appreciate the best of it.

Sweet revenge?

Her son was an excellent cyber investigator when he didn't have his ass in the clouds. Didn't Karl owe his mother some relief? The image of her little boy spun like a movie reel. And then she slowed it down and studied the fixed picture of him on the mantel. Why even think twice about Karl helping Laura recover what belonged to her.

The truth was, even if he could find her, he'd never go after Berta. His heart couldn't take it.

Laura's thoughts went in circles as she watched the splatters on the windowpane. Then with a sigh of relief, the answer came to her. Always in the rain. She opened a desk drawer and pulled out a burner cell that

Karl suggested they reserve for clients who didn't want calls on their personal phone. She felt the tension ease from her shoulders as she looked at the roses in the vase on the mantel. A dozen every month. A reminder of a contract she'd made with a former client. A private matter between them.

"Hello. How are you doing?"

"What a nice surprise, darlin'. Are the roses sent last week still blossoming?"

"As always. Again, a warm thank you."

"You're calling to tell me you're ready to come down to Texas for a long visit."

"I'm closer to doing just that. Very close. First, let's talk business."

"Fire away."

"I need to hire someone for a special job. Track some records, settle a matter. Not something this woman's investigator can handle."

"That can be arranged."

"It's about a person who stole money from me."

"That kind of activity costs a lot of money, darlin'."

"I'll pay half of what's recovered. No questions asked. Thing is, I don't have money for a retainer." Laura kicked off her Jimmy Choo shoes.

"Loyalty. The contact will take my word you're good to go. Just need the details, darlin'. Then I'll book a flight. Could sit in front of your fireplace with a little Jim Beam in hand before you and I head back to Texas, darlin'."

A Story of Unusual Interest
Karen Odden

London 1879

I looked about the music hall with the long tables of people chattering over their suppers, the elevated stage with the crimson velvet curtains, the pianist in his black coat, pounding away in the corner, and the trapezes above, their ropes attached to long metal beams suspended from the ceiling.

I'd gone doving plenty of times in music halls like this, back when I was thieving. Pickings were always good, here in London's West End, as it's the easiest thing in the world to slide your hand into a man's trouser pocket when there's a half-naked girl dressed in little more than feathers prancing on the stage. Or to slip a necklace from the missus, when she's a bit too far in her cups. Coming tonight, you can be sure I left my own jewelry at home and stuffed my reticule deep inside my pocket.

For the first time, I was visiting a music hall as a newswriter, a proper one, for the *Mirror*, a daily paper with offices on Fleet Street, like so many others. Mr. Murdaugh, the editor, had assigned me the task of reviewing music halls, providing a survey of the acts, the food, the drink, and the general pleasantness of the seating area. I'd have preferred something more exciting, but I was new the paper, only two months along, so I took the assignments offered. However, he must have seen my disappointment, for he added, "If you find a story of unusual interest, bring it to me."

"Unusual interest," I'd echoed.

"A story that'll sell more papers." He'd handed me a list. "For now, start with these five halls."

I'd glanced over it. "Could I add the Westonia? I've a friend who performs there."

He'd shrugged. "Fine."

The Westonia was my sixth music hall in as many nights, and I shook my head at the petty crimes that occurred in all of them. So far, I'd observed pickpocketing, prostitution, excessive drinking, the distribution of French postcards, swearing, doving, and—just now— what had every appearance of attempted adultery, with the man wearing a gold wedding band on the very hand that was slipping down the bodice of a flower girl twenty years younger. But though the Society for the Suppression of Vice would've been up in arms, none of this was a story worth bringing back to Mr. Murdaugh.

I looked down at the page of my pocketbook, half-full of penciled scribbles. Thus far, I'd seen a magician, a juggler of flaming candlesticks, a red-headed chanteuse, a short play with three men dressed as women, a violinist (who'd had dinner rolls thrown at him for being so wretchedly bad), and a man who sang the bawdy limerick that began, "Are your apples ripe for plucking, miss?" By the second verse, all the men had joined in. At last, that song ended, and then came the act I'd been waiting for.

My friend Margaret had introduced me to Antonia, one half of the trapeze duo, last month. We'd all spent several afternoons together, and I'd found her lively, clever company. Antonia—or Annie, as we called her—had come with her brother François from Paris, where they'd been trained by the great trapeze artist Jules Léotard himself at the Cirque d'Hiver.

All of us in the audience tipped our heads back to watch as Annie and François climbed the metal ladders, stepped onto their platforms, waved, and pirouetted, their costumes glinting in the lights. They unhooked the trapezes and, simultaneous to the second, swung toward each other, gaining height with each swing. Annie folded her knees over the bar, dangling upside-down, her hands reaching for François's—and he caught her! Amid cries and shouts, François flung her back to her trapeze in one smooth arc—

And then Annie's trapeze broke, one side of the bar torn from its rope. At the audience's gasps, the stage pianist halted, the music shorn mid-chord. The audience's gasps became screams of horror, as we watched Annie's desperate scrambling to gain purchase on the smooth bar as it swung about.

My heart in my throat, I watched as Annie's hands slid down. She jackknifed to catch the rope with her feet and then jackknifed again to grasp the rope with her hands. One grab after another, she climbed, the rope coiling around her bare ankle. As she reached the top, she swung herself over, walked the narrow metal beam toward the platform, and leapt down onto it. A true performer, she waved brightly before she began to climb down the ladder.

Wild cheering erupted, and François swung back to his platform and descended. Above, the broken trapeze swung back and forth, like a pendulum.

This was certainly newsworthy.

I watched them run to the stage and, hand-in-hand, they bowed. Then they vanished off stage right. As the next act—a woman with three trained dogs—appeared, I rose from the table and made my way to a door along the side wall. The man in front of it put up a hand. "Not allowed, miss."

"Annie's a friend of mine," I begged. "*Please.*"

His expression changed. "Ah, go on." He pushed the door open, and I slid through.

I hurried down the wooden steps and turned toward François's voice, strident and shrill above the muted noises coming from the stage. I didn't speak much French, but I knew what curses sound like. In the damp corridor, they stood together, François hovering anxiously over Annie, with her back against the wall, a cloth pressed to her hand. Three lanterns at intervals along the bricked corridor cast a strange, flickering glow.

"My God, that was terrifying! Are you hurt?" I asked Annie.

"Who are you?" François demanded, his face white to the lips.

"Kit Jimeson," I said.

"She's Margaret's friend. I told you about her," Annie replied and turned back to me. "Kit, what are you doing here?"

"I was in the audience, writing a story for the paper," I said. "Do you need a doctor?"

"I'm all right," she said, slowly pulling back the cloth on her hand to examine it. "A cut, that's all."

"What happened?" I asked. "Did the knot come undone?"

"I check the ropes every night, after the act," François said grimly. "The rope wasn't loose or frayed. I put all my weight on it to test."

Annie shook her head. "The metal loop pulled off the bar. The straight part had had been filed thin. The edge cut me."

"You think someone caused this on purpose?" I asked, dumbfounded. I turned to François. "Could it have been meant for you? Do you ever switch sides?"

"Never. The lengths are set for our different heights and weights," Annie said.

"Why would someone do this?" I asked.

"It could be Emmeline," François said.

"She's the singer," Annie explained to me. "And no, François. She's spiteful, but she wouldn't kill me."

"Why is she spiteful?" I asked.

"She's not paid as much as Antonia," François said. "She's been here longer, but Woodley knows she's not the one people are coming to see." His chin was set. "Someone's out to hurt you, Annie. This is the second time in a week."

My eyebrows rose.

"Someone set the fire to the women's dressing room," Annie explained. "Last Thursday, with a firebomb through the window. I wasn't there, though."

"You usually are," François said.

"Yes, but my costume ripped, so I went to see our seamstress first. And Emmeline couldn't have done that. She was on stage for the musical act," Annie reminded him.

He flapped a hand dismissively. "She could have paid someone to do it."

"Where's Emmeline now?" I asked. "She might talk to me, if I say it's for the paper. She might let something slip."

They pointed me to the women's dressing room. As I turned away, I saw a man of about forty, burly and with heavy moustaches, barreling toward François and Annie, his arms outflung. "What the devil happened? Are you all right?" he demanded.

"I'm fine, Mr. Woodley," Annie said.

The stage manager, or perhaps the owner, I guessed. At least his concern seemed genuine.

As Annie began to explain what had happened, I started down the hall.

* * *

Emmeline was the red-headed chanteuse I'd seen, although at the moment her flaming wig adorned a wire stand; her natural brown hair was cut short. She was alone in the room, crowded with tables full of finery, racks with shoes and hats, and costumes hanging on wall hooks. She stood before the tall mirror, adjusting her costume. When I explained that I was writing an article on music halls, she agreed to talk with me. I asked her how long she'd been singing, which other halls she'd worked in, and how she chose her songs, until I finally worked around to Annie's accident. "I've heard there are some here who are jealous that she's paid more than other performers," I said.

Her brown eyes became slits. "So that's why you're talking to me. Not for a feature."

"Did you have anything to do with the accident tonight?" I asked bluntly.

Her eyes flew wide. "No!"

"I heard there was a fire in the dressing room last week, too," I said. "Antonia could have been badly hurt."

"I had nothing to do with that either," she said, spinning around to face the mirror. She eyed my reflection. "For God's sake, why would I hurt her? It just makes her more precious." Her voice was thick with disgust. "Woodley'll probably pay her more, just to keep her. That's what happened at the Moorland, when that tightrope dancer almost fell. She told him she'd leave unless he gave her another five pounds a week, and he did it!" She shook her head. "Now, get out of my bloody dressing room."

She was unpleasant, but her logic made sense to me.

* * *

On the way back to where I'd left Annie, I walked past a closed door that might have stood open for how little it concealed the row happening inside between Mr. Woodley and a woman.

"Because they're going to shut us down!" he shouted. "The damned Society will take any excuse. They'll tell the bloody police we're a danger to the public!" He paused. "Perhaps we can keep it quiet, if—"

"You wouldn't have cared if it happened to anyone but her!" came a woman's shrill voice. "Prancing around in her sequins—"

"Oh, shut up, Mary! She's my best act. That's all she is!"

Seizing the moment of silence, I knocked. "Mr. Woodley?"

The door swung open fast enough I felt the gust. He scowled. "Who are you?"

"I'm a writer from the *Mirror*," I said. "I happened to be in the audience tonight."

His expression changed. "Oh, hell."

"I'm also a friend of Antonia's." I slid sideways through the doorway. "So my instinct is to tell the story to make her sound like a brilliant performer instead of making your music hall sound unsafe." I added pointedly, "If you'll talk to me."

"Fine," he muttered. "Come in."

With her mouth pursed, his wife plumped herself on a chair and took up her knitting.

"Why do you think this is happening?" I asked. "First the firebomb in the dressing room, and now the trapeze? Who would want to hurt her?"

He only ran his fingers into his hair and tugged, but his wife spoke up over her clicking needles: "There'll be another one soon. Mark my words. They happen in threes, and the next one will be worst of all."

"Oh, shut up, Mary." Mr. Woodley took my arm, opened the door, and drew me into the hallway. "I need some air." He strode along the corridor to the back door, threw the bolt, and stepped out into the yard. He tipped his head back and drew a deep breath. The yard smelled of tomcat piss and rubbish, but he didn't seem to notice.

At last, he turned to me. "It's George Wick behind this."

"Of Wick's Music Hall?" I asked.

"Aye." He sniffed and tipped his chin toward the east. "On the other side of Maywell's. When I opened four years ago, he lost business, and we had no end of rows over it. My acts are better because I pay more." He paused. "He won't talk to you. He hates the papers. Bad reviews."

The final number ended—the applause and cheers from inside reaching a crescendo that burst through the walls.

"Damn it." He stomped to the door, slammed it behind him, and threw the bolt.

I walked past Maywell's to Wick's. Apparently, their stage was dark on Wednesdays. The building looked a bit ragged and worn, with a shutter hanging awry and the door in need of a fresh coat of paint. With his business not prospering, I imagined Mr. Wick would be as surly as Mr. Woodley had led me to expect. As I walked home, I had an idea of how to convince Mr. Wick to talk to me.

* * *

The next morning, I walked down the street in the drizzle, pausing on the pavement opposite Wick's to study it again. The three buildings— Wick's, Maywell's, and the Westonia—were each separated by only a few feet. Hardly an alley, really—more like a snicket. I strolled one time around Wick's. Plenty of these places had illicit businesses operating out of them during the day, when the shows weren't on. The Octavian was caught running a thieving ring out of the basement a few years before.

At the back of Wick's was a low set of windows, with one cracked open.

I sniffed and paused, sniffing again to be sure. I knew the

significance of the odors of clay, ammonia, hot plaster, and burned charcoal.

I banged on the back door, my best hope of entry at this hour, and when a young man opened it, I asked to see Mr. Wick. "I'm writing for the *Mirror*, doing a story on music halls," I explained. "It'll be good publicity." He shrugged and pointed a thumb down the hall.

I knocked on the office door with its mottled glass, and when a man's voice bid me to come in, I pushed the door open to find a slender man with a pale face—as unlike burly Mr. Woodley as a canary from a walrus. He looked up from a sheaf of papers. "Who are you?"

"My name is Kit Jimeson, and I write for the *Mirror*."

He rolled his eyes and put up a palm. "Get out. I don't talk to papers."

"I think you'll talk to me." I stepped inside and shut the door. "You're counterfeiting coins on the premises."

His mouth opened and closed.

"I'm not interested in that, if you answer my questions about something else," I said, taking the chair across his desk. "There have been two near-fatal attacks against performers at the Westonia. Are you behind them?"

Two red spots appeared on his pale cheeks. "No! *I* don't stoop to that sort of thing! Who's saying I would?"

"Mr. Woodley says he's your competition, and according to him, he's winning," I said.

Mr. Wick gave a shrill bark of a laugh, like a wounded dog. "If he's winning, it's only because he's poached my best acts. Mr. Owens, the magician was mine. So were the trapeze duo."

"All the more reason for your resentment, isn't it?" I asked. "Come now, Mr. Wick, be honest, or I'll be talking to the police about—" I waved a hand toward the hall.

He sat back, his gray eyes sparking, his slender hands clasped over his flat stomach. "You're completely misinformed."

"Then inform me," I retorted.

"I don't give a damn about the Westonia. Why would I? I've already sold up."

That was not what I expected. "Sold the music hall," I said, to be sure I understood.

"My wife is ill, Miss Jimeson. My son lives in Shropshire, and we're going to live with him." The anger that had lit his eyes had dimmed, and his expression showed only sadness.

"I'm sorry to hear about your wife," I said, and I meant it. "Who did you sell to?"

He gave me a look. "Woodley, of course. He offered years ago to buy my place."

I shook my head in disbelief. "Woodley? Are you certain?"

Mr. Wick spread his hands. "Well, it was a private buyer, all done through a solicitor. But who else would it be?"

I considered. "Is that legal? For a solicitor to keep the buyer secret?"

"Aye. He had papers to say he was designated to act on the buyer's behalf. And once Amelia got sick—well, I don't really care who bought it. I have my money. I'm vacating at the end of the month." He looked down at his hands and then up at me. "The reason Woodley thinks it was me is because that's what *he* did. He broke my windows, had two of my performers attacked one night, and sent threatening letters to my wife. He's measuring my oats in his half-barrel, like most people do," he concluded sourly.

"But are you sure it was Woodley?" I persisted.

He blew out a sigh. "The man who beat up my juggler said it was a warning from Woodley. He's a thug." His hands reached for some papers on his desk. "Now, if that's all."

I stood. "Thank you, Mr. Wick, and—well, good luck to you."

He nodded, and I left.

Outside, I reached the pavement and stood looking at the three buildings—Wick's, Maywell's, and the Westonia. The assaults on Mr. Wick's establishment sounded a good deal like those that happened at Mr. Woodley's, and the man who attacked the juggler could have falsely named Woodley to create acrimony between the two music hall owners. What if both men were mistaken?

Maywell's department store was tall and narrow, with shining plate glass front windows, brass fittings on the door, a neat green awning with the name emblazoned in gold script, and upper stories with dormers that looked like high-and-mighty eyebrows.

I could think of someone who might want to buy both music halls, to expand his holdings.

* * *

The next morning, I donned my nicest dress and set off for Maywell's.

I'd spent plenty of time thieving in West End department stores, and this one was no different from the others. Wood cabinets and shelves, with clerks standing at each one, ready to remove merchandise to be examined by customers—and to be slipped by me into the long thieving pockets that lay against my crinolines.

I took a turn through the store. Out of habit, I identified the private detective trying to be inconspicuous, eyed the ceiling mirrors, and observed the single cam locks at the back of the cabinets, easily picked. The store was crowded, with narrow passages between the different displays, and certain departments that I'd seen in other shops were missing for want of space. Yes, I could see Mr. Maywell wanting to expand.

At last, I approached the plainclothesman in the corner with a smile. "Could you tell Mr. Maywell I'm here, please? I'm Miss Jimeson from the *Mirror*."

He frowned. "Do you have an appointment?"

"Oh," I said thoughtfully. "It's for an article about the better West End department stores. I don't think he'll want to be omitted, do you?"

His expression changed, and he beckoned to one of the clerks. "Take this newspaper lady up to Mr. Maywell's office."

I followed the man up the stairs. Thirteen steps to the landing, nine more to the upper floor. A right turn and the clerk opened a door. A young man at a desk looked up. Beyond him, if the bronze sign was correct, was Mr. Maywell's office, the door cracked.

"How do you do. I'm Kit Jimeson," I said, smiling. "From the *Mirror*.

My editor has asked me to write a piece on the better department stores, and although he left this one off the list, I was hoping to speak Mr. Maywell before the story goes to print tomorrow. Would it be possible?"

He blinked behind his spectacles. "Please have a seat."

I sat on the bench, and the young man entered Mr. Maywell's office and pulled the door closed. I eyed the lock; it was a simple one. Two voices muttered. Then the young man reappeared. "Mr. Maywell will see you now," he said pleasantly.

I entered his office and paused. Mr. Maywell was perhaps one of the most handsome men I'd ever seen. Tall, with a wave of wheat-colored hair, blue eyes, a firm jaw, and a pleasing smile. I stepped forward and held out my hand—we newspaperwomen were supposed to be brash and modern, after all. "Good afternoon, Mr. Maywell."

He shook my hand and gestured across the desk to a brown leather chair large enough to fit two of me. "I understand you are a newspaper writer."

"I'm from the *Mirror*," I replied promptly. "Writing on department stores here in the West End."

"I think it's an excellent idea, allowing ladies to write on certain topics—those suited to their interests, of course."

"Kind of you," I said sweetly. I took out my pocketbook and pencil. "Could you tell me a bit of the history of your store?" I licked the tip of my pencil and waited expectantly.

He sat back, folding his hands and looked out the window, as if remembering. "My father opened this store nineteen years ago ..."

As he talked, I scribbled random phrases in my pocketbook and darted my eyes around the room. Two cabinets, locked. His desk, heavy wooden, likely with locks. A tall cupboard, no lock. Windows that opened from inside. A carpet with a telltale curl at the corner. Three paintings, all large enough to conceal a hidden cupboard or safe.

"And for the future?" I asked, as he wound down. "Will you expand? I've noticed you don't have some of the departments that other stores have—linens, draperies, housewares, china, larger leather goods. Of course, they take a good bit of room."

Mr. Maywell stiffened. "We do plan to expand at some point, but not quite yet." He took out a silver pocket-watch on a matching chain. He was hinting that I'd overstayed my welcome, but I couldn't help smiling at the chain. People thought they kept their watches safe; any pickpocket worth their salt knew how to take the silver chain along with the watch, for an extra few shillings from an Ivy Street fence.

Clearly, Maywell wasn't going to reveal his plans for expanding the store. Finding the truth would require a visit to his offices, later, when he wasn't in them.

I thanked him and left, double-checking the number of stairs and planning a route to reach the upstairs office after the store was closed. From the bottom step, twenty-six steps to pass the display of scarves, a left turn and I estimated twenty more to a side door that opened to the alley, where constables didn't patrol.

* * *

I waited until well after dark. At half-past eleven, the bells of St. George's tolled twice. Along the street, the gas lamps still shone at intervals, the yellow light blurring at the edges in the damp. The patrolling constable passed Maywell's front door, lifting his bull's-eye lantern to peer in, as he did with each building, rounding every forty-five minutes or so. Behind his retreating back, I slid into the alley, making my way to the side door and setting my lamp in the dirt. I removed the lockpicking kit from my pocket. I didn't need much light for this; I closed my eyes and let my fingers work. A small snick, a turn of the knob, and I was in.

The department store was a peculiar place, vacant. It smelled of woolens and the linseed oil used to polish the cabinets. I stood for a moment with my hand on the knob, waiting for my eyes to adjust. The only dim light was from a gas lamp some distance away, and I was glad I'd studied the room earlier. Nineteen steps to the scarf display, twenty-six to the steps. I climbed the stairs with one hand on the banister.

Thirteen to the landing, nine more to the upper floor.

The door to the outer office was open. Light from the gas lamp below helped me find my way to the inner office. I used my picks again. Once inside, I pulled every shutter closed, hung the sheet I'd brought to conceal any sign of light, and lit the lamp, setting it on the desk.

Where first?

I tried the cabinet doors, but none were locked, and after a cursory examination of the contents, I closed them. I tugged at the desk drawers; all opened readily save one that was locked, and I tackled that next. It opened easily with my picks, and I sifted the contents. Ledgers, letters, recent bills of lading, and correspondence, but nothing pertaining to the purchase of the music hall.

Next, I rolled back the corner of the rug and ran my hand along the floorboards. I felt the unevenness of one and inserted one of my picks between the boards, prying gently. It eased upward, and I lifted it. Below was a metal box—my heart leapt with satisfaction—but when I opened it, there were only banknotes and coins inside. I resisted my impulse to filch some. With a snort of frustration, I replaced the box and rolled the rug back down.

Next, the paintings. I lifted them each from the walls to find no secret compartments behind. But as I set the third one back in place, I heard a faint flutter. I examined the back. Ah! An envelope, taped. Carefully, carefully, I removed it and slid the pages out.

By the lamplight, I could see one copy of a deed of sale, signed by John Brighton, a solicitor in the Temple, and naming Wick's Music Hall, with the address and the price of purchase. Witnessed by two law clerks in Brighton's office, it had been notarized by a Mr. Sanders. I made a note in my pocketbook of all four names. Maywell might have Mr. Brighton in his pocket, but would he and the other three men all lie to cover up his purchase? I would guess they didn't know he'd coerced Wick into selling.

With care, I slid the papers back into the envelope. I examined the room to be sure it was exactly as I left it, doused the lamp, removed the sheet, locked the door behind me, and slipped away.

* * *

The next morning found me doing something quite unlikely for a former thief. I was sitting on a bench at Scotland Yard, waiting to see Inspector Gordon Stiles.

When he arrived, I asked him to take a walk with me, which he obligingly did. Mr. Stiles was an agreeable sort, about twenty-five years of age, well-mannered and better schooled than most of the Yard men, and we had an understanding. He knew I had been a thief, knowledgeable about safecracking, fencing, and such matters, and as such I had helped him solve a jewel heist not long ago. I could tell that he never quite trusted that I'd left off thieving for good, but we were friends, after a fashion.

I explained everything I'd learned, and all that I suspected. He walked with his hands in the pockets of his black overcoat, his head down, eyes on the pavement as I talked, but I knew this meant he was listening hard. We walked in a large square around Whitehall, until we returned to stand beside the grand stone arch that marked the entrance to the cobbled yard behind the police division.

"And how did you find these papers of sale?" Mr. Stiles asked. I raised an eyebrow, and he rolled his eyes. "Never mind, I didn't ask." He sighed, his expression concerned. "If Maywell has used violence to intimidate Wicks—and possibly Woodley—this is a serious matter, Kit. Promise me you'll stop detecting and let me look into this. I'll speak with the solicitor. He'll have kept a copy of the deed to be filed in the Land Registry Office, and we'll try to discover the truth of it."

"And you'll tell me what you find?" I pressed. "I want to write it up for the paper."

"When I know all the facts," he promised. "I'll tell you what I can."

* * *

Three days later, true to his word, Mr. Stiles appeared at the *Mirror* offices. He offered to buy me coffee at Croom's in Fleet Street, and over our cups, he gave me the pieces I had been missing from the story—

how Maywell had planted the idea in Mr. Wick's mind that Mr. Woodley was trying to force him out; how he'd hired a thug from the Bludger gang in Bethnal Green to threaten both music hall owners; how a change in law that was coming next year would prevent Mr. Maywell from purchasing adjacent buildings for expansion without submitting architectural plans to a committee; and how the solicitor was unaware of his client's scheming. Mr. Maywell had been arrested and was in gaol awaiting trial.

That afternoon, I went to the music hall to see Annie, swearing her to secrecy but telling her everything I'd learned. Her eyes were wide with dismay. "So this had nothing to do with me. I was just … someone Maywell put to use, like a broom—or—or a mop."

I understood how it felt to be a tool for someone else's gain, the means to someone else's end. I touched her arm gently. "He's a terrible, wicked, greedy man," I said. "But it's over, and I'm glad you're all right."

"And he'll go to prison?"

I nodded. "I think so. Mr. Stiles said the evidence would hold."

Her eyes flashed resentfully. "Good."

The next morning, my story about Mr. Maywell's scheme ran on the second page of the paper, Mr. Murdaugh having conceded, rather grumblingly, that it was a story of unusual interest.

Lies of Omission
John W. Salvage

Sean Doyle

Jessica Dupris was not what I expected from a private detective, though honestly, I don't know what I did expect. She was in her late thirties or early forties, attractive because of her confidence and intelligence. She wore a business suit not unlike what Jeannie wore, except she wore loose-fitting slacks instead of knee-length skirts.

"My consultation fee is for a half hour, Mr. Doyle," she said.

"I'm sorry," I replied, a nervous laugh escaped my throat. "I don't know how to start."

"Let me guess. Troubles with your wife?"

I nodded.

"You suspect her of infidelity?"

My silence was all the answer she needed. She jotted down some notes on her yellow legal pad.

"I don't know anything," I said at last, my eyes never leaving the cup of coffee I had requested but still hadn't sipped. "But yes, I suspect she's sleeping with her boss."

"And who is her boss?"

"Herman Rothchilde." I felt more confident now that I was letting it out. "He's a partner at..."

"Rothchilde, Rothchilde, and Wilkes. I know. I've seen the ads."

"Then you know how handsome he is."

"Yes." She looked up from her page and fixed her eyes with mine. "But working with an attractive man doesn't mean she's cheating on you."

"No, it's not that. Or it's not just that. I'm not a jealous person. Not usually anyway. It's just that..."

Just what? How could I explain?

"Why don't you just start at the beginning?" she said at last, her tone consoling now, though she never lost that professional distance that made me feel like I was under a microscope.

"She got the job about eight months ago. She'd been looking for what seemed like an eternity. Fresh out of Law School, fantastic grades, passed the bar on her second attempt. It seems like it should have been easier to get a job, but with the job market like it was, she had a hard time even getting an interview.

"She was ecstatic when they hired her. She went into law because she wanted to be a criminal defense attorney. She kept talking about what a big deal Rothchilde was."

"And what does she do?"

"She's an Associate."

"What kind of cases do they have her working?"

"They started her off doing research, but then she started getting her own cases. Small stuff mostly. DUIs, shoplifting, minor drug offenses. No big clients. She wasn't expected to win any of them, just work plea deals."

"And she enjoyed this?"

I shrugged. "She looked at it as getting experience. The money was nice. We'd been living on the edge for so long. With her in school full time, I was the only one paying the bills. I mean, I do okay, but a nurse's wages aren't enough to cover living expenses for two adults along with student loans for two undergrads, nursing school, and law school.

"But lawyers make good money, and I figured that once she was in, we could start paying all that crap down. Then we could start saving. Maybe even start a family."

"So, you don't have any kids?"

"No. We wanted to wait until we were in a better position financially."

"Smart." She circled something on her note pad, but I couldn't see what it was. "Please, continue." She looked up at me, her expression blank. When I didn't start right away, she gazed at her notes. "You said she was getting new cases, earning experience and money."

"Right. So, after six months or so she comes home bouncing off the walls because she just landed a case she thinks she can actually win. Rothchilde wants her to make a deal at first, but eventually he lets her run it her way. Long story short, they end up going to trial and she wins the case."

"Good for her."

"Yeah, it was awesome! We went out and had a fancy dinner to celebrate. She was over the moon." I slipped into silence. Was that night really the last night we made love?

"Her career really took off. She was called into more important cases. Not running them, mind you, but she was in the loop, going to strategy meetings and the like. Of course, the smaller cases didn't stop. Her caseload was really something. She worked late every few nights at first. Then every night. Then weekends.

"I guess I should have expected that, but I didn't expect it to be so relentless.

"I mean, my work in the ER is relentless too. Twelve-hour shifts, overtime, always on the move. But, when my work's done, it's done."

The detective nodded while she scratched down notes. "Was it these long hours that made you think she was being unfaithful?"

"Not at first. I just figured she was busy. But then, things got worse. Everything that used to make her happy irritated her. She spent more time at the office. Instead of just being disengaged around me, she would wall herself up in her study and sit there for hours. She said she was working, but when I walked by her door, I could hear her whispering on the phone. I walked in on her once and she rushed to get off the phone, then lit into me. That was hands-down the biggest fight we ever had."

"So, is there anything in particular that happened to make you think she is sleeping with her boss?"

I swallowed. Here it was at last. I drew a deep breath and let it out slowly, rubbing my sweaty palms on my pant legs.

"About two weeks ago we had one of those rare moments when we were both going to work at the same time. We had breakfast together. It was fast and quiet, but at least it was cordial. I remember her outfit. A tan skirt and blazer with a white top. I remember thinking how much even her clothes had changed. She dressed so conservatively now. Buttoned up practically to her chin. She used to be more daring. I figured she was trying to look professional. Law firms are like that, you know?"

Jessica nodded as she continued writing.

"Anyway, it made an impression on me, so I remembered it. That night I ended up getting home before her, so I saw her when she arrived."

"And?"

"And she was wearing a completely different outfit. Black skirt and blazer instead of tan. Dark blue shirt."

"I see."

"I asked her about it. I admit, I probably came off more accusatory than I wanted."

"What did she say?"

"Told me I was crazy. Seeing things." I laughed. Not because it was funny, but because it wasn't. "That's the worst thing about being married to a lawyer...you never can win an argument.

"Anyway, another fight. Another nail in the coffin." I quickly wiped a tear from my cheek. Talking about it made it too real. The more I said, the more hope drained from my heart.

"Is there anything else?"

"Yeah. A couple days later I had the day off work. While she was asleep, I went to her car and popped the trunk. Inside I found a big suitcase packed with clothes."

"What kind of clothes?"

"It wasn't lingerie or anything. It might have been better if it had been. At least then I would know." I sighed and shook my head. "No. It was business suits. New stuff. Designer. A dozen of them. Maybe more. Isn't that strange?"

"Mmm." Jessica nodded absently, reviewing her notes as she chewed on the end of her pen.

"I expected her to take off after that. To disappear and not be heard from until she sent the divorce papers. She didn't, but the situation at the house hasn't gotten any better. She is more closed off now than ever before. And now...I just need to know."

"What are you going to do if you find out she's being unfaithful?" Jessica looked up and studied me.

"Do?"

"Confront her? Confront him? File for divorce?" And then she said what she really meant. "Take revenge?"

"Revenge?" I honestly hadn't thought that far ahead. What would I do? "I don't know. I don't think so. Really, I just want to know if it is worth pouring any more into this relationship. If there's a chance, then maybe we can work something out. If not...I want a divorce. And I'll take my revenge by having her pay me back for all the years she milked me while I paid the bills."

"Do you think that's what she's doing?"

"I don't know. It doesn't seem like her. Not the woman I know...knew... Whatever."

Jessica handed me a Kleenex.

"I just need to know her secret."

Jeannie Doyle

I held him close, my arms wrapped around his waist as he hugged me tight. His breath was hot and short on my neck, his body quivering with the release of so much tension.

Then he was gone, throwing his arms around his mother and sisters. They hugged me as well, his mother thanking me so quickly in Spanish that I could only make out one word in ten. The message was plain enough. 'Thank you for helping my boy.'

It was anticipation of moments like these that kept me going through Law School. When I was frustrated with the tedium of contract law and secured transactions, I would daydream about the innocent people I would help free.

I basked in that moment. The glory of finding justice for one wrongly accused person felt greater than the radiance of the sun.

My eyes fell to the back of the courtroom. Herman Rothchilde's self-important smile melted all that joy.

He pushed through the dwindling crowd as I packed my briefcase. He spared a smile for the family, but no words, as they passed him. His congratulations would mean nothing to them. He had never met them. A pro-bono case was not worth his time.

"Congratulations, counselor." His voice was commanding, loud enough to draw the attention of the few law students still hanging around at the back of the court.

"Thank you," I replied. Months ago, I would have added "sir," but no more.

"We need to meet our client," he said, his voice quieter.

I froze, the last folder hovering in the air above my briefcase, suspended as if some alien force prevented me from moving. Though we worked many cases, there was only one "our client."

I took a calming breath, forcing my heart to slow. I'm not sure that was truly comforting, but it broke the spell. I put away the last of my case notes and fastened the metal clasps. "I thought we were done until next week."

"Something came up."

I set my jaw in a way I hoped seemed like professional resolve. "Let me freshen up."

He led the way out of the courtroom, speaking to me as I neared the ladies room. What he said didn't penetrate the sound of blood rushing in my ears. I excused myself and entered the bathroom. As soon as I closed the door, the dam burst. I sprinted toward one of the stalls and spilled my lunch in a series of violent retches. When I was done, I shook, every nerve in my body tingling and alert.

In the mirror my eyes, red and puffy, stared back at me with loathing. I rubbed away the running mascara with a tissue. When I looked back my eyes had changed. Still red and puffy, but now filled with the calm facade I trained myself to project.

Stepping back into the stall I closed the lid and sat upon it. Lifting my briefcase onto my knees I unbolted the clasps and reached into the back pocket. Feeling around the soft leather, my fingers touched a pencil, a few paperclips, a loose staple. Then I felt the long, thin cylinder.

I pulled out the container and looked at the device laying inside the clear plastic tube. So small. So powerful. I placed the tube on top of my casefiles and unbuttoned my shirt to the navel. I removed the red plastic cap from the tube and slid the transmitter onto the palm of my hand. I wove the antenna into the lace of my bra as Agent Bremen instructed and tucked the body of the device into the underwire.

'Activated as soon as you remove the cap.' That is what he told me. I hoped to God it was true.

After buttoning myself up, I pulled the burner phone out of the same pocket and entered Bremen's number. "Meeting him now," I typed and hit send.

I stepped out of the stall. Thank God I was still alone. I looked at the phone again, the little message under my text read "delivered." I opened the battery compartment and slid out the battery and the sim card. The battery and phone went into one trash can and the sim card another.

"You've got this," I told the woman in the mirror.

She looked back and nodded. "I've got this," she replied. I believed her, so I grabbed my briefcase and headed out.

"Everything alright in there?" Herman's voice made me jump. I turned and saw him standing next to the women's restroom door just on the other side of the hinges, so the door blocked him from view as I emerged.

"Yes," I smiled, and touched my hand to my belly. "Just some nerves."

"You're doing fine," he replied and then led me to the black Lincoln town car waiting outside the courthouse. The driver opened the door for us, and we slid into the back seat. The driver walked around to the front and climbed in, then wordlessly pulled out onto the street.

"Where are we going?" I asked, more for Agent Bremen's sake than my own.

"I'm not sure," Herman replied absently. Then, turning to face me he said, "Remember what I said about questions."

I nodded. It was one of the first lessons he had given me after I joined the firm. *A good defense lawyer should only ask the questions to which they really want an answer.* At the time he said it Jeannie laughed, her boss still someone she respected.

"Look Jeannie, I know this is more than you wanted. It's more than I wanted, but you've got to know this isn't forever. Once the trial is done you can relax. Take a vacation. Take a couple of those pro-bono cases you love so much."

"I thought you didn't like the pro-bono cases."

"Well, I don't like losing money, but I want to keep you happy." He shrugged. "Besides, your successes win attention for the firm. That can attract paying clients. So, it's not all bad."

We sat in silence as the car drove through downtown, the skyscrapers shrinking and flattening as we left the business district and delved into the industrial sectors near the docks. Street vendors and sharply dressed professionals were slowly replaced by cracking concrete and rusting metal.

"How's Sean?" Herman asked.

The question brought a stab of guilt. None of this had been fair to Sean. It wasn't fair to either of them, but at least she understood the stakes. She yearned to tell him, but she never crossed that line. It was better to retreat further into herself than let him know she was neck-deep in shit and sinking. Still...she was losing him. At this rate she might never get him back. Even if she told him everything...when she told him everything...would he understand? Could they ever reclaim what they once had?

"He's fine," I snapped, fearing that I had taken too much time. "He doesn't know anything." That was the answer he really wanted.

"Good. You two should take a nice vacation when this is all over. I have a place in the Caymans I could let you use. Beautiful view. Quick walk to the beach."

"That would be lovely," I replied coldly, "but let's take this one step at a time."

The car turned and stopped before the gate of a high chain-link fence. A man dressed in a black suit stepped out of the guardhouse and unlocked the fence. Pulling it open he nodded to the driver and ducked his head to look in the back seat. The wind caught his jacket, tugging it to the side and exposing the handgun slung into the holster under his arm.

The driver pulled up in front of a garage door. A heartbeat later it rolled up and the car proceeded into the warehouse's dark maw.

The door rolled back down as soon as we passed through. A chill crawled down my spine. I had never done well in enclosed spaces, and though this vast warehouse contained nothing but a card table and a few men sitting around it, my claustrophobia had never been so acute.

The car stopped and the driver exited. He opened the door and stood back for us to emerge.

Two of the men from the card table approached. Leo Caracappa took the lead, his wide grin and oversized belly ambling over to us. His greedy eyes looked me up and down, making me feel even dirtier than the grimy floor on which we stood. When he got to us his eyes shifted at last to my boss.

"Herman," he said taking his hand firmly and shaking it with both of his. Then he embraced me, pulling me tight against him. "Jeannie," he said, his hug lasting too long, his hand moving down to the small of my back. "Thank you so much for coming." He parted, his hand lingering on my hip.

"You are our number one client," Herman said, clearing his throat and shifting his feet nervously.

"And you're my number one attorney." He paused, looked to me and then back to Herman. "Well, number two."

I forced a smile and his eyes twinkled. "I brought you a present, my dear." He extended one hand to the man behind him. The man handed him a garment box.

"Mr. Caracappa," Herman interjected, shaking his head and shrugging his shoulders. "I told you. It isn't appropriate."

"Nonsense. I'm just trying to make up for ruining her suit."

"You've already made up for it," I said, refusing to take the box. "There is no need for more."

"It does my heart good to give." He continued to hold the box in front of him, his smile fading. The twinkle in his eyes turning dark as the corners of his mouth curled downward. "Is my generosity not appreciated?"

I swallowed and forced another smile as I reached for the box and thanked him. His smile and the twinkle returned.

"You're welcome, my dear," he said, patting me on the cheek. His hands were big, his palms sticky. I wanted to pull away but forced myself to stay put. He turned to speak to the man behind him, but his eyes lingered on mine. "What did I tell you, Stevie? This girl's unflappable. Guy gets capped right in front of her, and she barely blinks an eye."

The image, always lurking, sprang up from my memory. Caracappa's face twisted with rage, the gun in his hand as bolts of fire thundered from the muzzle. Red holes appearing in the Victor Seville's chest before his head exploded, splattering brains all over me. I stood hyperventilating, unable to move, unable to scream while gore soaked through the fabric of my lucky green suit.

It was Herman who snapped me out of it. His finger to his lips, blood splattered across him, his glasses smudged red, his lips twisted in terror.

"Is she going to be a problem?" Caracappa had asked. The iciness in his voice stole the breath from me. The implications were clear.

"No, no problem, Mr. Caracappa," Rothchilde had said cupping my cheeks between his hands. "Just calm down, Jeannie. Everything will be okay."

But it wasn't okay. It would never be okay. After soul searching over many sleepless nights, I reached out to the FBI. Though I had imagined the weight of the world would fall from my shoulders after that, the pressure only increased. Being a witness was one thing, but the FBI needed more. They needed me to wear a wire. They said attorney-client privilege wouldn't matter because I was looking for confessions to crimes I had witnessed, not crimes for which I was defending him.

"This one's yellow," Caracappa said, his deep voice bringing me back to the present. "With a silky blue shirt. You'll look fantastic."

"Thank you," I replied, but the words hitched in my throat. "I'm sorry. My throat's a little dry. Do you have any water?"

"Yeah," Caracappa said gesturing with his head to the left side of the warehouse. "There's a sink in the can."

I walked to the bathroom and stepped inside. It was as dirty and stained and stank, but with the door locked behind me I could breathe. In that moment the air seemed fresher than springtime at the Park of Roses.

I thought of Caracappa's words. 'Guy gets capped right in front of her, and she barely blinks an eye.' That's what we'd been waiting for. Mentioning Victor Seville's murder on tape. Had Agent Bremen caught it? Would it be enough?

The water ran yellow out of the faucet, so I let it keep running until it turned clear. I wet my hands and dabbed them on my face and the back of my neck.

I studied myself in the mirror. I looked strangely calm, as though my heart were not pounding, my mouth not about to open in a long, terrified scream.

"Showtime," I said to myself and whoever else might be listening.

Please Agent Bremen. Please be listening.

I opened the door and prepared a smile. I expected Leo Caracappa to be standing a few feet from the door, his arms wide, his eyes lascivious. There would be a few comments I would have to laugh off, and then finally we could discuss his case.

Instead, Caracappa's lips were pulled tight and frowning. Sweat beaded on his forehead. Behind him Rothchilde was tied to a chair. Rothchilde's eyes screamed at me in blind panic over the duct tape covering his mouth. A drip of crimson ran from his nose, over the tape and onto his Armani suit.

"Have a seat, sweetheart," Caracappa said gesturing to the chair next to Rothchilde's. "We have to discuss a few things."

Jessica Dupris

I should have listened to that little voice telling me to get out of there. When the guns came out, it was too late.

I watched from the warehouse's dormer vent, camera in hand, while Caracappa's men bound and gagged Rothchilde to the chair. Caracappa stood over him, talking as if it were a game. Then his face curled up into an ugly snarl and his meaty fist slammed into Rothchilde's nose.

"Shit," I cursed under my breath, then raised my camera and snapped a few more pictures. This was important evidence.

Mrs. Doyle stepped out of the door and came up short. She didn't scream, or run, or fight. Instead, she moved to the chair Caracappa's men had set out for her and sat.

One of the men unwound a length of rope. Mrs. Doyle turned to Caracappa and said a few words. The mob boss shrugged and said something to his goon, who dropped the rope to the floor.

I snapped a few more photos. It was enough. I let the camera hang from the strap around my neck and pulled out my cell phone. I thumbed the button, but nothing happened. "Damn!" My phone had been acting funny for the last couple of days. I had plunged deep into the dark web working the Rockera case and who knew what viruses my phone had picked up.

A low rumble brought my attention back to the warehouse. Three of Caracappa's men entered through the open garage door holding two men between them. A goon stood to the side of each man, holding him by the arm and neck. The third walked behind, his gun pointing at the captured men's backs.

The men were dressed in dark suits and ties, their hands bound behind their backs. The one with light hair and glasses twisted his head in all directions, searching for an escape route. The one with salt-and-pepper hair held himself with more reserve, scowling at Caracappa as he squared his shoulders.

Who were these guys? Cops? No, Feds.

I snapped off a few more pictures while my phone reset.

Caracappa's men brought the captives even with Rothchilde and Doyle then forced them to their knees.

I tried my phone again. A brief flash of light, the screen appeared, a point of light wound around in an infinite loop.

The man with the gun stood behind the four prisoners, a second goon stripped down to his cotton undershirt. His shoulder holster and side arm lying on top of the folded shirt and jacket. He put on a pair of black gloves, pressing them tight onto his hands. Caracappa paced before his captives. His gesticulations where terse and pointed, his mouth set in a snarl.

Where had the fourth man gone?

My phone finally popped to life. The Dupris Detective Agency logo blinked on. Painful moments later the icons popped up one by one. I pressed the phone icon as soon as it appeared. I dialed 9-1-1 and connected the call. The screen went white and pulsed. The word "dialing" appeared at the top of the screen. The image froze. The screen went black.

BOOM!

The Fed with the glasses was lying face-first on the ground, a crimson halo spreading around his head. The man with salt-and-pepper hair screamed with rage. The lawyer turned his face away, straining to leave his seat. Mrs. Doyle watched wide-eyed, her fingers digging into the metal chair, holding herself from fleeing.

My fingers snapped pictures before I could even make the conscious decision to do it. The agent tried to stand, but the gunman swung the pistol, knocking him down. He fell beside his partner's twitching body. The other goon was on him in a second, kicking him in the gut twice before coming down with a hard punch to his face.

Time to go.

I rushed down the catwalk to the fire escape. I searched the grounds below. The door next to the fire escape's exit was still closed. My car was parked out of sight on the other side of the neighboring warehouse.

I scurried down the ladder, my feet light on the rungs. The cold metal passed through my hands in the quick, precise rhythm I had learned at the Great Lakes Naval Station. My feet hit the ground and I was off. I poked my head around the corner, my heart pounding in my chest.

Shit!

The fourth goon stood by my car looking through the driver's window. He turned around, already moving back to the warehouse. I pressed my back to the wall and drew my Ruger LC9S from its holster in the small of my back. Small and light enough to not draw notice, its 9mm rounds could still stop a man. I chambered a bullet that I dearly hoped I wouldn't need. I've already killed enough people in my life.

I straightened and held my sidearm at shoulder height. There was a chance he would just run by me. He might go right to the door, run inside, and disappear. That would give me time to run.

But what about Jeannie Doyle and Rothchilde? And the Fed?

The footfalls approached, echoing down the long narrow passage between buildings. Staring at the blank space in front of me, I waited for him to appear. *Please don't look. Please don't look.*

He emerged past the wall, so close I could see the acne scars along his cheeks. He took two steps past the opening, already reaching one hand for the doorknob. He turned. His eyes wide at the sight of me.

"Freeze!" I brought my other hand up to support my weapon and squared my feet.

The goon stopped, raising his hands in front of him.

"Turn around, asshole. Keep your hands up."

His eyes narrowed as he searched my face. He nodded and turned.

"On your knees."

"You're going to regret this," he replied.

I swung the weapon and brought down the butt just behind his right ear. He stiffened, a grunt escaping his lips before he fell to concrete. I knelt above him, my knee firmly on his back as I pulled my handcuffs from their case.

I snapped the cuffs around each wrist and stood.

A cry of pain and fear escaped the warehouse. Mrs. Doyle. I looked at the man beneath me then back to the closed steel door.

Could I just run? If I did, they were all as good as dead. What about the pictures? If I went in all cowboy and things went bad, the photos would disappear along with the rest of us.

I ran to my car, pressing the button to pop the trunk. I threw in my camera and was about the slam the door closed, then paused. I pulled out my phone one more time and pressed the power button. It turned on, slowly, but it turned on. I pressed the phone icon and typed in 9-1-1. Dialing...dialing...dialing...

"Fuck it," I muttered, throwing the still-dialing phone into the trunk, and slamming it closed.

I ran back to the warehouse door. I knelt beside the unconscious goon and reached under his jacket, extracting his handgun. His Glock held more rounds and had better stopping power than my Ruger, so I put mine back in my holster and locked and loaded his weapon.

No sounds came through the heavy metal door, so I grabbed the handle and eased it open. The light shining through the door illuminated a small, disheveled back room. Distant voices spoke somewhere through the gloom.

"I told you, I don't know anything." The woman's voice was calm and sincere.

"Yeah, you keep saying that. And he keeps saying that. But if that's true how come these assholes was listening to everything we said? Now, I know lawyer and liar are pretty much the same thing, but I got my own truth detector."

I darted to the next doorway and peered into the warehouse room. The man with his shirt off and the man with the gun stood behind the three prisoners. Both were facing me, but neither saw me in the shadows.

Rothchilde sat limply in his chair, his bobbing head the only proof he still lived. One of Mrs. Doyle's eyes was blackened and swelling. Blood dripping from her lip stained her suit. Still unbound she pressed one hand against her wounded eye. The agent was kneeling, his face as swollen and broken as Rothchilde's. The fourth man, the dead one, was gone. Only a bloodstain marked where he once lay. The town car was parked behind them, a red-blotted plastic sheet visible within the open trunk. Caracappa stayed seated in front of the three, his back to me as he continued the interrogation.

"It's alright," he said, his voice regaining an inner cheer. "I figured it out." He turned his attention back to the man with the gun. "Ronnie, shoot this piece of shit." He nodded to Rothchilde and the man raised his gun even with the lawyer's head."

"Freeze," I yelled, stepping into the open.

All eyes turned to me, but I only had eyes on the man with the gun. The smooth motion of his raising hand took the gun past Rothchilde's head and flowed toward me. I squeezed the trigger and the .45 jumped in my hand. The bullet smashed into the center of his chest, a red spray exploding behind him. He dropped to his knees, already dead, his gun clattering to the ground.

The gloved man dashed back to the table where he had left his sidearm. Caracappa rose from his chair and ran. He only got two paces before Mrs. Doyle shot out her foot, entangling him mid-stride.

He landed hard on the concrete.

The man in the gloves crouched as he moved, keeping himself low with the prisoners seated between us. I stepped forward, yelling for him to freeze. He reached the gun and yanked it from his shoulder holster. He spun. I fired. The bullet caught him in the left shoulder. He brought his gun level. I put him down with another bullet, this one catching him just below the throat.

Caracappa struggled to stand. Mrs. Doyle sprang from her chair and kicked his feet out from under him. He slipped and fell once more. I ran up behind him. "Stay down, asshole!"

He turned and looked at the gun in my hand then back to Mrs. Doyle, hate filling his face.

"Mrs. Doyle," I said watching Caracappa for the slightest move. "Go free the FBI agent."

She stepped over to him as I moved to Caracappa. Maybe it was because she was moving that I missed the other guy, the one who'd been watching the front gate.

It was like being hit by a baseball bat. My breath was knocked out of my lungs. The world teetered and suddenly I was seeing the world on its side. I opened my mouth to speak, but I coughed instead. A crimson Jackson Pollack appeared on the floor in front of me.

Two more shots rang out, then a third. Bullets whizzed around me. Caracappa stood and ran. I raised my hand, focusing on his back, my vision wavering. I couldn't breathe through the blood in my lungs. I should have panicked, but instead a strange peace eased over me.

More gunshots. Distant. Remote. A warm pool closing around my ears.

I squeezed the trigger. The kick from the .44 jerked my hand to my face, the cloud of gun smoke obscured my view. Through my fading vision and the clearing smoke Caracappa dropped to one knee, then fell prone.

Then I was swimming in a dream. Faces looked over me, hands held me still, lifted me. Voices whispered. Voices yelled. Sirens screamed.

The last thing I saw before I blacked out was Mrs. Doyle in a gurney next to me. There was blood on her face, a blood-soaked bandage over her right arm, tears on her cheeks, and oddly...a smile. A nurse stood next to her, holding her hand, kissing her lips.

I remember thinking, 'wow, she really is cheating on her husband.' Then it dawned on me that this was her husband. Her lips moved and their tears fell as he held her hand and caressed her cheek.

Hunted
From the Podcasts of Summer Cum Laude, College Detective
Michael J. Ciaraldi

Rain pattered down on the campus as bells chimed the hour.

In her dormitory room, a young woman sat, speaking into her recorder. "A rainy night on campus. But on the top floor of Founders Hall, one young woman sits in her room. She's ready for mystery."

The telephone on her desk rang.

Excitement started to show in her voice. "She's ready for danger."

The phone rang again.

More excitedly: "She's ready for *anything*!"

Another ring.

"She's—"

One last ring cut off as she lifted the receiver and spoke crisply, "Summer Cum Laude, College Detective."

A voice came from the receiver. "Hello, I'm looking for my dog."

Summer thought for a second, then said, "I've never tried to track down a dog, but I suppose I could use my detective skills for that."

"Detective skills? Isn't this the Humane Society?"

"No, it isn't. And before you ask, I don't know their phone number. Goodbye."

Summer laid the phone down, then raised the recorder to her mouth. "Where was I? I was sitting at my desk, listening to the rain on the window, and reading my name on the glass pane in the door. 'Ed-you-all Muck Remus.'"

The phone rang again and she picked it up. "Summer Cum Laude, College Detective!"

A woman's voice came through the line. "Hello, Summer? I need your help."

"Oh, hello, Prof. Ipcress, what's on your mind?"

"Remember when I asked you to find those missing files a few months ago? I seem to have lost them again."

"What do you remember about them?"

"These are grant proposals I'm submitting to the National Science Foundation."

"So the phrase 'National Science Foundation' would be in them?" asked Summer.

"You know, it would, at that."

"One more question," said Summer. "Are you still running Windows 2000?"

"I think so. It's been a long time since I changed anything."

"All right, Professor, we'll get you updated later. For now, try this. Click on the Start button."

"Left or right click?"

Summer sighed. "Left. These are all going to be clicks with the left button."

"Got it."

"All right. Count up about five lines in the menu and click on 'Search'".

"OK."

"When the new menu appears, click on 'Files or Folders'. Let me know when the new window appears."

"It's there," said Prof. Ipcress.

"Do you see where it says 'Containing text'? Click in the box underneath it and type 'National Science Foundation'".

"OK, I did that. Nothing's happening."

"We're almost done. Click on the button marked 'Search now'".

"All right. Hey! Those are my files! You're amazing, Summer! What do I owe you?"

"No charge for my oldest client, Professor. Have a good evening."

"Thanks, Summer. Talk with you later."

As Summer hung up the phone, there came a knock on the door. She called out, "Come in, it's unlocked!"

Susan "Scooter" Capriati and her boyfriend Harry Deighton entered. Scooter spoke. "Hi, Summer."

Summer greeted them. "Hi, Scooter, Harry. What's up, my loyal assistant?"

They sat down, then Scooter asked, "Did you hear that Jennifer Arrowsmith is coming to campus?"

"Really? The author?"

"Yes, she'll be writer-in-residence this semester."

"Wow. I think I've read all her books. It's amazing how she travels around the country, solving murders and then writing about them."

Harry spoke up. "And I even hear they're going to make a TV show about her. They'll call it 'She Writes About Murder', or something like that." He thought for a second. "You know, there's one thing I've always wondered about her. It seems that everywhere she goes, there's a murder. She solves it and then gets to write a book about it."

Summer said, "Well, we do live in a violent society. Anyway, I suppose it's just a coincidence. After all, if there *is* a crime, people know she's an amateur detective, so they naturally turn to her. And who knows how many places she visits where there aren't any murders? She just never writes about those times."

"I suppose," Harry said. "I wonder if we'll get to meet her."

Scooter broke in. "That would be great. Maybe we can compare detective techniques."

Summer said, "Let's see what we can do. I have an idea. Come on."

"I'm game," said Scooter. "Harry?"

"Sorry, Piglet, I have to get back to the lab," he said.

"OK, Pooh Bear, I'll see you later," said Scooter sadly. Then she and Harry kissed.

Summer laughed. "Enough mush. Let's go see President Queeg!"

* * *

Queeg and Jennifer Arrowsmith were talking in his office.

"We're all excited, Ms. Arrowsmith, about your being on campus this term."

"Please, President Queeg, call me Jennifer."

"Thank you. And you can call me Admiral. All my friends do."

"Uh, all right," said Arrowsmith. She gestured toward the water pitcher on the side table. "Do you mind?"

"Help yourself."

Arrowsmith was setting her glass down as there was a knock on the door.

Queeg called, "Yes?"

Summer poked her head in the door. "Mr. President? I hope we're not disturbing you."

"Not at all. My secretary Marjorie is out sick today, I'm afraid. Come in, there's someone I'd like you to meet."

Summer and Scooter entered, then Queeg made introductions. "Jennifer, I'd like you to meet our campus's own student detectives, Summer Cum Laude and her assistant, Scooter. Summer, Scooter, this is Jennifer Arrowsmith."

Summer shook Arrowsmith's hand. "It's an honor, Ms. Arrowsmith. I'm a great fan of your work."

"Thank you. Summer, is it?"

"That's right." Summer nodded.

Scooter then shook Arrowsmith's hand. "And congratulations on your latest bestseller, *The Nun Wore Black*."

"Why thank you, Scooter. You know, it seems to me I *have* heard about the two of you. You captured that physicist, Prof. Moreau, didn't you?"

Queeg broke in. "That's right. He stole the strawberries from the dining hall."

Scooter added, "And tried to blow up the campus nuclear reactor; don't forget that."

"Oh, well, yes, that too," said Queeg.

Summer asked, "What will you be doing on campus this term?"

"I'll be leading a seminar course on true crime writing, and giving occasional special lectures."

Scooter said, "That sounds great. I hope the two of us will be able to take your course."

Summer said, "And who knows? Maybe you'll find a mystery to solve."

"You never know," said Jennifer Arrowsmith. "I've never solved a murder on a college campus before."

Queeg pointed out, "Our time is limited. I need to take Jennifer to meet the Provost, so if you two will excuse us..."

Summer started to say, "Of course–" then began to cough.

Queeg gestured toward the pitcher. "Have some water."

Summer poured herself a glass, then drank it and set it down on the desk. She said, "Thank you, Sir. And again, welcome to campus, Ms. Arrowsmith."

"Oh, yes, I'm sure I will find it most rewarding," said Arrowsmith. "You know what they say, 'When opportunity knocks, be prepared to answer.'"

As they all exited, nobody noticed that Jennifer Arrowsmith had picked up Summer's glass as she returned hers to the table.

* * *

Two weeks later, Summer and Scooter listened attentively as Jennifer Arrowsmith continued her lecture. "Now class, the assignment for today was to read my bestselling true-crime book from last year, *The Lawns Were Burned*. What did you think? Was it easy for me to track down the killer? Anyone?" She looked out into the classroom expectantly.

Scooter and Summer looked at each other, then around the classroom. They were the only two students in the room. Finally, Scooter timidly raised her hand.

Arrowsmith called on her. "Scooter. What do you think?"

"Well, Ms. Arrowsmith, after someone burned a giant question mark on the front lawns of each of the victims, it seemed obvious that the killer was a crazed Unitarian. And since this happened in Texas, and there was only one Unitarian in a hundred-mile radius, there really was only one logical suspect."

"Yes, but this alone would not be enough for a conviction, or even for an arrest. How well did this ruthless killer cover his tracks? Anyone?" Again she looked out expectantly.

Summer sighed and raised her hand.

Arrowsmith pointed. "Summer."

"I would say that he did a mixed job. There were those dozen gasoline cans you found in his garage, and that in itself is suspicious since he didn't own a lawnmower or any other gasoline-powered equipment. And when he went to fill the cans, he apparently drove to the gas station at night in his electric car, and this is the only gas station in town where the attendant on duty is blind; so that would make it hard for anyone to identify him. But *then* he made his fatal mistake; he paid for the gas with his credit card. So once you had all those clues, it all seemed pretty conclusive, even though he claimed the card had been stolen. Too bad he never admitted his guilt; he was still protesting his innocence up to the time he was executed."

"Yes, that was a shame. But you know what they say, 'Justice delayed is justice denied.'"

Summer continued. "But this all seems so strange. Why would the killer take all those precautions to avoid being recognized, and then use his own credit card? It's almost like he wanted to get caught. If someone had acted like that in a novel or a play, nobody would believe it."

Arrowsmith replied, "Who can understand the mind of a madman? And you know what they say, 'Truth is stranger than fiction.'" She looked at her watch. "We're almost out of time for today. Now, class, for your next assignment, I want you to work in groups. So divide yourselves into teams of two or three, and send me an email to let me know who your partners will be."

Summer raised her hand.

"Yes, Summer, what is it?"

"Uh, Ms. Arrowsmith." She looked around the room. "Seeing as everyone else has dropped the course, and that Scooter and I are the only two students left, do you think maybe we could be a little less formal in class?"

"I'll have to think about that. After all, discipline is so important, in the classroom and in everyday life." Arrowsmith looked at her watch again. "Now we really are out of time. Class dismissed. See you all next time."

* * *

Summer narrated into her recorder. "We headed to Honest Mike's Electronics to pick up some new equipment."

Summer and Scooter entered and found the proprietor behind the counter.

Scooter called out, "Hi, Mike!"

"Hi, Scooter, Summer. What's up?"

Summer replied, "We're here to pick up that gear I ordered."

Scooter asked, "What is it, anyway? You've been pretty secretive about it, Summer."

"Oh, you'll see..." she replied.

"Here's that new cell phone you ordered, Summer," said Mike as he handed it to her.

"Does it have all the features I asked for?"

"Of course. And a few little extras, too."

"Good. Well, I guess we'd better be going." Summer started to turn away, then turned back. "Oh, is there anything else?"

"Well, there is one more thing." Mike reached under the counter and brought out a gift-wrapped package, then looked at the tag. "What's this on the package? 'For Scooter, From Summer and Mike. Happy Birthday.'" He smiled and presented the package to Scooter.

"Happy birthday, my loyal assistant!" cried Summer.

"I don't know what to say..." Scooter unwrapped the package. "Wow! My own recorder! Now I can narrate our adventures myself!"

Summer said, "That's right."

"I don't know how to thank you both," Scooter said excitedly. Inspiration dawned, and she raised the recorder to her mouth. "As I recorded my first narration, I pondered the future. What adventures await our intrepid pair? What dangers would they face?"

Summer and Mike looked at each other, then rolled their eyes.

Scooter kept narrating; she was on a roll. "What moral crises will they confront? What crazed villains will threaten the safety and stability of the campus? What–"

Summer interrupted. "Scooter, I think that's enough for now."

Mike chimed in. "Yeah, the, uh, batteries aren't, uh, fully charged yet. Yeah, that's it. Need to conserve those batteries."

"Oh, right. I guess I'll have to continue this later."

Summer agreed. "That sounds good."

Mike asked, "Say, Summer, there's something I've always wondered. Why do you narrate your adventures into that recorder?"

"All the great detectives do that. Sam Spade, Philip Marlowe, Nick Danger, Guy Noir..."

Mike continued. "But isn't that just a literary device? You know, so the readers or the audience would know what's going on?"

"It is?" Summer said.

"Think about it," Mike continued. "When Philip Marlowe was active in the 1930s, the tape recorder hadn't even been invented yet."

Summer hesitated. "It hadn't?"

"The Germans invented it, and they kept it a military secret until the end of World War II," said Mike.

"They did?"

Scooter added, "Now that you mention it, I remember reading about that."

Summer's face fell. "You did?"

"Yeah, the Allies couldn't figure out how Hitler could broadcast speeches from two different cities on the same day," said Scooter.

"They couldn't?"

Summer took her recorder out of her pocket, contemplated it for a few seconds, and then raised it to her mouth. "As we left Honest Mike's, I pondered the history of recording technology..."

* * *

Summer and Scooter were walking across the quad when they saw Harry and waved to him. Harry saw them and walked over.

"Hi, Susan. Hi, Summer. How is that course with Jennifer Arrowsmith going?"

Scooter replied, "OK, I guess. It's certainly been interesting, but there's something strange about Ms. Arrowsmith."

"Oh?" asked Harry.

Summer joined in. "I suppose you could call her..."

"Eccentric?" asked Harry.

Summer relied, "Maybe..."

"Weird?"

Scooter said, "Yeah..."

Harry was getting into it. "Crazy as a soup sandwich?"

Summer said, "That might be a little strong..."

"Detached from reality?"

Scooter said, "Well, yes, there is that..."

"Bonkers? Mad as a hatter? Off her rocker? Nutty as a fruitcake?"

Summer and Scooter looked at each other, then nodded.

Nodding, Summer said, "That about sums it up."

"I see." Harry sighed and shook his head. "So, where are you two headed?"

Summer said, "I need to get to the campus bookstore and pick up some supplies for an art project."

Scooter said, "I'm free for the next few hours. How about you?"

"I don't have anything scheduled. Want to get some coffee?" asked Harry.

"Sure," replied Scooter.

"Then I guess I'll see you both later." Summer took out her recorder and looked at it, pondering.

"Something wrong with your recorder, Summer?" asked Harry.

"Don't go there," warned Scooter.

Summer wandered off, still looking at the recorder. As she did, she started to raise it to her mouth, then lowered it again.

Scooter and Harry looked at each other, shrugged, and then walked off hand-in-hand.

* * *

President Queeg was sitting at his desk as Jennifer Arrowsmith entered. She greeted him. "Admiral?"

"Come in, come in." Queeg gestured toward a chair.

Another man, wearing the uniform of the campus police, entered and addressed the president. "Sir?"

"Come in. I don't think you've met Inspector Doppler from the campus police. Tom, this is Jennifer Arrowsmith."

They shook hands.

"An honor, Ms. Arrowsmith. You're quite popular down at the station house."

"Why, thank you, Inspector."

Scooter walked in, followed by Summer, who said, "Mr. President?"

"Have a seat."

Scooter asked, "Why did you call the four of us here, sir?"

"Inspector Doppler here has informed me that Professor Bedrosian is dead. It happened a few hours ago."

Summer addressed Arrowsmith. "You probably hadn't met him yet, but he taught courses for the major in Interactive Media and Game Development."

"How did he die?" asked Arrowsmith.

Inspector Doppler explained. "The autopsy should be complete shortly, but early results say he drowned..."

Scooter broke in. "Drowned? In the university's swimming pool?"

Queeg replied, "No, in his office."

Summer asked, "What? How could he drown in his office?"

"That's what I want you to find out. The campus police are looking into it, but they can use the expertise of our campus' two, now three, resident detectives."

Arrowsmith asked, "Did Bedrosian have any enemies?"

Summer replied, "None that I know of. I had a rather public disagreement with him last term, but it wasn't serious."

"What was it about?"

"I told him that a detective game he and his students were designing wasn't realistic."

"How so?" asked Arrowsmith.

"There were several weaknesses. Let's see." Summer started ticking off points on her fingers. "The plot relied on too many coincidences. The heroine knew all sorts of trivial facts, which naturally were just the ones she needed to crack the case. She was incredibly lucky. She was always telling people things they already knew. The authorities were totally incompetent. Things like that."

Scooter agreed. "That's right. It was just totally unrealistic. Wouldn't you say so, Inspector?"

Everyone looked at Doppler. "That's right. Not true-to-life at all," he said.

"So what happened?" asked Arrowsmith.

Queeg continued. "Summer and Bedrosian exchanged some rather heated letters in the student newspaper for a few weeks, but then it died down."

"The argument was never resolved," Summer replied. "But I suppose you could say that we agreed to disagree."

Arrowsmith took charge. "I see. Well, we'd better get started. 'Strike while the iron is hot,' as they say. Why don't we divide up the investigation? Summer, you could try to find out if Prof. Bedrosian had any enemies." Arrowsmith laughed. "Other than you, of course, Summer. Inspector, contact the state police and see if any other unusual deaths have been reported. Scooter and I will wait for the autopsy results, then start looking into the forensic evidence."

Summer said, "All right. I'll get started on that right away."

Queeg offered, "Good luck."

"Thanks. I'll let you all know if I find anything," said Summer.

Doppler said, "So will I. Summer, I want to discuss some ideas with you..."

Summer and Doppler left, engrossed in conversation.

Queeg mused, "I wonder when we'll get those autopsy results."

The telephone rang and Queeg picked it up. "What? Where? Hold on!"

He turned to Scooter and Arrowsmith. "It's the coroner." He spoke into the phone. "Yes? Yes? I see. Thank you."

Queeg hung up and addressed the others. "Well, the autopsy results are in, and we know how Prof. Bedrosian drowned."

"How?" asked Scooter.

"His lungs were filled with...India ink!" Queeg replied.

"India ink?" asked Scooter incredulously.

"Yes, that's the kind of ink used in drafting and art," replied Queeg.

"I know what India ink is, sir. What I meant was: how could he drown in ink?"

"Apparently he was first rendered unconscious by a blow to the head, then his assailant put a funnel into his nose and poured in a gallon or so of ink. With his lungs full of ink, he suffocated."

Scooter said, "That's bizarre!"

"I agree," said Queeg.

Arrowsmith pointed out, "But no more bizarre than some of the murders I've investigated over the years. Now it's time to really get to work. Scooter, you check with all the stores in the area which sell India ink in bulk, and see who recently bought a large quantity. I'll go and examine Bedrosian's office."

"All right, I'll let everyone know what I find," said Scooter.

"Good luck," said Queeg.

"Thank you, Mr. President," said Scooter. She left.

"How long do you think your investigation will take, Jennifer?" asked Queeg.

"Oh, I don't think it will be long at all. I'll see you later, Admiral."

"Yes, we've had enough deaths on this campus. Let me know what you find."

"Of course, sir. I'll be in touch. Goodbye."

* * *

Several hours later, the group reassembled in President Queeg's office. They passed around a pitcher of water and started their meeting.

Queeg opened the discussion. "I hope you all have something to report."

Summer led off. "All I can report is a negative, Mr. President. I interviewed the Provost, Student Affairs, Human Resources, and even the editor of the campus newspaper, and they all agree that Prof. Bedrosian was liked and respected by everyone on campus. In his personal life there wasn't anything suspicious either. No significant debts, sudden wealth, jealous husbands, anything like that."

Scooter laughed. "I guess that leaves you as his only enemy, Summer."

"I suppose, but I know that I didn't kill him. What could the motive be for his death?" Summer got up and started pacing.

Doppler went next. "I checked with the state police, but they didn't have anything. The last time this state had a death this bizarre was five years ago. It's funny; you cracked that case, Ms. Arrowsmith."

"I remember it well. The victim was run over by a lawnmower."

Summer said, "That sort of accident happens all the time, doesn't it?"

"Yes, but usually on the lawn, not in someone's bathroom," said Arrowsmith.

"Really?" Queeg pondered for few seconds. "Anyway, what did you find out, Jennifer?

"I searched the area around Bedrosian's office, and found an empty gallon bottle of ink in one of the custodian's closets. I dusted it for fingerprints, but then I'm afraid I dropped it and it shattered. Fortunately, I had already preserved the prints. I'll bring them by later."

"Good work," Doppler said. I'll send them to the police and FBI.

What did you find, Scooter?"

"With so many engineers and art students on campus, the local stores sell a lot of India ink. But it's usually in small bottles. In fact, if you wanted a whole gallon, you'd have to special order it."

"Did anyone order some recently?" asked Doppler.

"I asked the manager of the campus bookstore to make up a list of recent special orders; I picked it up on the way here." Scooter took out an envelope and removed the list. "Let's see...F. Smith: Some software. Dr. Wu: a centrifuge. J. Carter: an embroidered sweater. President Queeg: a rocking chair. Ah, here we go. Gallon of India ink: S. C. Laude."

They all turned and looked at Summer.

"It was for my art project," Summer said weakly.

They continued to stare at her.

Summer looked at each of them in turn. "You don't think..."

Doppler took out his handcuffs. "Maybe you'd better come with me, Summer."

Summer started edging back toward the door.

Arrowsmith cried out, "Summer, how could you?"

"I know this looks bad, but I didn't do it," Summer protested.

Doppler spoke soothingly. "Just stay calm and come along quietly."

Summer looked wildly in all directions, then dove out the door.

"After her!" yelled Doppler.

Doppler and Scooter ran out the door. Arrowsmith took out a handkerchief and used it to pick up Summer's glass, then walked toward the door. She turned back as she left. "I'll be in touch, Admiral."

Queeg looked down, shaking his head.

* * *

Later that day, Scooter and Harry walked across the quad. He asked, "Any news?"

"Apparently Summer got to her dorm room before the police could set up a stakeout. She picked up her laptop computer and some other equipment, then went into hiding."

"This campus has so many places to hide that it's like Swiss cheese. How are you going to track her down?"

"I don't know. Just search systematically, I guess. I did get an email from her protesting her innocence."

"Sent from her laptop?" Herry asked.

"Yes."

"Where did she plug into the campus network? She'd have to go into a building for that."

"Apparently she used the wireless network. Maybe from the library parking lot or something; the signal reaches there."

"That gives me an idea," said Harry excitedly. "Let's head to my lab, Piglet."

As they left the quad, Doppler and Arrowsmith entered from the other end.

"Any news?" Doppler asked.

Arrowsmith smiled. "I think you'll find this really interesting." She reached into her purse and handed him a card. "Here's a copy of the only fingerprints I found on the murder weapon, the bottle of India ink." She handed him another card. "And *this* is a set of prints I lifted from a water glass which we know was handled by a certain person."

He held up both cards and examined them closely. "I'm no expert, but even I can see that they're the same. So, whose prints are they?"

"Summer Cum Laude." She smirked. "The so-called College Detective."

"That's pretty conclusive. I guess I'd better ask the local police to issue an A.P.B."

"Yes, I suppose you'd better." She turned away so Doppler couldn't see the smug look on her face.

* * *

Harry sat at his lab in the Physics Department tinkering with the array of electronic equipment that covered it. Honest Mike looked on as Scooter entered.

"Hi, guys," she said. "How's it going?"

Harry replied. "Oh, hi, Susan. We're making some progress."

Scooter came over and kissed him.

Mike protested. "Hey! No kiss for me, Scooter?"

Scooter laughed. "Sorry, Mike, you'll have to find your own significant other."

"Oh, well. Any news?" asked Mike.

"We've had a few reports of sightings, but nothing definite. Finding Summer's fingerprints on the murder weapon is pretty damning."

"I still don't feel right about this." Mike said, shaking his head. "Summer and I have been friends for years, besides the fact that she's my best customer."

Harry joined in. "And she's responsible for you and me getting together."

"I know, but if Summer's gone rogue, we have to help track her down," said Scooter. "With her knowledge of criminal techniques, she's a danger to everyone."

Mike sighed. "I suppose..."

"So, what have you got?" asked Scooter.

Harry handed Scooter a device. "We rigged up this tracker. If Summer uses her cell phone, it will lock on to the signal."

"Is that legal?"

Mike laughed, "Who's going to turn us in?"

"Good point," said Scooter. "Can it access the GPS unit in the phone? Most new phones have that, so the emergency operators can trace 9-1-1 calls. That should tell us her location to within a few feet."

Mike looked embarrassed. "Well, no, actually. When I sold Summer that phone last week, I installed a switch so she could disable that feature. I call it my 'stealth' capability."

"That's not legal either, is it?" asked Scooter.

"Well, no," said Mike.

Harry chimed in. "But you can still get a directional fix, and an approximate range from the signal strength. That should help."

"What else can it do?" Scooter asked.

Mike started pointing. "You can push this button; that will give you range and direction if Summer uses the wireless networking features of her laptop. And this one will detect any bugs or other listening devices. I built one of those for Summer recently, by the way."

"This is great," Scooter said. "How about her recorder?"

Harry said. "Hey, even if we're willing to skirt the law, we still have to obey the laws of physics. The recorder just doesn't put out enough of a signal to detect. Sorry."

"That's all right," said Scooter. "You guys have done great. I guess I'd better start putting this to use."

"Well, good luck," said Mike.

Harry's expression turned serious. "And watch yourself."

"Hey, Summer would never hurt *me*," said Scooter. "I think...I think..."

As Scooter left, Harry and Mike looked at each other thoughtfully.

* * *

The clearing in the forest at the edge of campus was dark as sirens sounded in the distance. Summer entered, looked around warily, then set her laptop computer down and started it. She pulled out her recorder and spoke into it. "I've managed to elude the police for the last two days, but how long can I keep this up? I must gather the evidence I need to clear my name."

When the computer finished booting, Summer started to type. The sound of sirens was getting closer. A helicopter approached. A searchlight swept across the clearing. It went past Summer, then reversed and came back toward her. She flattened herself on the ground, trying to burrow under the leaves. The searchlight went past her again, then came back slowly. It finally stopped on her.

Doppler's voice came from between the trees. "There she is!"

Summer jumped up, grabbed for her computer, but stumbled and dropped it. She scrambled to her feet and rushed from the clearing, leaving the computer behind.

Doppler entered from the other side of the clearing and looked around. He grabbed the computer, looked on the ground for tracks, then gestured. Over his shoulder he called to the other searchers. "This way!" He ran after Summer.

* * *

The next day, Doppler and Arrowsmith were walking across the quad. He spoke. "It's been three days. We've come close a few times, but we just can't seem to catch her."

Arrowsmith gestured with her coffee cup. "I'm sure you'll find her soon, Inspector. With campus security, the local police, the county sheriff, and the state police all searching for her, there's no way Summer will be able to escape." She took a sip. "In fact, I'd say–"

She choked and collapsed to the ground.

"Ms. Arrowsmith!" cried Doppler.

Doppler crouched next to her, felt her pulse, then leaned over and sniffed her lips. "The scent of bitter almonds," he said. "Cyanide!"

* * *

That night, Summer entered the alley between two campus buildings and looked around. She took out her cell phone and punched in a number. After one ring Scooter's voice came from the phone. "Hello?"

"It's Summer."

"Summer, how could you do it?"

"I already told you; I didn't kill Prof. Bedrosian."

"I don't mean that. Why did you kill Jennifer Arrowsmith?"

"What? Arrowsmith is dead? How?"

"Cyanide in her coffee."

"Maybe the real murderer killed her. Once I proved my innocence, I'm sure that Arrowsmith would have gone after the real killer. Hmm...Have they done an autopsy yet? Maybe they'll find some clues."

"They won't be able to. Her body is missing from the morgue. Some kind of bureaucratic slip-up, apparently."

"This is getting crazier and crazier. Look, I'd better hang up before someone traces this call."

Scooter entered the alley with her cell phone in one hand and the detector in the other. "You mean like this?"

"What is that thing?"

"Just something Mike and Harry whipped up. It let me track your computer and now your cell phone. It detects bugs, too. So, are you going to give yourself up?"

"I can't," said Summer. "If I'm in jail, I'll never be able to find the evidence to clear my name."

"You can't hide forever. The police are closing in. The way they feel now, if they see you they'll shoot first and ask questions later. If you turn yourself in, at least you'll be safe."

Summer walked up to Scooter and put her hands on Scooter's upper arms, looking her in the eye.

"Susan, we've been through a lot together. Do you trust me?"

"I want to, but I don't know any more."

"Look. I think I know a way we can get to the bottom of this. Will you let me try? If it doesn't work, I swear I'll give myself up."

Scooter thought for a long moment, then nodded. "All right. What do you want me to do?"

Summer put her arm around Scooter's shoulder as they walked out of the alley. Summer said, "Thank you, dear friend. First, you need to go see President Queeg..."

* * *

There was a knock on the door of President Queeg's office. "Yes?" he called.

Scooter stuck her head in the door. "Mr. President?"

"Come in, come in. Any news?"

"Yes sir, I have some important news. But you must promise me that you will keep it confidential until tomorrow morning."

"Of course."

"Summer has agreed to give herself up to the police."

"Good work!" Queeg exclaimed.

"There's more. I promised to meet her tonight at midnight at the football stadium. Then we'll go to the police together."

"Why do I have to keep this secret?"

"If the police are there, that would scare her off. It has to be just me."

"I understand. You can count on my discretion," replied Queeg.

"Thank you, sir. I'd better be going." Scooter pulled the tracker out of her pocket, flipped a switch, looked at it, and smiled. "Oh, and you might want to call the physical plant people and ask them to spray some pesticide around your office."

"Thanks for the advice. And good luck. I won't rest until this killer is brought to justice."

"Don't worry about that. I'm sure that tonight everything will become clear."

* * *

Summer walked onto the darkened gridiron, narrating into her recorder. "The campus football stadium can be an eerie place at midnight. As I stepped out onto the 50-yard line, I knew that my fate depended on two things: my detective skills and Scooter's loyalty."

Scooter entered at the far end of the stadium, then walked toward Summer. "So, are you ready to give yourself up to the police and face the consequences, Summer?"

"Oh, I'll be going to see the police, but not to give myself up."

"Oh?"

"You see, I know who the real murderer is. I knew it had to be someone respectable, a citizen above suspicion. Someone with a detailed knowledge of crime techniques."

"And that's who committed the two murders here on campus? It sounds like a description of you, Summer."

"Well, that's the really interesting part. You see, there was only one murder on campus this week. And it was part of a string of murders all over the country for many years. But that string stops here, tonight."

Jennifer Arrowsmith stepped into the light, aiming a gun at Summer and Scooter.

Arrowsmith spoke. "What did Raymond Chandler say? 'When in doubt, have a man come through the door with a gun in his hand'? Will a woman do? You know the drill: Don't move."

Scooter gasped. "Ms. Arrowsmith! You're alive!"

"Of course," Summer said. "With her knowledge of chemistry and meditation, she was able to fake her own poisoning and death."

"But why?" asked Scooter.

"It's very simple. Years ago, I happened to be visiting a small town when a murder occurred. I was lucky enough to figure out who the killer was, and alerted the police. When the book I wrote about it became a bestseller, I knew I was onto something."

Scooter said, "So you really did catch the murderer?"

"Oh, yes, that first time. But you see, I couldn't count on there being a murder whenever I visited a town. I mean, what are the odds of that?"

"So you decided to help the odds a little, right?" asked Summer.

"Of course. All I had to do was show up in a town, pick a victim, kill him or her, and then frame somebody else for the murder. It was quite simple, really."

Summer said, "And with the great Jennifer Arrowsmith testifying for the prosecution, the accused would never stand a chance. Right?"

"Exactly. I kept writing bestsellers, and the money rolled in. Then, when I had the chance to come here for an entire semester, well, there would be so many opportunities. A whole campus full of victims, of both kinds: people to kill, and people to frame."

"So what made you decide to frame Summer?" asked Scooter.

"As soon as I met her I knew that Summer was the only one who might expose me. So she had to be the first to go. I could have just killed her, but then I knew that her loyal assistant would stop at nothing to track down the killer. So why not eliminate my nemesis and destroy her reputation at the same time? It was easy to lift her fingerprints from a water glass and claim that I got them from the murder weapon, which I conveniently destroyed."

Summer asked, "But why fake your own death, rather than choosing someone else to kill?"

"I knew that I couldn't continue my killing spree indefinitely, much as I enjoyed it. So, with the bulk of my wealth in numbered Swiss bank accounts, plus arrangements for a little plastic surgery and a new identity, I could head off for a very comfortable retirement. And if I wanted to kill a few people every now and then, well, I could always do that too. You know what they say: after you retire, you really should have a hobby. That's the best way to keep your mind sharp." Arrowsmith laughed softly.

"You planted the bug in President Queeg's office, didn't you?" Scooter said. "That's how you knew we'd be here tonight."

"I was never a Boy Scout, but I follow their motto, 'Be Prepared.' You never know what tidbits of information you might find through a little covert surveillance."

"So what happens now?" asked Scooter.

"It's a tough decision. I could just shoot you both, but then the police would keep looking for the killer."

"How about not shooting either of us?" Summer asked.

"Sorry, not an option. Hmm...I know. Tomorrow morning the stadium groundskeeper discovers a tragic murder-suicide. Summer Cum Laude has shot her faithful assistant and then, filled with remorse, has taken her own life. Yes, I think that will do very nicely."

Scooter said, "And you think you can get away with this?"

"Why not? You two are the only ones who know I'm still alive, and that I'm the real murderer."

Summer said, "Ah, but what if someone else heard your little confession? I suppose that everything is ready, on the dark side of the moon..."

The first three haunting notes from *Close Encounters of the Third Kind* rang out over the stadium's public address system: Dooong, dooong, dooong. Arrowsmith looked around, puzzled.

As the stadium lights blazed on, the final two notes sounded at full volume: DOOM, DOOM. As Arrowsmith clapped her hands to her ears, Summer and Scooter rushed forward and grabbed her, snatching the gun.

Harry and Mike rushed onto the field as Doppler ran in from the other side. Mike was carrying a shotgun microphone and wearing headphones.

Harry hugged Scooter as Doppler handcuffed Jennifer Arrowsmith. "This is the first time I've ever had to arrest a murder victim," he said.

"Did you record her confession?" asked Scooter.

Mike replied, "No problem. I got it all with my trusty directional microphone."

"You gave us quite a scare," said Harry. "I thought you were never going to say that code phrase."

Summer said, "Hey, in detective work, as in comedy, timing is everything."

Arrowsmith objected, "You'll never be able to use my confession in court. If the police record a conversation without a warrant, it's inadmissible." She struggled with the handcuffs.

Mike and Harry grinned at each other. Mike said, "Harry and I did the recording, and we're not with the police."

"But Doppler knew you were recording, so the rule still applies."

Doppler's face was a model of innocence. "I had no idea they were recording anything. I was way over there by the switch for the stadium lights."

Harry said, "And we were very careful not to mention to him that we had the recording equipment with us."

Mike chimed in. "And we have a recording of *that* conversation to prove it. Your plan worked perfectly, Summer."

"All right, Ms. Arrowsmith. Let's go," said Doppler as he led her away.

* * *

In her dorm room, Summer sat at her desk, narrating into her recorder. "Besides her taped confession, I'm sure that the police will be able to find enough physical evidence to convict Jennifer Arrowsmith for the murder of Professor Bedrosian. And if the authorities in other states want to prosecute her, I'm sure that all the clues they need are in her books.

"The university had offered rewards for finding the killer or killers of Prof. Bedrosian and Jennifer Arrowsmith. I split the one for Bedrosian with Scooter, Harry, and Mike, but since Arrowsmith is not actually dead, we didn't get anything for that.

"And so another case ends, probably my most dangerous to date. No one knows what the future holds. So, on the top floor of Founders Hall, a young woman waits. She's ready for mystery."

Summer's desk telephone rang.

"She's ready for danger."

The phone rang again.

"She's ready for *anything*!"

The phone rang again.

"She's—"

The phone rang again, then cut off as Summer took the recorder from her mouth, picked up the phone, and spoke crisply into it. "Summer Cum Laude, College Detective."

None of Your Farbin' Business
Shannon Lawrence

The scent of burnt gunpowder was cloying, sticking in Mariska's nose and throat in a gritty nightmare. This was by far the most irritating job she'd taken to date. Surely, any case should be solvable without the investigation taking place at a Civil War re-enactment.

Even worse, she'd been forced to be on the side of the Confederates.

Now here she was, fleas nipping at her ankles and everything else just plain coarse and itchy. Far too many layers of fabric were required for her role as seamstress (heaven forbid a woman be dressed as a soldier, despite the fact that there had been documented female fighters in the War of Northern Aggression, as the last guy to pass through with a tear in his jacket had called it). Yet here she sat, covered in calico, complete with an apron and underclothes that mocked the bright sun above her as if to say, "Hit me with your best shot." The wool pants draped over her lap didn't help, and sweat slicked her hands as she plunged the needle in and out of the filthy fabric to create a hideously crooked pattern that might or might not hold the fabric together.

They hadn't bothered to ask if she could sew, too intent upon putting her in her place.

As soon as these pants were patched, a *closed* sign was going up on the outside of the tent. Food and investigation time.

The job–the real one–was to find out if one Colonel James Jackson was committing the sin of adultery. According to Mrs. James Jackson (actually Liza Pomeroy, who was married to Sebastian Pomeroy, who was playing Colonel James Jackson), the Colonel had a Civil War Wife. Much like a work wife, this involved an emotional attachment between one married man and one female co-worker that could cross lines, but

Liza was certain those lines were being crossed at the various battle re-enactments her salesman husband attended. After all, he was away in various cities among the battle states, sleeping in tents for days at a time. How better to get time away with a mistress?

Tailing of Sebastian outside of the re-enactments had produced zero proof of adultery. If he was having an affair at home, he hid it well. His only female co-worker was a wizened older woman of robust age and girth. Not that Mariska would kink shame if that was his thing, but there was no evidence of any such thing. A client? Not that she'd seen, but it was always possible. Only he did his selling online, via email, and by phone. The days of the traveling salesman were long past, especially for people like him who sold software products. There was no reason to spend gas and airfare costs to sell a digital item in this digital world.

A shock of pain went through her finger as she jabbed it with the needle. She let out an inadvertent "Oh!" The man whose pants she was mending poked his head into the small tent.

"What was that?"

"Uh, almost done! Give me about two more minutes and your pants will be as good as new."

Good as new. Mariska eyed her handywork and hoped he wouldn't look before putting his pants back on. Hopefully, he'd be too eager to get back to the action. One could hope. If this uniform was a rental he wasn't getting his deposit back.

Not her fault; he'd been the one to tear them.

She snipped the thread and tied an ugly knot, shook out the pants, and ducked through the tent opening. "All ready."

He started to shift the pants to examine them, and she said, "I hear they're putting on fresh ears of corn as a treat. With butter, even."

"Hot damn!" On went the pants and off went the Rebel in hot pursuit of buttered corn that didn't exist. There'd be plenty of beans and salted pork, though.

"God speed," she said with a smart salute in his general direction.

There was no paper and no pen, so she'd have to do without a closed sign. They'd figure it out if they came calling. It's not like they were paying her to be a seamstress. They could at least throw her a tip.

She had it on good authority that the Colonel wasn't too far away. He was to the east of the battleground and had one of the biggest tents, which was supposed to be a different color than the others. Something about liking to stand out. "The dipshit's a peacock," had been his wife's exact words. "You'll always be able to find him."

It was Mariska's understanding that the east was directly left from her tent, so she walked clumsily over the dry, clumpy ground, the tall grass scratching her legs and catching at her dress. There were small, light tents in the shape of inverted Vs all around. Men in uniforms of gray and a brownish color they called butternut sat around in clumps, some on wooden chairs, others on rocks or logs they'd pulled over. A smattering of women tended small fires with pots and kettles. Some folks glanced her way, but no gazes lingered.

Then she saw it. The peacock's tent.

It wasn't just a different color from the others. It was a Confederate flag, the bright red a beacon in the sea of off-white tents. The absolute absurdity of it wasn't lost on her. There's no way everyone could be okay with this. Yet no one seemed to be paying the tent any more attention than they were paying her.

She continued on past the tent, glancing back once to be sure she could see the entry from her current angle. Up ahead was a food station. She hadn't eaten since early that morning, and it was positioned just right to keep an eye on the Colonel.

He didn't make her wait long. As she sat in the grass eating cornbread and a bowl of beans with bits of salt pork he came out of the tent in a fancy uniform that included a long coat, a wrap the width of a scarf around his waist, and a big hat. He turned to the tent opening and reached inside, helping a young blond woman out. It was a complicated process, as she wore a hoop skirt and the opening wasn't big enough to easily squeeze it through. At one point, he had to grip her upper arms and pull, and Mariska imagined her feet inches off the ground, kicking as he yanked her through.

The struggle gave Mariska plenty of time to take pictures. Her bowl settled on the ground, she drew her phone out of her apron pocket and snapped away. She even got a picture of the giddy blond kissing him after he'd saved her from the vicious tent, him bending her backwards in a "romantic" way.

"Farb!" yelled a woman nearby.

Mariska looked around, wanting to see whatever a farb was.

Those nearest her all stared at…Mariska. One woman with decorative combs in her hair pointed a damning finger Mariska's way. "She's got a phone!"

Mariska shoved the phone back into the pocket and stood up, indignantly swiping blades of grass off the back of her dress. She pointed back at the woman, who looked far too excited to be making accusations, and yelled in an equally loud voice, "J'accuse!" for no reason other than having wanted to do it ever since she heard the phrase for the first time. Then more quietly: "Mind your business." She still had no idea what the woman was yelling at her about other than having a phone. "Rude," she muttered.

A Confederate soldier working the food table who looked like cannon fodder, according to the simplicity of his uniform, sidled over. Quietly, he explained, "Farb is what they call someone who isn't all in on the re-enactment. It's an insult. People are expected not to bring their phones or other tech."

"Well some of us have jobs."

"Hey, no judgment here. I've already been called a farb by about a dozen people who can afford better costumes. Also," and here he paused to look around, "I applied sunblock where others could see me doing so. And bug spray."

"That just seems like taking proper precautions."

"Sure, but it's not authentic. To be a real soldier, you have to fry in the sun and be eaten alive by insects."

"I'm currently doing enough of those things for the both of us," she said, rubbing one foot over the opposite ankle to assuage the horrific itch of the flea bites there. She was certain if she searched her scalp she'd find a tick. At least one. "I like your uniform just fine. Looks more real than the Colonel over there." She nodded toward where he still stood, fixing his uniform. The blond had disappeared into the crowd of tents, but another man stood talking to him, gun slung over his shoulder, jacket the butternut color that stood out against the grey. He had a single white feather poking out of his dark cap.

"Oh, that guy. He's just here to get his dick tickled. His tent has a revolving door."

This was good. "You don't say? It's not just the blond?"

"She's the second of the weekend so far, and his primary, I think, but there will be more. He always does this. He's a real piece of shit. Probably been with most of the women out here, at least the unmarried ones. Some of the married ones, too, but most of them are here with their husbands."

"Gross."

"Yep."

"Well, thank you for the information. I'll be sure to give him a wide berth."

The soldier tipped his hat and walked away. In the meantime, she studied the Colonel, who was now engaged in an argument with the man he'd been talking to, in an attempt to see what could so compel women that they would tent hop to be with him. Nobody was bathing here, so they were being exposed to each of the women before them. It seemed to pay to be Visitor Number One. Mariska shuddered at the thought. Even if he'd been conventionally attractive, which he wasn't, it would have given her the ick. As it was, he looked pretty rough. Maybe if she got closer she'd discover some sort of magical pheromone. Now she was intrigued.

Feather man turned abruptly and walked away. The Colonel flipped him the bird behind his back. Ballsy, that one.

Intrigued or not, it was time to text those photos to the Mrs. and see if they were good enough. Wanting to avoid being yelled at again, she meandered a little ways toward a smattering of trees and turned her back on the rest of the camp. The signal wasn't great, but the photos went through after a brief delay. Almost immediately, three dots appeared, showing Liza was sending a reply. Mariska looked around as she waited, which is why she saw the lithe redhead in a much simpler outfit made up of a skirt, shirt, full apron, and an armband with a red cross on it ducking into the Colonel's tent. He was nowhere to be seen, so she assumed he'd gone inside already.

Her phone chimed.

I'll need better than that to get what's mine. That piece of shit.

It wasn't like they were in a hotel room where she could try to peep through the window. Tents weren't see-through. Especially not his. Mariska sighed, sent a text in return–*Understood*–and strolled toward the tent, figuring she could wait until she heard noises that indicated the Colonel was getting busy then poke her head in and get some photos to close the deal. She was more than ready to be done with this job.

As she approached his tent, the blond did, as well. She had a look of determination on her face–lips clenched tight together, eyes squinted– and swept past people, her hoop skirt smacking a few in her passage. "Hey!" yelled one guy as he toppled off the log he'd been perched on after being clobbered from behind by the aggressive clothing. "Watch where you're going." She didn't so much as glance at him.

Mariska held back, waiting to see what would happen. She snuck her phone out, tucked it into her sleeve, and started recording.

The blond did not disappoint. She shoved her upper body into the tent and shrieked. The tent shook around her, skirt wiggling, feet moving against the earth in a constant forward push that got her nowhere. Another scream joined hers as the tent pegs gave up the ghost in the front of the tent, sending the blond plummeting forward. A loud smack sounded. A rending of fabric occurred, the tent tearing. And then the blond drew herself backward, dragging the now less than dressed redhead out of the tent. She was still wearing the basic undergarment, indicating they hadn't been fully engaged yet. Just a little third base, over the underclothes action. Or was that second base? She never could remember.

A frantic slap fight ensued. The surrounding men held back, always happy to watch a girl fight. One guy slugged the arm of the man next to him and pointed, laughing. The Colonel crawled out of the now half-collapsed tent, tugging his pants up as he went. Before he did, Mariska got a glimpse of the anaconda in his pants and realized why this guy was so popular. It was surprising that puppy could be contained. Liza had been holding back.

The woman who had yelled *farb* and pointed at Mariska earlier as if she expected her to be strung up as the tech-witch she was approached the mayhem with a couple other women. They pushed their way through the crowd of men that now encircled the two fighters, one of whom was getting pummeled, the other who was doing the pummeling. The redhead wasn't really fighting back, but she did have a handful of the blonde's hair clenched in a long-fingered fist. One thing was for sure, the redhead could take a pounding.

The yelly lady arrived at the action and shoved the two women apart. "You should be ashamed of yourselves!" Always yelling, this one.

"He's mine." the blond said.

"You can keep him," the redhead said. Both panted after their crazy workout.

Now that they weren't throwing themselves bodily at each other, the men fell back. This kind of drama was more entertaining for the women than the men. They hadn't even gotten to see a breast in the mayhem. What a disappointment. There'd been ankles, though. Was this the right time period for that or was that a different one? She couldn't remember.

The redhead slinked away through the crowd, despite the fact that the bulk of her clothing was in the tent. The blond and Ol' Yelly rounded on the Colonel at the same time.

"You bastard, you said I was the only one!" yelled the blond.

"You cheapen these re-enactments with your sluttery!" yelled the Ol' Yelly. Mariska took a moment to wonder if she could actually talk in a normal tone of voice or if this was it for her. Imagine living with that.

The blonde's shoulders sunk, and she grew quieter. "You said we were going to get married, that you were going to leave your wife for me."

"I'm going to, baby," the Colonel said. "This isn't what you think it is. She's from the medical tent."

Seldom do the stars align so perfectly, but Mariska was catching this entire exchange on video. Liza would be delighted. This was even better than just catching him having sex with someone.

The yelly lady shook her head and walked away.

The blond let out a single sob then slapped the Colonel so hard across the face that his head jerked to the side and his body stumbled after it. She turned and stalked away, once more battering those surrounding her with the hoop skirt.

The Colonel hurried to fix his tent, getting it propped back up in a short time. No one bothered to help him. In fact, everyone was back to their own business, side-eying him here and there. He didn't seem to be particularly well-liked, which didn't surprise her at all. She stopped recording and put her phone away in its hidey-hole on her apron. No one had busted her this time. *They* were all farbs, the lot of them! Saying that in her head felt oddly satisfying. Snobs.

Mariska hurried back to her own tent with the intention of sending the video to Liza. If the photos had taken a moment to send, the video would take longer, and no one likes being slurred, even if it's with words they don't understand. Better to send it privately and make sure Liza was okay with her packing it in. The battle was due to start soon, and she wanted to be gone before the air filled with gunpowder again. Before had just been from the drills.

Just as she stooped over to enter the tent, a woman's screams sounded. They carried across the field and voices called out to ask what was going on. "Murder!" came the response. "He's dead!"

With a sigh of resignation, she backed out before she'd even fully entered the tent and went toward the screams. Sure enough, the crowd surrounded the one red tent. The blond stood outside the tent, still screaming, but with sobs interspersed throughout. Her hands covered her mouth and tears poured from her eyes, spreading mascara in angry waves that created a crazed raccoon look. A man ducked into the tent and came hurriedly back out.

Mariska worked her way through the crowd and past the blond. Before she even poked her head in, the smell of feces blasted though the flaps, a common smell around death. The Colonel lay partially splayed across a solid cot that definitely didn't look to be authentic to the Civil War time period, though it was certainly big enough for two…in certain positions. He wasn't wearing the jacket anymore, and his white shirt showed stains of deep red in multiple places, the fabric torn. His arms were also bloodied as if he'd tried to ward off his killer. She snapped several pictures, paying close attention to his wounds and the ground around him.

The wounds seemed strange, so she bent closer. They weren't straight like a knife stab wound or even a slash. Instead, they looked to be almost clawed, with multiple prongs. None were terribly deep except for the one on his throat, which had finished him off. Someone had been feeling a lot of rage when they did this.

It hit her that she should probably contact Liza and let her know what had happened. For now, she wanted to ensure no one else entered the tent until the authorities arrived. She shouldn't have to begin with, but it was too late for that now.

Stepping out of the tent, she asked, "Has anyone contacted the authorities?"

A man stepped forward, looking somewhat chagrined. "I did." He held up a cellphone, then quickly put it away when a few glares shot his way. "They'll be here soon."

"Great. Everyone needs to clear some space and leave room for the investigators. They'll want to check for evidence, and you're all trampling some of it, I'm sure."

"Who are you to tell us what to do?" asked one man in a nice uniform.

"I'm a private investigator, and I have some familiarity with working crime scenes." Mariska looked pointedly around at the crowd. "Any other questions?"

They collectively backed up a few feet, though they didn't disperse. Eventually they'd get bored, she hoped. For now, she'd stay in front of the tent to at least make sure it stayed empty of all but the body and evidence. Pulling her phone out with a challenging brow raised around at the crowd, she auto-dialed Liza and waited three rings before the other woman picked up.

"Did you get the evidence?" Liza asked.

"I got more than that. Listen, Liza, I have some shocking news. Your husband's been killed. I'm waiting for the police to arrive now."

A wail sounded from nearby, emitting from the blond, who'd plunked herself down on the ground, the hoop skirt jutting up into the air in a most unladylike position.

"What was that sound?" asked Liza.

"Evidence. I'll call you back when I have more news. Do you have someone you can call to be with you?"

"No need. He had it coming. I'll await your update. In fact, I'll pay you double if you can tell me who did it. I'll send them a gift."

Liza really needed to work on her delivery when the police got there, but that was a Liza problem, not a Mariska one. The Mariska problem was what to do now? She'd been *this* close to getting away from this place, but double the funds (and let's face it: curiosity) meant sticking around and asking some questions. It couldn't hurt to try for a bit, though she wished she could put on some more comfortable clothing so the sweating and itching could be held at bay. She also, in general, was not a dress person to begin with, leaving her feeling oddly exposed.

Best get to it then.

The blond was still a sobbing mess, and everything in Mariska felt repelled by that, but she was suspect number one, for sure. Plus, she was close by, which meant double duty of questioning her and guarding the tent was possible. The crying didn't mean she couldn't be guilty. Regret could be a powerful thing, and people could still feel grief after they killed someone. Sidling over, she braced herself to deal with the now very soggy woman who had recently cleaned another woman's clock.

"Excuse me, can I ask you some questions?" she asked the quaking woman.

The blond looked up at her, eyes red and unfocused, mouth in an open pout. "What about?"

"Your fiancé." She figured leaning fully into the relationship might make her responsive. "I'm gathering information for the police."

The woman just looked at her and did one of those shuddering sobs overtired toddlers did.

"Okay, how long have you been seeing him?"

"We've been madly in love for two years. He was my everything."

"Did you see him after your fight with that other woman?"

"That slut? No, I went to calm down. Relationships are forged and strengthened in peace and understanding." A hiccup followed this proclamation.

In Mariska's understanding, problems were typically not solved by beating another woman either, but she had no desire to get in a battle of sayings. "Why did you come back to his tent?"

"I was c-c-calm." This came out as a wail.

"So you weren't mad at him anymore?"

The blond looked surprised. "Why would I be mad at him? It was her that led him astray. She's nothing but a disgusting temptress."

Oh, lord. Once again, Mariska bit her tongue. Was every woman he'd had sex with a temptress? Did this woman really not know what he'd been doing? Everyone else at camp seemed to.

The blond returned to full-scale wails and threw herself backward to lie prone on the ground. "My loooooove," she scream-wailed.

Mariska took this as her excuse to duck out of the conversation. She really hadn't gotten anything useful, but at least she'd know how to handle relationship issues in the future because of the wise words of this hysterical sage. She felt her eyes roll.

Her next step should probably be the redhead. She thought back, trying to remember if she'd seen her around the scene when the Colonel was discovered. She thought not, despite the fact it had seemed like the entire encampment was there. So where could she have been? Certainly no one could have missed the screams. And what about her clothes? Had she ever gone back to get them?

Mariska pulled out her phone and opened the photo app, examining the photos. There was no sign of the clothing the redhead had been wearing when she entered the tent, which indicated she'd likely gone back for it, but when? There'd only been a small window of time between the fight between the two women and the screams notifying everyone of his death. Did that leave time for both a woman fetching her clothing *and* a murderer, or were they the same person?

Police arrived as she ruminated, and she told them what she'd seen. After getting one of the officer's numbers to text them the photos and the video she'd recorded she headed out with the intent of finding the redhead. Instead, she ran into the Cannon Fodder Confederate she'd met earlier, figuring it wouldn't hurt to talk to him, as well. Farbs should stick together, after all. And he'd had some strong opinions about the Colonel.

"Hey there, fellow farb. Did you hear about what happened?" she asked.

He chuckled. "Sure did. While it couldn't have happened to a nicer man, he didn't deserve to die."

"Yeah, it's unfortunate. Do you think they'll cancel the battle now?"

"Oh no, it would take an act of God to stop the battle."

"You don't happen to know who the blond was who came out of his tent, do you? Her name?"

"I don't know her, but she was a frequent flyer. I think I heard her called Samantha at one point? Don't quote me on that."

Mariska made a mental note of the name. "There was a redhead that visited him afterward, tall and thin. She had a cross on her arm. She and Samantha got into a fight. Any idea who that might be?"

His cheeks flushed and he pressed his lips together for a moment. "Yeah, that's Rebecca. We dated for a while, but she wasn't interested in commitment. I guess he's a good choice if you don't want anything serious." His knuckles whitened as he tightened his hand on the rifle he held.

She hadn't expected to find out he had a motive, but there went another mental note.

"Do you know where I could find her?"

"She should be at the medical tent."

Ah yes, the red cross. That made sense. Honestly, what kind of a PI was she if she hadn't put two and two together? She was so used to seeing them on medical marijuana establishments that she'd spaced their other uses.

"One more question: did you go to his tent at all? Maybe to confront him about your ex?"

"He's a jerk, but my ex's actions...her feelings...weren't his responsibility. If I was going to confront anyone it would be her, and I have no desire to do that. I've moved on."

See now, here was someone who got it. "Thanks! Stay safe out there during the battle."

The medical tent was actually near her seamstress tent that had been empty all afternoon now. She wondered if there were any soldiers walking around with their underwear hanging out because they couldn't get their pants sewn up. You'd think people could make it one day without tearing their clothes. During the short walk, she kept an eye out for the guy with the feather in his cap and Ol' Yelly. She winced at the thought of the loud conversation she'd have to have with that woman.

Behind her, men headed toward the field. The battle was starting soon. Reaching into her apron pocket, she took a peek at the time on her phone, which showed it was 2:47 PM. The battle would be at 3:30. That gave her a little time to track down the folks she wanted to talk to, but Feather Man might have to wait until after if she didn't find him before. She added a little more hustle, anyway.

The medical tent was longer and slightly taller than most of the other tents, including her seamstress one. A couple of the "nurses" sat outside smoking, all with the armband on their mismatching uniforms. Rebecca was not among them, but there were voices in the tent, one man and one woman, telling Mariska she might be inside. She stopped in front of the smokers and asked, "Has anyone seen Rebecca?"

One older, raspy-voiced woman nodded and pointed toward the tent entry with her cigarette. "Yep, she's in there with a patient."

"Am I allowed to go in to talk to her?"

"I guess. It's just a sprained finger, so he should have his pants on."

"That's reassuring," said Mariska.

"You never know around here," said the woman. She and the other nurse laughed.

"Thanks."

There was a faint smell of antiseptic inside the tent. It made sense that there had probably been a lot of cuts coming through that would need to be cleaned and bandaged. These men were using real antique weapons for their drills and the upcoming battle. Supposedly, they would be carefully checked before each exercise to ensure no one had loaded theirs up, but somehow a bunch of men playing pretend with real weapons made her nervous, anyway.

Rebecca knelt in front of a man who sat on a cot, hand held out in front of him as he clutched the wrist to steady it. She put the finishing touches on a wooden splint setup, then patted the man's knee. "You're good to go, Jim. Just be careful and try not to use it much. At least it's not your trigger finger."

"That would suck," he said. "Thanks for the help."

"Of course! That's what I'm here for."

He stood up and headed out of the tent, hand held carefully in front of him.

"What can I help you with today?" asked Rebecca, as she washed her hands with sanitizer. Mariska looked at the bottle in surprise. "Oh, this? Medical safety has to come before authenticity sometimes, and sanitation is one of them. I wish we could have a working sink, but this will do in a pinch."

"Are you a real nurse?" asked Mariska.

Rebecca laughed. "Actually, I'm a doctor. We do get some serious injuries at these, so they encourage people with medical experience to come along. I can't say every group is like that, but this one's good about it."

"What do you see most at these?"

"Honestly? Diarrhea. Got a whole chest of anti-diarrheal meds and electrolytes. Most people aren't used to eating just beans and pork; it's not great for the guts. Other than that, cuts, scrapes, sprains, broken bones, infections, and sunstroke. But we've had strokes and heart attacks, things like that. Anyway, did you come to ask questions or is there something I can help you with?" This last was asked in a curious tone, rather than a rude one.

"I witnessed your fight earlier and wanted to ask some questions about Sebastian Pomeroy. You've heard the news?"

The smile fled Rebecca's face and she looked away. "I heard." She busied herself tidying up.

Mariska figured getting right to the point would serve her best, so she said, "I notice you've got your clothes back. When did that happen?"

"I went back as soon as I saw Samantha had left, so pretty quickly after."

"Did you guys talk about anything?"

"Not really, no. We weren't really in it for the conversation to begin with."

"Gotcha." Mariska noticed a light smear of blood on the other woman's sleeve. She pointed to it. "What's that from?"

"What?" asked Rebecca, looking at her sleeve. When she saw the smear, she raised one eyebrow. "Seriously? Do you know how many people I've bandaged today? I can show you the trashcan full of bloody wrappings if you want."

"Can any of the women outside attest to when you got that stain?"

"Since they've mostly sat on their asses smoking, I'd say no, they would not be able to. I can't even say exactly when it happened." She threw down the cloth she'd been using to clean up. "And who the hell are you, anyway? You're not a cop."

"I was a cop, but no, I'm not anymore. I'm a private investigator working for his wife."

"His wife? Already? Did the police even arrive yet?"

"I was already here when it happened."

She smirked. "What are you, the PI equivalent of an ambulance chaser? You contact her and offer to work for her as soon as you smelled the blood?"

She was pretty snarky for someone who'd gotten creamed in a fight an hour or so ago by a tiny blond woman. "As I'm sure you're aware, the smell of feces is typically the strongest scent with a newly dead corpse. And when I say I was already here, I mean I was investigating him for other reasons before he was killed."

"So he *was* killed then? It wasn't just something like a heart attack?"

"It was definitely murder. How long had you been sleeping with him?"

That smirk again. "We both know there was no sleeping involved, and not long. I was definitely under no confusion about our relationship or lack thereof. He was good for some fun at these events and that was all."

"So you knew he was married?"

"Yes. I don't think there's anyone who doesn't know that."

"Tell me, did you see anyone else approaching the tent as you left?"

"Not a soul."

Mariska eyed her, deciding whether to ask her next question. Finally, she decided this woman hadn't done it. It had been obvious during the fight that she wasn't that invested in him. "If I show you photos of him, could you tell me what you think?"

"Show me and I'll let you know."

Mariska busted out her phone once more and handed it over with the last photo of him open. Rebecca expanded the photo, eyes and fingers moving over the screen. She held it up close to her face at one point, brows furrowed. Finally, she looked up and said, "I'm not a coroner, so they'll have a much better idea, but it looks to me like he was stabbed with something that had multiple tines or teeth." She turned the phone toward Mariska. "See here? There's a row of small punctures, and it explains the multiple parallel scratches, as well."

It made sense now that Mariska was looking at the punctures. Immediately, her mind jumped to something she'd seen earlier. But she needed to talk to two more people before she could be sure. "That's a huge help, thank you."

"You're welcome. Glad to help."

Shots fired as Mariska exited the tent and she almost bolted back inside before her logical brain reminded her of the time. Feather Man was probably out of the question right now, but she could still find Ol' Yelly and that was by far the most important conversation at this point. The problem was getting around the battle. It was like walking along the outskirts of a football field, except they had guns. Men ran at each other, knelt to shoot, fell fake dead onto the ground. One man almost collided with her as he tried to get around a group of men in combat. "Get off the battlefield, lady!" She *was* off the battlefield, but lo and behold it was Feather Man, only without the feather."

"Oh, hey, can I ask you some questions about Sebastian Pomeroy?"

He looked dumbfounded. "Are you serious right now?"

"As serious as a murder."

His face fell. "Yeah, okay. Make it quick. I'm in the middle of a battle here."

"What were you arguing with him about earlier?"

"He has…had…one of my guns. He was supposed to get it valued by a friend, but he hasn't returned it and he never sent the information either. I think he sold it himself when he found out how much it was worth."

"What did he say when you confronted him?"

"He called it a piece of junk and said he'd mail it to me."

"What do *you* think the gun's worth?"

"I think it's got to be a couple thousand. My dad left it to me. I wasn't going to sell it, just wanted to know what it was worth."

"Did you return to his tent after your argument?"

"I didn't see him again. Chances are, I'll never get that gun back now. Why would his wife return it? She wouldn't even know which one was mine."

His logic might be sound, but I figured I'd put in a word for him with Liza anyway. "Find me after the battle and give me your name and information. I'll pass it along to his wife."

"I'll do you one better." He reached into his pocket and pulled out a business card. "Here you go."

He ran into the battle with a yell, aiming, firing, then promptly dying. Figuring her questions had kept him alive longer than he would have been otherwise, she felt a sense of accomplishment as she detoured to walk around the back end of the first row of tents to get farther away. Sure enough, the gunpowder was thick. She sneezed twice in a row, irritated that she hadn't left before this started. What sounded like a cannon went off with a massive *boom*. Men yelled and cried out. The air filled with smoke.

Ol' Yelly sat in a wooden chair by a fire, arms crossed, watching the battle intently. Though her hair had been up earlier, it was now down around her face, just past chin length. She looked up at Mariska, not appearing to recognize her from earlier. "Can I help you with something?" No surprise that she yelled this.

Mariska had only one question. "What happened to your hair combs?"

The older woman's face went from belligerent to enraged, eyes moving from a narrowed position to an almost crazed wideness. She bared her teeth in a sneer, her nostrils flaring. Her voice got quiet, which was far more ominous than the yelling. "That's none of your business."

Mariska nodded. "You're right. It's police business."

Now fear registered. She was as expressive as she was loud. Her mouth twisted as she chewed on her cheek. "I just took them out is all."

"And then used them to stab a man to death?"

"I didn't!"

Mariska looked into the fire where the woman had set up a small pot on a frame. Just visible under one of the logs were the tines of one of the combs. Whatever they were made of, they hadn't melted yet. She picked up a long fork Ol' Yelly had been using and shifted the comb until it sat beside the flames.

"What do you think are the chances there's still some DNA on these combs?" she asked.

"Damn it. I didn't do it on purpose. He ruins everything, all this." She waved her hand at their surroundings. "Every time. He has cheapened this for years now, bringing his whores into his ridiculous tent, flaunting his money. He never even fought in the battles, just climbed onto one of the horses and directed from the back. He was a coward!" She huffed, breathing heavily with her rage.

Mariska waved at the police working around the red tent until someone looked her way. She crooked a finger and gestured to the officer to come her way. When he stepped up next to her, she said, "You'll want to talk to this woman about her hair combs and her history with the victim. I pulled one of the combs out of the fire." Looking at the woman one more time she threw out one final warning. "Just to let you know, she yells."

Then she dashed off a text to Liza: *You'll want to cut that double check. I'm on my way.*

Backyard Blues
Elle Higgins

"I could kill him" rang out, accompanied by metal jabs scraping earth and stone.

Emma jerked up from her examination of the foundation of a Cape Cod house, turning to follow the sound.

"I could just kill Robb." The statement personalized this time.

The person exercising the voice and the garden spade was a young woman, maybe twenty-five, not much younger than Emma. She was in the adjoining yard, a few feet beyond a rickety picket fence dividing the properties. The thrusts repeated, each one harder and harder.

"Everything okay over there?" Emma called out.

The woman jerked up, whipping her head to face Emma. "I didn't know anyone was there. The Johnsons are at work during the day." She whisked a tarp over a pit.

Emma walked to the fence. "I'm Emma Grant, Empire Assurance. We hold the homeowner's policy here. I have permission to investigate for water seepage."

"Laura Peters," the woman said, ramming her shovel near a border of elderly lilac bushes. The branches, nearly laid flat, recalled Amy Lowell's poetry: "wind-beaten, staggering under a lopsided shock of bloom."

Approaching the fence, the woman stepped around mounds of dirt and dead plants. "We just moved here in January. Is the area prone to flooding?" she asked, glancing back at the rear of the house behind her. Her backyard abutted the Johnson's side yard, both lining Oakwood Place. Her house faced Adams Place, a cross street forming a corner with the two roads. "We're renting with an option to buy. The conservator patched up the garage wall where some corner bricks were separating. Claimed it was cosmetic, not structural. Could seepage be the cause?"

"I'd have to examine it." Emma walked the length of the fence to Oakwood and turned left to join Laura, who met Emma at the driveway.

"In the Johnson's case, the house sits on an underground portion of a stream that runs between the houses. It's above ground in the right of way for the utility wires that connect power to their rear." Emma said, pointing to a dense green space with mature trees. "It resurfaces again across Oakwood in the outlet between the two homes opposite." She motioned to a bungalow and a Cape, mirroring those of Laura and the Johnsons.

Emma scrutinized Laura's face. "But honestly, are you OK? You sounded distressed. Who's Robb?"

Laura started, but stood mute, looking everywhere but at Emma.

Emma was about to repeat her question, when the air was pierced with a crackle, and then some whimpering, followed by a full-throated yowl.

Laura jumped. "My baby's awake. I must go." She dashed into the house, closing the garage door behind her. It seemed to be the only access to the interior at this point.

Another squawk sounded, followed by a sustained whimpering cry, until Laura's voice and cooing sounds replaced it, a murmuring of "Amy, Amy, Amy."

Emma looked for the source. The sounds came from a tan and brown device looking like a chunky transistor radio. A baby monitor.

* * *

Dismissed, Emma retraced her steps up the driveway, noting that the garage sat at the bottom, making it the lowest point in the property, a level below the main floor. The driveway descended from Oakwood, which in turn sloped downhill from Adams, giving even more momentum to any water washing downward and seeking a nadir. No wonder the blocks of the foundation had shifted.

Scanning up and down Adams, she marveled at how quiet the neighborhood was. But not deserted. Across the street, in a driveway almost directly opposite Laura's bungalow, two elderly women sat in lawn chairs, sharing beverages. They waved Emma over. Neighbors were a good source of information. Emma accepted their offer of a chair, but declined a beer since she had to drive back to her Albany office.

Drinks with conversation seemed a regular ritual for the matrons. Between them lay a copy of today's Times Union, its headlines shouting the declining health of Erastus Corning, mayor since 1941. Details were meager this spring of 1983, Corning having been hospitalized since June of last year, first in Albany and now in Boston. Speculation abounded about who would take over running the city and his lucrative insurance company.

The women, who had lived there several decades, recounted that the two Capes historically suffered from flooding—and sometimes mold— conditions Emma had anticipated.

They had also known only one owner of Laura's house, a Mrs. Eva Booker.

The woman named Frances said, "She kept pretty much to herself. Of course she was working as a stenographer for the State, no children. While I had a couple kids and my jobs at area drugstores."

The other woman, Doris, said. "Frances was one of the first lady graduates of the Albany School of Pharmacy."

Frances glanced down, smiling. "I loved the field, and I had family— and later Doris, to help with child care." Turning to her friend, she said, "I couldn't have juggled it all without your help, Doris. And you had your hands full, with raising five kids and helping out at your husband's deli."

Doris grinned broadly. "Even after the kids went off and we retired, we didn't see much of Eva. Then things got bad as she got more confused."

"Senility." Frances tapped her forehead. "She'd wander around the yard, muttering and burying garbage."

Emma could only imagine what Laura was uncovering with her digging. She looked across at Laura's bungalow. It was dark, drab, buried behind massive fir trees that nearly sat on the house, a source for insect infiltration her insurance appraiser mind noted. What would the interior be like?

"A conservator moved Eva into the nearby old-age home," Doris said, "But the house was full of junk. The renters had to hire a dumpster to clear it out."

"There's still an awful lot to do. Tough for a young couple with a new baby, a new city, and a new job for him. We're hoping they'll stay."

Emma wished the women good day and headed to her office.

* * *

Back on Oakwood for the internal inspection of the Cape Cod, she looked for Laura. She wasn't in the yard, so Emma wandered to Adams Place and spied the elderly women again sitting together having drinks. Laura had joined them, relaxing in a lawn chair, while Doris was rocking Amy. A stroller stood nearby with a diaper bag and books.

Still in working hours, Emma declined a beer, but pulled up a chair and joined the conversation.

"We were just talking about Eva Booker," Frances said. "She was the original owner of the house, built in 1920. Old-timers here spoke of her renting the house out while she worked in New York City. And when she returned, she took in boarders. This was before the War."

"Was there a Mr. Booker, too?" Emma asked.

"No one left on the block remembers him," Doris said. "It's rumored he traveled for work. Maybe why Eva lived in the City?"

"By the forties, he wasn't around. Not something to ask a casual acquaintance," Frances added.

"I don't think it was a happy marriage," Doris said. "The people next door heard yelling and sounds of things thrown, glass breaking . . .."

Laura fidgeted, then jumped up. Emma recalled the first words she heard the woman speak.

Thanking the matrons, the young mother took the baby. "I must put Amy down."

"We're just a few feet away if you need anything," Frances said.

"Any time," Doris said, slow to release her bundle.

Emma said, "I'll walk you back so I can tell you about the garage damage."

Laura started. Then rousing herself, she said, "Won't you come in for a cup of coffee? I need your advice and I don't know where to turn."

* * *

While Laura took the baby upstairs, Emma looked around. The rooms were cut by doorways and arches. One door apparently leading to the basement must be the route Laura came up to get Amy. The top half was glass, common in older homes to provide light into the lower level and to see who was approaching the door. The old-fashioned deadlatch allowed the door to be locked from the inside without a key. Seafoam bathroom tiles and melamine kitchen cabinets with lemon laminate countertops screamed 1960s vintage. The young couple had a lot of work ahead if they bought the house.

Over coffee, Laura explained she had been working in a biology lab and studying for the Medical College Admission Test when Amy came along.

"A surprise, but we had family to help. Then Robb got a job for the Session in Albany. The pay is phenomenal, but Amy and I rarely see him. He works long hours and takes our only car. I can walk to the post office, the library, some shops, but I don't know anyone here."

She looked down at her mug. "I know how to do science, not mothering. And people said babies napped a lot so I'd have plenty of time to study. Not my baby." Whimpering came over the monitor. The mother tensed, letting out a deep breath when quiet resumed.

"With warmer weather, I'm outside a lot." Laura produced a Kodak Kodachrome photo showing fresh stone paths and perennial beds. The lilacs and peonies bordering Oakwood were untouched. Dated "1963," it matched the vintage of the interior. Perhaps a time of renovations?

"It was once beautifully landscaped. Reclaiming the backyard is a physical outlet, but junk is buried everywhere, so gardening has its own frustrations."

And, Emma imagined, a means of getting out her frustrations, recalling Laura's anger the day they met.

Laura leaned towards Emma. "I need help."

Now Emma held her breath, bracing for a declaration of marital conflict, possibly emotional abuse or at least neglect.

Instead, Laura removed a paper bag from the diaper pack, withdrawing a bunch of tissue. She peeled back layers, exposing a bone. It looked like the carcasses she'd seen after her aunt made stock for chicken noodle soup. Emma raised her eyebrows.

"I know. It looks like a chicken bone, but I just consulted some books on the human skeleton at the library."

"You think it might be human? Where did you get this?"

"Found it in the back while moving some peony plants by the old lilac bushes. Can you recommend someone to verify it?"

"But if you think it's human, shouldn't you call the police?"

"Even though I studied comparative anatomy, I'm not an expert. I would feel very foolish if it's animal—"

A crackle, then a wail, signaled that Amy was getting up. The nap had lasted less than a half hour.

* * *

While Laura went up to get the infant, Emma dialed Dr. Elizabeth Fox, Chief Clinical Pathologist for Albany Medical Center. She also did forensic pathology for Albany County and conducted her own research—currently a study on veterans with major cognitive disorders. These men with traumatic brain injuries—fractures in the face and skull—developed dementia in greater numbers than other vets. They had collaborated on the Burmese kitten case involving arson and asphyxia victims in a house her company insured. The sole heir, Emma continued her family's insurance business, but preferred investigative work, earning a master's in criminal justice.

"I don't really work with random bones," Fox said. "I advise you determine if it's human ASAP." She referred them to a colleague, a forensic anthropologist at SUNY Albany who worked in his lab afternoons.

Excited, Laura cried, "But I don't have a way to get there."

Knowing it was over an hour trip one-way by bus, Emma said, "I can give you a ride. But we don't have an infant car seat."

"I'll ask Doris to babysit." Laura dashed over and Emma informed the office of her schedule change.

* * *

As they neared the Anthropology forensic lab, its door burst open. A young man scampered out, red-faced and breathless, followed by a shouted, "And don't come back."

The door still ajar, they saw Dr. Winters, scowling and standing over an upended tray, its contents littering the counter.

The professor shook his head. "Clumsy undergrad assistant. Not only late to work, but sloppy in methods and handling."

Emma explained their errand, citing Dr. Fox's referral.

Pulling on latex gloves, Winters said, "Let me see."

He nodded approval as Laura put on gloves and retrieved the tissue-wrapped bone from the paper bag. "At least you know how to handle artifacts."

"I used some acid-free wrapping materials left over from our move," she said, pink suffusing her face. "It was near a wishbone."

"Furcula," Winters murmured, as he took the bone. "Chicken bones, the thigh or femur and also phalanges, are sometimes mistaken for human bones, particularly the thumb or first finger."

Putting the bone under a microscope, he said, "Chicken phalanges can look similar, especially when missing the proximal epiphysis—the wider end closest to the body—like this one." He scrutinized the object. "In fact, there's a break at this end. Made shortly before death, since there are no signs of repair." He looked up. "It's definitely human, probably male, given the size and the angle of the joints. And it's remarkably preserved. You say you found this buried in your garden?"

"I was moving some peonies near a grove of lilac trees. It's slow work with the garbage and the clay-like nature of the dirt."

"That explains it. Both a clay-rich soil and an alkaline soil that lilacs prefer can protect bones from decay. Still I'd say that the bone has been in the earth some 40 years, way before you were born."

He jumped up whipping off his lab coat. Just then he noticed that during his examination, Laura had been picking up the scattered specimens and replacing them on the tray, matching number IDs on the objects with the labels. His eyebrows raised again. "You know your way around a research facility."

"I was a biology major, Pre-med."

He studied her, then said, "We must call the authorities, but first I want a look at the site."

* * *

They met in the backyard, the anthropologist again showing approval at how Laura covered the hole to keep out animals and the elements. "This is remarkably intact." After probing with a small trowel and soft brush, Winters said, "There are more human remains here." He faced Laura. "Before we call the police, I want assurance that you'll let me run the dig."

She returned his look. "On one condition. You let me assist both here and in the lab. I've got proximity and the skills, as you've seen."

Laura seemed in her element as the pair began to rope off and document the area while waiting for the authorities. Soon the streets were congested with police cruisers, lights flashing, and neighbors watching from nearby sidewalks and lawns. Frances and Doris, with baby Amy, were there.

A man, face pale, rushed up. The husband, Robb Peters. Standing close to Laura, he began protesting, citing private property and permissions, brandishing his arms, his face growing as heated as his arguments.

Laura pulled Robb aside, and the couple talked, her gestures animated, the husband frowning and running his hands through his hair. Then they waved Doris and Frances over. Robb clasped Amy to his chest while all four talked. Returning, Laura announced that she would divide her time between the excavation and the lab. Doris would watch Amy during the daytime digs. Neighborhood teens and Robb would take over during her afternoons and evenings at SUNY Albany. Robb even agreed to let Laura have the family car—after Emma explained his bus trip downtown was only 15-20 minutes. Laura beamed, but Robb still clutched Amy, his eyes, those of a deer in headlights.

It took some convincing to exonerate the current occupants from suspicion. Winters reinforced that it wasn't a recent body. The remarkable preservation was due to the clayey loam and the plantings nearby. Roots can damage a bone's integrity, but peonies and lilacs had shallow root systems. Once the county coroner signed off on the remains, the excavation could begin. The police would await any discoveries, but had little hope in solving this very cold case. Even missing persons reports wouldn't help when so many had disappeared during the Great Depression and World War II. What they had was an unidentified skeleton with no contemporaneous suspects or witnesses, except maybe a senile former homeowner.

* * *

While Laura conducted the excavation and forensic analysis, Emma pursued her own investigation. Following up on tidbits from the Adams Place matrons, Emma tracked down Eva Booker at the adult home, a small, family-run affair.

An aide noted that visitors were welcome, but Eva may not respond. On her bad days, she babbles, even hallucinates. And refers to herself by name, as some Alzheimer's patients do.

"She is really sensitive to loud noises. A busboy dropped a tray of mugs today, and Eva started screaming, was inconsolable."

She recommended Emma come another day. "She tells great stories about being a working woman in the 30s and 40s. Imagine. Supporting herself. Owning a house. All without a husband."

But Emma knew Eva had had a husband, gossip confirmed by a visit to the Albany County Hall of Records, where she located a marriage certificate between Eva Staneck and a Raymond Tasker. But the deed she tracked down was only in Eva's name, justifying the aide's praise here. To explain Raymond's absence, she also consulted the divorce index, listing just cases since the actual files were sealed to the public. She found neither name there. They might have gotten a divorce in New York City, but without knowing the year and borough, the search would be arduous.

* * *

A week later, Emma returned to Adams Place hoping to see the progress of the excavation. She was pleased to find Laura there, enjoying a beer. Amy was on a blanket nearby content with her toys. Emma told the women about what she had learned at the County records office.

Frances said, "Getting a divorce in New York back then was very difficult. Adultery was really the only reason, and proving infidelity was hard and expensive."

"Even if both people wanted it," Doris said. "Some staged compromising scenes, with a so-called detective taking photos, just to end the marriage."

"Though people with money could go to other states which were not so strict, like Nevada," Frances said.

Emma had seen those Hollywood movies with quickie splits in Reno. "What if they couldn't afford to go to another state or to court?

"There was the 'poor man's divorce'—desertion or abandonment," Doris said.

Laura shifted in her chair. "What if the couple isn't getting along, if they were incompatible?"

Frances said, "Cruelty, desertion, or a mentally ill partner were sometimes allowed but not often."

"That's why people, both men and women, just up and left. They would start again, without admitting they'd left a spouse behind,"

Doris added.

"Divorce was stigmatized, too," Frances said. "Not recognized by many churches, and divorcees, male and female, were avoided, sometimes ostracized."

Had this happened to Eva? No wonder she had kept her marital status vague, keeping the "Mrs." but using her maiden name.

Noticing the shift in tense in Laura's question from the present "is" to the past "were," Emma said, "Plus an ill-used or abused spouse may be too controlled or terrified to report it—on paper or in court."

Laura squirmed in her chair. "Let me catch you up with the dig. The field work is nearly complete. We've excavated the entire skeleton." She stopped to take a swig of her beer, then continued.

"The skull and the long and narrow pelvis confirmed it is male. These also provided an approximate age for the victim, about 50. But there are complications—a perimortem fracture in the occiput, the back of the head. And nearby was a rock whose shape conforms to the indentation, another potential fatal agent. Either injury might be the cause of death."

"The fractures of the finger and the skull suggests violence, but was it inflicted by another or by accidental trauma?" Emma asked.

"And how did the body get there?" asked Frances.

"Somebody put him there. There was a definite hole in the ground," Laura said. "The soil next to the hole had clear striations of earth built up over time, but the earth around the skeleton contained coarse grain soil and native dirt."

"That sounds like a ditch," Emma said. "From my seepage research, I learned the original storm drainage system consisted of trenches along the property lines. Many were filled in after storm sewers were constructed alongside sanitary ones beginning in the 1930s."

"When a ditch is closed up, backfill material would be like the earth we found," Laura said.

Frances asked, "Could the poor soul have stumbled into the ditch and the walls caved in?"

"But wouldn't he be missed?" said Doris.

"Not necessarily. Itinerant day or casual workers were common then as they are in all bad economic times." Emma looked at each woman. "But whether the death was accidental or intentional, someone filled in the pit, a cover-up suggesting foul play." On that somber note, the women packed up and parted.

To check on the history of residents at 189 Adams, Emma headed to the Bethlehem Town Hall for contemporaneous street directories. Eva was initially listed as housekeeper, but later her occupation changed to typist. So she had obtained her secretarial diploma before marriage. In the early 1930s, Raymond Tasker, occupation brakeman, was listed as living there, with "Eva S." in parentheses as his wife. From the mid to late 30s, both names disappeared and other people were recorded— probably the renters. Emma did find two directories from 1941 where just Eva's name reappears as "Mrs. Eva Booker." Had the couple divorced in another state or had they chosen the poor man's option? And had Eva retained the "Mrs." as a way to maintain respectability?

* * *

On Emma's next visit to Adams Place, Laura was again sitting with the matrons—with no Amy in sight. In answer to her raised eyebrows, the women laughed.

"Robb took the afternoon off to be with Amy. Since his regular babysitting, the two have become quite attached." Laura smile broadened. "And we're going out to dinner tonight—a real date."

Her work day over, Emma accepted a beer and settled in for updates.

Enjoying the lab work as much as the archeology, Laura reported, "Shards of glass from the grave might explain the severed finger. Identified as wavy glass, predominant in windows in the early twentieth-century before float glass manufacturing took over. Some were large enough to amputate the finger, especially if impacted."

Frances added, "Blood loss from a cut off finger could make the person disoriented enough to fall into the hole, maybe striking his head."

"After all these years, no trace of bleeding-out would remain—if the amputation occurred near the pit," Laura said. "Again, either the severed finger or bashed skull might be the cause of death."

She continued. "We also recovered nickel buttons with the embossed initials 'NYC.'" Turning to the matrons, she asked, "Didn't you say Eva Booker lived in New York City? Maybe these are souvenirs of that time. Of course, since synthetic fabrics were not widely available then, the natural cloth would have decomposed." Laura was beaming, confident and assured, so different from the stressed woman Emma had encountered just a few weeks ago.

Laura hurried on, her voice animated. "I have personal news. After this Session, we're returning to the City. Robb will work in the district office, and I'll do in a post-graduate in forensic anthropology—with Dr. Winters' recommendation. Our families are eager to help care for Amy."

The elderly women looked stricken. Doris said, "We'll miss you, especially that sweet baby Amy."

"Here we go again," Frances said. "Who will buy the house now?"

After congratulating Laura, Emma had decided not to share what she learned from the directories. Laura was full of the future, while Emma was focused on finding answers in the past. According to Frances and Doris, Eva's husband traveled for work, which would fit a train brakeman. And nickel buttons were common on railroad uniforms, particularly those of brakemen. On further research, Emma discovered the "NYC" stood for the railroad line, the New York Central. It not only ran trains between Albany and the City, but was also founded by Erastus Corning, the great-grandfather of the current mayor.

Raymond Tasker had lived for a time at the Adams house, and most importantly he had disappeared from the records. Had he been a casualty of the hard times, especially with the many railroad strikes of that era which left workers idle? But how explain these railroad buttons in a makeshift grave with a male skeleton from then?

* * *

She returned to see Eva, hoping she was lucid this time. The institutional paint depressed Emma, despite color theorists claiming green had a calming effect. The strong antiseptic odor barely covered the stink of human bodily waste and even that of near death, a sickly sweet undertone of nail polish or ammonia.

She found the frail woman sitting looking out at gardens with peonies, roses, and lilacs. Emma knew lilacs could represent love and remembrance, but also resistance and renewal. Which emotions did they stir in the elderly woman?

She pulled up a chair beside her. "Mrs. Booker. I'm Emma."

"Eva. Call me Eva. Eva, Eva, Eva."

"Are lilacs your favorite flowers? They are mine."

"My flowers, mine," said the elderly woman. "Bad flowers, Raymond called them. Bad Eva. Eva, get back here. Take that." The woman recoiled as if avoiding a blow.

"You used to have them in your garden at home." Emma pulled out Laura's photo of the backyard of 189 Adams.

Eva grabbed the photo and stared at it for several minutes, then dropped it. Tears overfilled her eyes.

"Does it make you sad to see what was once your garden? Sad to see what's lost?" Emma patted Eva's hand. "You're safe. Raymond's gone."

Less agitated, Eva smiled, chanting, "Raymond is gone. Raymond is gone."

Emma asked, "Where's Raymond gone?"

"Raymond went away. No longer here. No one cares."

"But where did Raymond go? Why did Raymond go?

"Raymond safe, Eva safe. No more hurt Eva. Not hurt anyone." The resident leaned back in her chair, her eyes closed. The wrinkles in the old woman's face smoothed. She looked years younger.

Just when Emma thought Eva might be sleeping, the woman jerked up, again looking down at the photo. "Pretty lilacs. Eva loves lilacs. Raymond don't love lilacs. Don't love Eva. Hurt Eva." She shrunk in her chair and began whimpering, "No, no." She became increasingly agitated.

"Open the damn door, Eva. See what you've done? Take that, Eva. Take that."

Emma wanted to ask Eva more, but certain the old woman was spiraling into a hallucination, she called in the staff, who took over calming the sufferer.

The care home owner walked Emma out, reassuring her that these switches from senility to more lucid moments occurred with dementia patients, particularly as the end of life approached.

Emma asked if she could tell her a bit about Eva's medical history, especially if there were signs of fractures on the skull or face.

Surprised, the director admitted that x-rays had revealed some fissures around the head and face, including the nose and eye sockets, but these were ancient and had healed—attributed to a long-ago car accident.

At a loss, Emma was drawn back to the Adams Place house. Two couples had shared this residence but had not shared similar outcomes. Standing by the original grove of lilacs, she contemplated the mound of fresh dirt covering the trench, closing up what had been the final resting place of a man gone some forty years ago. The forensic discoveries as well as circumstantial evidence suggested a story of backyard blues, a violent death for the buried victim. Was Raymond Tasker the skeleton in the Adams house grave? Had he himself been violent?

Eva's ramblings hinted this—and that she was the most likely suspect in the disappearance of her husband. They also suggested domestic violence, usually occurring behind closed doors. Reports of yelling and other intimidation, like striking walls, even a glass window on a basement door? The path Eva might have fled the garden just as Laura had that first day?

In the 1980s, the young mother had more options, but still experienced pressure to fall back into gender roles and expectations, with the potential for emotional abuse and neglect in her isolation and relegation to child-rearing at the expense of her career. Robb was not a bad man, just driven, and himself a victim of gender roles. Laura was one wife who found a way to escape and still save the marriage.

Would Emma's reporting her suspicions be a matter of justice? Or were Eva's actions a matter of just desserts? Whatever the extenuating circumstances, his actions had led Raymond here. Wasn't Eva's fate—an elderly woman lost in Alzheimer's after the abuse from this man—punishment enough?

Over the mound, the Peters had planted pink rose bushes. Red roses symbolized love, but its paler cousin also represented love—and gentleness, grace, and new beginnings. A line of poetry surfaced:

> In my garden, a blush of pink unfolds
> A rose of dreams, a story to be told.

Here marked a fresh start for today's couple, with a happier ending than the previous one.

Shattered Melody
Bonnar Spring

I steered around another sweeping curve with views of the heaving Atlantic Ocean a hundred feet below us. Two boring hours on I-95, then this twisting stretch along the coast—the only things making the drive tolerable were Alice's companionship and Vic's snazzy new BMW.

I glanced at the nav system. "We should be at Roxy's place in fifteen minutes."

"This thing—" Alice pointed to the screen. "—won't detect where to turn, Mamie. Watch for the 'Entering Cedar Isle' sign. Just beyond is a four-foot-tall granite post on the right that marks her driveway. The house is at the top of the hill."

"So, she's rich?" *Not that I was greedy.* While we usually work for a cut of the proceeds, Roxy and Alice go way back. So, I figured this would be a minimum-wage job—plus a semi-vacation on the Maine coast.

Alice shrugged. "As rich as a struggling musician with a CEO dad can be. Roxy tries to strike a balance between accepting help and making it on her own."

The road veered inland into a pine forest. I flipped on the headlights. "Besides the vandalism and graffiti, what did she tell you that has us rushing off to Maine?"

"Only background—Roxy's the headliner at the Cedar Isle Music Festival next week. Her dad's having chemo in Philadelphia, so her folks haven't used their cottage all summer. When she arrived this afternoon, the house had been trashed."

"And spray-painted threats, you said?"

"Yeah, creepy stuff. All about her." Alice laid her hand on my arm.

"She sounded scared to death."

We found the granite post and ascended a tree-covered hill on a winding driveway. The last turn revealed a three-story white clapboard house with steep gables, glowing pink with the setting sun. The second our headlights curled into the turnaround, a slight woman with wild auburn curls ran down the front steps.

I parked behind a pearl-green Mini Cooper. Alice jumped from the BMW and threw her arms around her friend. "We got here as fast as we could."

"I'm so glad to see you." Roxy was wide-eyed and quivering. "The police only left a few minutes ago. They took fingerprints and photographs all afternoon. Scraped paint samples for evidence." After another shuddering breath, she turned to me. "You must be Mamie. Alice has told me so much about you."

I must've made a face because Alice laughed. "I only shared how good you are at helping folks solve their problems."

A group of us have been doing this for three years now—taking jobs to return items to folks who'd been ripped off and lacked the time or money to go through endless legal hoops. Or, as in Roxy's case, working under the radar to unravel mysteries. "Our other partners are working a case in Baltimore this week," I said.

"So your partners? That's...Vic? Alice said you'd take his car."

"Yeah, Vic plays chauffeur," Alice said. "We met him doing a job in France a few years ago. Also Evan, who's Mamie's main squeeze and a computer hotshot, and Gina. She cooks when we don't need her for kick-ass intimidation."

"I can only pay the minimum you asked." Roxy grimaced. "But I'll owe you forever."

Alice squeezed her friend again, tossing me a mischievous grin over her shoulder. "Just remember who I am when you're a big star."

Just what I thought.

"Let's go in. I'll show you."

We trooped up to a wide porch with a one-eighty view of the open

Atlantic. Hidden by the trees at ground level, the water glistened in the violet evening light.

Roxy paused outside the door. "Most of the damage is downstairs. I haven't told my parents." Her eyes flooded with unshed tears. "I just want to fix everything. Fast. So my folks don't freak out and insist I leave…"

I took one step into the living room. "Oh. My. God."

Walls, furniture, rugs, floors splashed with paint, like a demented Jackson Pollock composition.

"The paint had dried solid on the walls but was tacky on fabric surfaces. The detective who caught the call is a local man we've known forever. Charlie Dalton. He's going to check with the state crime lab about having an expert estimate when the damage occurred."

"How did they get inside?"

"They disabled the alarm." Roxy's tone was flat. "Then cut the wiring. No one can come out to repair it until Tuesday."

"Someone who knew the code." *Uh-oh.*

To avoid the debris, we walked single file along the only untouched stretch of floor.

The kitchen was worse: cabinets open, contents spilled on countertops. Paint covered walls and surfaces here, too. We peered into the dining room—more of the same. Even the Lenox crystal bowl filled with seashells was splashed with paint.

"They used paint from our storage shed. Leftover from remodeling last year."

Which is why the destruction is in tasteful muted colors—blues, greens, and grays.

"Charlie said it pointed to someone who'd worked on the remodeling. Someone who knew about the paint and had watched us key in the door code." Roxy tiptoed to the corner of the kitchen. "These back stairs are less messed up."

We followed her up a wide-board pine stairwell. "There are three bedrooms here, and one on the top floor."

"Which is yours?" I asked.

Roxy opened the nearest door. And sighed.

Instead of splattered paint, scrawled messages covered the walls: *Sellout. Not good enough. Payback's coming, bitch. Wannabe headliner. Nepo whore!* And more, each more vicious than the last. A squiggle that could've started as a music note was transformed into a skull and crossbones. A gigantic black X covered the bed quilt.

Roxy stayed by the door. I didn't blame her. Like Alice had said, *creepy*. The threats weren't even aimed at me, and still I wanted to get away.

"And then there's my bathroom." Roxy pointed to the adjoining room. Alice and I walked in. On the huge mirror: *Leave NOW—or this will only be your first warning! If you stay, I'll be back.*

When we returned to the hallway, I asked, "Any other damage in the house?"

Roxy's long curly hair swung side to side. "No."

I didn't want to freak her out further, but sugarcoating my observations wouldn't be honest—and not alerting her was dangerous. "So, there's general destruction downstairs to get attention, but the threats are directed at you. Whoever trashed your parents' house knew you—at least well enough to know which was your bedroom—and wanted to leave a message."

This time, she winced.

"What are you going to do?" I asked.

"I'm *not* leaving, if that's what you want to know. The Cedar Isle Festival is the most important gig I've had. Absolutely everyone will be there. It's my big chance."

No surprise there.

Despite her resolute words, Roxy's head bowed and she leaned against the wall, looking half-dead from exhaustion. I guessed our arrival had punctured the nervy tension that kept her going after her gruesome discovery.

Alice must've spotted Roxy's fatigue, too. "How about getting out of here and finding a B&B in town for the night?"

Her head snapped up. "I said I'm not leaving. Charlie Dalton, the detective, lectured me about it, too. They won't run me out of town."

"Are there other bedrooms so we all could stay here?" Not in *this* room with the ugly messages.

"My brother's suite on the third floor?"

Suite? "What's up there?"

"It's like a studio apartment—sitting area, kitchenette, bath, extra beds." She perked up a little. "I could heat up the minestrone I brought from home."

"Soup sounds perfect, but first, Vic asked me to keep his BMW out of the salt air. Is there room inside your garage?"

"Sure, the right-side bay is empty."

I left them trudging up to the third floor and retraced my steps to the car. The sun had set, and silvery light flickered through the forest. I didn't want to project too far ahead without more information, but the intruder having the code narrowed the possible suspects. And because of the venomous personal attacks in the graffiti and the malicious destruction of the security system, I doubted the detective's supposition that it was a disgruntled former workman.

By the time I rejoined my friends, Roxy was half-asleep, curled up on an oversized chair. Alice cajoled her over to the tiny bistro table, where she managed a few bites of soup between yawns. The evening concluded the second our bowls were empty. Roxy downed an Ambien and crashed on her brother's bed. While Alice made up the two twin beds by the rear windows, I went through the house, checking every lock.

I fell asleep to waves breaking on the shore.

I woke to breaking glass.

* * *

"Alice? Alice?"

"Unh."

"Listen."

Alice sat straight up—she always woke up ready-to-roll. Feet to the floor, she peeled off her silk sleep mask and peered through the window. "It's too dark to see anything, but the sun-room—right below us—has glass walls."

"They don't have motion detector lights?" I asked.

Another crash, this one louder. "Her dad got rid of them years ago because every time the wind blew, tree branches activated them."

I slipped into my shoes and picked up my phone. "Come on. If that didn't wake Roxy up, let her sleep."

Misty gray light filled the second floor hall. I sniffed the air. "Something's burning!"

Alice and I ran down the last flight of stairs. She swerved left when we got to the ground floor and motioned me to follow.

Smoke and shattered glass everywhere. And on the floor, tiny fires— some glowing bright, some winking out.

Something flew toward a window near us. "Duck," I yelled.

Alice and I dropped to the floor. The window exploded. A projectile crash-landed a few feet away. I stuck my head around the corner of a sofa. No new fire, and several that had been burning bright were now smoldering.

"Count to one hundred," said Alice. Our mantra for not rushing headlong into harm's way.

When time was up, we crept along the floor. I activated my phone and shone it around. The smoke had thinned; we were alone in the room.

Alice stood and kicked at one of the smoky lumps. Brown paper surrounded a canister like a soft drink can. "Smoke bomb." She kicked again. "Like those things you set off at gender reveal parties. Someone stuck it inside a paper bag. Looks like there was other material inside the bag—cotton, at a guess—to create a small flame. Scary, but unless the perp got lucky, not flammable enough to set the house on fire."

We counted five more canisters on the floor, one that landed on the coffee table—alarmingly close to a big stack of newspapers—and a different seventh projectile. A piece of paper tied around a brick. I took pictures first, then cut the string with scissors Alice retrieved from the kitchen and spread open the paper. Where there's smoke, there's fire—next time!

"Hmph," Alice said. "Next time."

"I wonder if anyone besides Roxy knows we're here."

Alice thought a minute. "Vic's car is out of sight. Only Roxy's is in the driveway."

"Maybe we can use that to our advantage," I said, "for next time."

Alice retrieved a broom from the kitchen. "Can't do anything about the shattered windows right now, but at least we can sweep the debris."

Dawn was breaking by the time we'd cleaned up the mess.

* * *

Although a good night's sleep had revived Roxy, we waited until she was fortified with a cup of coffee before telling her about the excitement in the night. She sagged, head in hands.

Whether she was ready or not, it was time to get serious. "We need to alert the police about last night's attack. First, though, to get a clearer idea of how to help you—who most wants to keep you away from the music festival?"

Roxy chewed her fingernails before replying. "Samantha."

"Who's she?"

"We're friends—or I thought we were. Sam and I perform on the same music circuit. Small clubs and coffeehouses. Sam's doing a set at the festival, but I heard she was on the short list for headliner."

"And they picked you."

Roxy bobbed her head. "I can't believe she'd trash my house, frighten me like this…"

"She knows where you live, though? Which bedroom is yours?"

"Yeah, she's visited a few times." Roxy sat forward in her chair with more intensity than she'd shown earlier. "But there *is* someone else. Not so much about the festival, but he's such a bastard that he'd target me because I'm the only one who'll be here this summer." She screwed her face into a scowl. "And use my fear as leverage to get to my parents because he knows how sick Dad is."

"Who's that?"

"Dwight Randall. He lives next door—his house is halfway up the drive."

"Along the driveway? I didn't see it."

"It's a tiny place. He bought it when he was just starting out."

I ran the slightly-familiar name through my memory. "Oh, wow, you mean the block-chain guru? *That* Dwight Randall?"

"I guess." Roxy dragged her fingers through her curls. "He's a major pain in the ass. He's approached my parents dozens of times about buying our land. My great-grandfather bought thirty acres, back when a regular person could afford it. This house sits on the south edge of the property."

"Your folks don't want to sell?"

"Not really, though my brother's been making the case lately that the estate is too much of a burden for them now that my dad's so sick, and they should sign it over to us." Roxy rubbed her thumb along her fingers. "Theo would sell in a heartbeat."

"He's your only sibling?"

"Yep."

"What's he like?"

"Alice has met Theo." Roxy elbowed her friend with a laugh. "Why don't you ask her?"

I pivoted to Alice, raising my eyebrows.

"Theo is an entitled jerk who can't keep his hands to himself." Alice concluded her pronouncement with a decisive last slurp of coffee.

"O-kay. I get the picture."

Alice set down her cup and patted Roxy's hand. "We need to ask you about Doug, but I really don't want to upset you."

"I haven't seen him in almost six months." Roxy pinched her lips. "Doug's my ex-husband, Mamie. We met in college—so Alice knows him, too. We got divorced last fall. It wasn't...amicable."

Alice jumped in. "He wanted Roxy to give up performing."

"He gave me an either-or. Music or him." She exhaled a puff of air. "I didn't have to think about it."

"Where's your ex now?"

"He bought a house in Pelham Harbor." When I looked blank, Alice said, "That's about forty-five minutes north of here."

Roxy's phone buzzed. "It's a text from Charlie Dalton, the detective."

> *He's on his way over to ask more questions about yesterday.*

Alice and I have worked together so long it took only a single let's-do-it nod. She shot her finger at me, so I took the lead. "Detective Dalton doesn't know about the fire yet, so you'll tell him when he arrives. *But* because Alice and I will work more efficiently if no one knows we're here, this is how I want you to play it."

After I said my piece, Roxy's eyebrows knit together. "I'd feel much better if you stayed here with me all day."

Alice jumped in. "If *anything* at all worries you, text me, and I'll come running. Like Mamie said, though, we get better results when we work behind the scenes."

I slugged down the last of my now-cold coffee. "Come on downstairs to see the damage and how we cleaned it up. You'll tell Detective Dalton *you* did it, of course." I hoped my smile was encouraging. "Since we don't want to run into him coming up your driveway, we'll hide out on the third floor until he leaves."

"You were a great natural actress and singer when we were in school." Alice wrapped her arm around Roxy's shoulders. "I've seen you put on your performing face."

Roxy straightened. Chin high. "You're right—I need to think of this as psyching myself up. Getting ready to knock 'em dead at the festival."

Alice and I barely had time to get into position before tires crunched on the crushed-shell driveway. A burly man in jeans and a plaid flannel shirt stepped out of a police cruiser. Through an open third-floor window, we heard him call out for Roxy. She rushed down the front steps. "Charlie, thank goodness. Come see what happened last night!"

She might be running on caffeine and adrenaline, but Roxy knew how to put on a good act.

Once they went inside, we moved to the rear windows. The shattered sun-room glass allowed snippets of their conversation to filter up.

Roxy ran upstairs the second the detective drove off. "Could you hear?"

"Most of it," I said. "That was nice of him to nail in your storm shutters."

"Yeah, Charlie's a good neighbor."

"Don't you want to find a place to stay in town?" Alice asked. "At least until you get the windows replaced and your security system back online."

"No, no, no. I already told you that. Charlie kept insisting I get out of harm's way, too, but it's important to me to make a stand." Roxy enveloped us both in an embrace. "And with you guys around, I feel surer about that."

"Be careful this afternoon. Maybe stay up in Theo's room," Alice suggested. "We'll stay in touch by text."

* * *

We set up at a café in town and split Roxy's list. Alice took the rival musician, Samantha, and Roxy's ex, Doug. I picked the block-chain guy, Dwight. *And* Roxy's brother, Theo. A disproportionate number of the cases we've taken involve conflicts between siblings for parents' possessions. That, plus Alice's distaste for him, meant I'd vet Theo. Just in case.

We worked phones and social media all morning. By noon, Alice had made progress. "I know this is only the first elimination round— Samantha or Doug could've hired or enticed someone to do their dirty work—but I don't see it. Doug's got a new girlfriend. She's already moved in, and they spent last weekend with her parents in Connecticut."

"This, despite his over-the-top *it's me or music* ultimatum?"

"His new girlfriend's family has megabucks, and it sounds like all she aspires to is a humongous diamond and the wedding of the season."

"Loser." I rolled my eyes. "What about Samantha?"

Alice clapped her hands to her cheeks in mock-astonishment. "It just so happens she's in LA, doing a demo tape for Warner."

I laughed out loud. "Wow, so probably not holding a grudge about losing out on a small-town summer festival."

"What'd you learn, Mamie?"

I took another bite of my excellent chicken pesto panini while I sorted out the tangled strands of information. "First of all, the blockchain guy is such a techie that he keeps everything in an online calendar." I flashed a quick grin at Alice. "Which I hacked into. He arrived in Cedar Isle two days ago and was home last night. Because it would've been dead easy for him to sneak up the hill to Roxy's and throw the smoke bombs, he'd top our suspect list—except he was in Phoenix last week, speaking at a conference."

"Even if analyzing the paint samples says the graffiti happened longer than two days ago, it doesn't matter." Alice sipped her iced coffee. "With his money, Dwight could've hired someone."

"True, so I'm using his online calendar to monitor his movements and calls. He apparently injured his knee playing tennis this morning. Called an Uber to drive him to the hospital and is there now getting an MRI."

"Hey, if he's our guy and he hurt himself that badly, maybe the attacks will stop."

"Or he'll just change MO." I tapped my fingers on the table. "A more puzzling possibility is Theo. He's staying with his girlfriend in Camden, less than a half-hour away..."

When I trailed off, Alice scratched her ear. "What did Roxy say that made you suspect her brother?"

"Her dig about how his being eager to sell their land. And guess what? Theo has an appointment with a land broker today at three."

Alice's eyes widened. "We'd better split up this afternoon. Theo will recognize me, so trailing him is your job."

I gave her a thumbs-up. "Good call."

"You keep the BMW to follow Theo but drive me over to Roxy's first."

"You want to check out Dwight's place?"

"Yeah, he's the biggest unknown, has the deepest pockets, and might be stuck at the hospital for a while. Besides, I want to stay close to Roxy. I don't really expect an incident in daylight. The whole point seems to be spooking her anonymously. Still…"

* * *

I dropped Alice off at the foot of Roxy's driveway and returned to town, cruising the crowded streets until I found a parking space. With time before Theo's appointment, I waited on a bench in the main square, studying recent pictures of him that Roxy texted me. Hard to believe this skinny-faced sourpuss was her brother. I wondered if he just didn't photograph well—but then, there he was, strolling along the center of the sidewalk so others had to dodge out of his way. Blue blazer, tan khakis, loafers without socks. Talking on his phone. I already didn't like the guy.

I dashed into the real estate office ahead of him.

A young woman approached me. "Good afternoon, I'm Bianca. May I help you?"

"Just looking."

I didn't miss her glance down at my (really good knock-off) Prada espadrilles—probably all that kept her from sneering at me as inconsequential. The large open space featured the usual real estate décor of walls covered with glossy photos. In an alcove at the back, an older man was on the phone.

When Theo entered, Bianca didn't bother with gatekeeping. "Mr. Grayson is in the conference room. I'll tell him you've arrived."

"I'll wait for Doug out here."

Doug? I hid a gasp by coughing into my elbow.

I texted Roxy. *Send pic of your ex.*

Theo wandered over. Too close. He pointed to the photographs of a cedar-shingled Colonial I'd pretended to study. "That home is not in a stellar location."

I stepped away but remembered to smile. Alice is better at 'demurely sexy' than I am, but I try. "What would you suggest?"

He took my arm and escorted me several paces to images of a waterfront McMansion. "Much nicer."

"Is that *your* house, by any chance? The one you have on the market for—" I squinted at the fine print—"a cool ten mil?"

"I wish!" His exaggerated laugh would have put a game-show host to shame.

"So, what are you doing here?" That's what passes for flirting *chez moi.*

Theo waved his hand like an orchestra conductor. "A friend and I have some ideas we want to talk over with a broker."

Nothing for it but to ask. "What kind of ideas?"

"Well, there's nothing definite yet..." He leaned into my space again. "If you'll be around later, I'm heading over to the Time &Tide after this meeting. Perhaps you'd like to join me for a drink. We can talk more about it then." Theo's arm had snaked around my waist. I was pretty darn sure he didn't mean *talk.*

The door opened.

With Theo so near, I hadn't dared to check my phone for Doug pictures, but the guy who entered was *old.* Gray hair and wrinkled old. Not a likely ex-husband for Roxy.

I turned my attention—my charm—to the newcomer. "Hi! Doug, right? Don't I know you?"

He blushed scarlet. "Yes, Doug Hobart—and you are?"

"Margaret Longwood." Margaret's my real first name so I wasn't lying. "I b'lieve we met at that yacht club party?"

He was wearing a cap with their sailing-ship logo, so it was a safe guess. He had no idea who I was, of course, but shook my hand with old-world cordiality.

In a stroke of luck—or possibly the mere arrival of the other attendee—Bianca called Theo over.

I flashed my A-game simper at Doug. "Interesting, what you and Theo have in mind."

"Well, if we can get all parties to agree to terms, it would be a game-changer."

A game-changer. I needed to know more.

But my phone picked that exact second to chime. *Roxy.* Not a text but a call. *Damn.* "I've got to take this."

I moved to the front window. "What's up?"

"I've been texting Alice for a half hour, and she hasn't replied." Roxy rushed her words together. "Do you know where she is?"

Ice filled my stomach. *That's not like Alice.* "Was something wrong? I mean, why were you trying to get in touch with her?"

"Two guys came with a delivery." Her voice rose from its normal alto to a piercing soprano. "They'd dumped a ton of gravel beside the driveway by the time I got outside—and wanted me to pay for it. I told them I hadn't placed the order, but they showed me paperwork that specified where to leave it and that it was COD."

So, a daytime prank. "Did you get rid of the them?"

"Yes." A wail. "But not the mess they left."

With Theo and Doug not five feet away, I had to be careful about what I said, but Alice stayed near Roxy's to *be there* in an emergency. Even if she muted her phone while doing surveillance, Alice would never have failed to text Roxy once she saw a message.

Despite being so close to learning more about Theo and Doug's plan, Alice was my priority. Anyhow, in that brief moment, the older man from the office strode over to the waiting clients. Everyone shook hands. Meeting on. Nothing I could do here now.

"I'm on my way."

* * *

After the bustle of a seaside resort in summer, Roxy's hilltop was eerily silent. I zipped up the driveway. In a replay of last night, Roxy ran out to greet me.

"Still no word from Alice?" I asked.

She shook *no* with her whole body.

"I'm going to look for her. She's supposed to be checking out Dwight's house. How do I get there?"

"About halfway down the drive, by a big sycamore on the left, there's a path. I can show you."

Our job is to keep Roxy safe... "No, stay here. Keep your phone handy."

I ran down the hill. Found the sycamore. Took the path—still running—until I realized my haste was too noisy. Moving more deliberately, I edged along the dirt trail until I spied, in a clearing in the forest, a little Hansel-and-Gretel gingerbread house. Not what I expected from a tech bro. Of course, now that he was big-time, he must want the hilltop view.

Staying in the cover of the surrounding trees, I began to circle the cottage.

Movement—Alice, stumbling through the trees! I ran to her, and she sagged against me.

"What happened?"

"Dunno." Alice swiveled her head and winced. "A car drove up just as I got here. I was behind the house, but I heard someone open and close a car door, so I sneaked up to a window to try to spot who came in. Whoever it was must've seen me first because, a few minutes later, I heard a crackle of leaves behind me. And then—pow."

"Let's get you out of here. Can you walk?"

"With your help."

It took a while to hobble up the path to Roxy's, but by the time we got there, Alice was walking almost normally. We settled her on the front porch swing, and Roxy got ice for the bump on her head. Alice repeated her story.

Why would someone go out of their way to incapacitate Alice? "Do you have any idea who your attacker was? Or where he might've gone?"

"There was only that rustle before he hit me. By the time I came to, I was alone in the woods."

"I'll look around later," I said, "but let me tell you who Theo met in town."

"Doug *Hobart*?" Roxy's face twisted into concentration. "No, my ex is Doug *Witham*." She took out her phone and typed. "Is the Doug Hobart guy you saw sixty-something? White hair?"

I nodded.

She tilted her phone toward me. "This him?"

"Yep."

"He's a banker."

So, the son of a major landowner and a banker walk into a real-estate office... "Alice, if you're okay staying here with Roxy, I'm going to rush into town to have that drink with Theo."

* * *

Five p.m. and the bar was hopping. I entered, camouflaged by a noisy scrum of thirty-somethings. Theo was visible in profile at a corner table. A second person sat across from him. Not Doug Hobart, the banker. Someone else.

Shit. This was going to get complicated.

I eased out of the bar before Theo spotted me.

* * *

I told Roxy and Alice who I'd seen.

"You think they're working together?"

"I don't know what else it could be. It looked like a serious discussion—you know, not just folks hanging out after work."

"This pisses me off," Roxy shouted. "I want to be part of the take-down."

We all slapped hands. "You're in."

"We need to plan for their next assault," I told Roxy, "because it *will* come. Probably tonight since they haven't been successful in scaring you away yet."

"We'll take turns watching," Alice said.

I stood. "Right now, though, I'm going to Dwight's place to see if I can figure out why Alice was attacked." I didn't mention my lock-picks to Roxy.

His house sat empty and dark. No cars were around, so I let myself in. On the kitchen table, I found what I was looking for. Compelling evidence, though possibly not the sort the perp intended. I took pictures and left it in place.

* * *

It grew dark. The wind came up. I guessed tonight's offensive, like the smoke-bomb strike, would come closer to dawn, so I asked Roxy to share the first shift with me.

At two a.m., Alice came down to spell Roxy. "All quiet?"

"So far." Clouds covered the moon, and we hunkered in the dark by bushes at the corner of the house.

Time passed.

"Shh."

Footsteps coming up the driveway. We moved deeper into the shadows.

Two shadowy figures stood by the front steps. I checked to make sure my flex-cuffs were handy. Alice pulled out her night-vision camera and started recording.

"This is back-ass-ward," Theo said. "We want her to go, so we fuck up her car?"

"At first, I planned to seal the deal by destroying her guitars, but when I asked Roxy about them, she said she'd stored them in the theater's climate-controlled vault. No way to get at them in there. This'll do the trick, though. She loves her car—"

"And she never bothers to lock it when she's home," Theo finished.

His companion uncapped a bottle, then eased open the door handle.

"We've got to stop them," Alice hissed.

"The second we see a flame," I whispered, "we'll rush toward them. And keep recording."

As we watched, the man shook liquid into the car, rooted in a pocket, and pulled out—

"Matches," Alice mouthed.

"Ready, set..." An orange glow. "Go!"

We ran at them.

Theo bolted, and Charlie Dalton dropped the match.

I fastened cuffs on the detective before he could recover.

"You've made a mistake." He struggled against the restraints. "I was making sure Roxy was okay."

"We've got you on tape." Alice dangled the camera in front of him.

"After I saw you in the bar with Theo, I did some research," I said. "You've got money problems, Detective Dalton. Gambling. Alimony. A fancy new car. When Theo approached you—as an old family friend—about helping him persuade his parents to sell, you must've realized you could make a fortune, too. Being called in to investigate your own crime was a nice touch, but your gravel truck stunt was stupid. When you saw a woman was sneaking around Dwight's house, you were afraid she'd seen you. So, you knocked her out cold—then placed that gravel invoice in Dwight Randall's kitchen. You aimed to implicate *him*, but the invoice is clearly marked 12:33 pm. At 12:33, Mr. Randall was getting an MRI on his knee at Mercy Hospital." I grinned. "Sorry, Charlie."

Disappearance of an Easy Lover
N.M. Cedeño

Standing beside a thoughtless, twenty-two-year-old heartbreaker, waiting for a man who had resorted to torching vehicles to intimidate her, I decided I'd misjudged the danger I might be facing. As a private forensic genealogy detective, I usually work cold cases. I quit teaching to follow my passion for genetic genealogy and to become a private investigator in Dallas, Texas. Hunting for old documents and digging through archives matches my skills far better than facing villains. I'd knowingly violated my policy against accepting current cases because the matter seemed simple: find a girl and ask why she ghosted a guy. How could something that straightforward be dangerous?

The case started one Friday afternoon when my office door opened and an awkward, twenty-something man with red hair tripped through the doorway of Laster Genetic Genealogy and Investigations.

I stood to greet him, my voice sounding raspy as always, and not only because I hadn't spoken in several hours, "I'm Maya Laster. How can I help you?"

Flushing, the young man pushed his wire-frame glasses up his freckled nose. "I don't know if you can help, but I hope you're willing to try. The last two offices I visited refused me," he said in a rumbling baritone that was subdued, but not quite defeated.

"Well, I won't promise not to be strike three, but I'm happy to listen. Please sit." I pointed to the cushioned guest chair in front of my desk. "What's your name?"

"Sorry. My social skills are bad, but I usually remember to introduce myself. Today has been difficult." He introduced himself as Charlie Dunne and sank into the chair.

"Pleased to meet you, Charlie. People who come here are often flustered. Take your time." I sat behind my desk and waited for him.

He bit his lower lip and stared over my shoulder for a few seconds before speaking. "I met an incredible woman named Angel a few weeks ago. She was in Dallas, staying with a friend while she visited graduate schools—SMU and UT Dallas, plus some other places. She is the most amazing person: smart, funny, curious. I felt like our brains were on the same wavelength. We spoke and texted daily for three weeks. Then, three days ago, all communication stopped."

"She ghosted you?"

"I can't believe she would do that. If she wanted to stop seeing me, she'd tell me, probably loudly, to my face. Something happened to her. I called all the Dallas-Fort Worth area police departments and hospitals to see if she'd been in an accident but found nothing. I texted her, asking if she was okay, but she didn't reply. I'm so worried, I can barely think." Radiating urgency, he leaned toward me.

"If you only knew her for three weeks, how can you be certain you had a full picture of her character? Some people act a part for a while, can't sustain it, and drop the façade. Only then do you see the real person. Maybe ghosting you was a sign of her mask dropping." I felt sorry for him. Being treated like that hurts.

Charlie waved his hands in denial. "People who ghost other people are afraid of confrontation or they're massively self-centered. Angel's not like that. She said when it came to difficult issues, she'd rather face them at once—rip the bandage off—instead of prolonging the pain by tiptoeing around."

"You don't think cutting all contact with you could be her way of 'ripping the bandage off' instead of prolonging goodbyes?" I asked, knowing I sounded skeptical.

His hands tightened into frustrated fists. "You don't believe me any more than the police or the other two private detectives, but I know in my gut that something is wrong." Anguish crackled in his deep voice.

"What makes you think something is wrong? Is it only a feeling in your gut?"

"She was always looking over her shoulder. Watching for something. She said she was trying to avoid an ex. Now that she's vanished, I tried to find her online, and I discovered she's using an alias. The name she gave me, Angelina Renee DiRossi, belongs to a dead woman, someone who died in her eighties. I don't know Angel's real name. I think she's hiding from something or someone."

"What do you want me to do?" I asked, wondering what Charlie's goal was.

"Find out who Angel really is." He pushed a piece of paper across my desk. "I submitted a fast-food cup that she left at my house for DNA analysis with a friend who works at a private lab. The lab didn't identify her or any immediate relatives. The results only show cousins."

I took the paper and read the results. He had enough information for me to start researching, but I was suspicious of his motives. "Why?"

His eyebrows came together in confusion. "Because I love her. I want to make sure she's okay."

"If I find her and she doesn't want to see you, I won't tell you where she is," I said. I gave him the glare I'd perfected on students who were being less than truthful during my teaching career.

He didn't flinch under my piercing gaze. "But you can tell me if she's safe. If she left by choice, not because of coercion, threats, or fear for her life, I'll drop the matter."

I stared at the pale, freckled face that I'd judged to be young and naïve and reassessed. While still young, and possibly naïve, he had intelligence and determination. I still thought it was likely that the woman had ghosted him, and that she might have planned to do so all along, from the moment she gave him the name of a dead woman. While she might have been trying to avoid an ex, that didn't mean that she didn't ghost Charlie.

I brushed aside my plan not to take current cases. This was an affair of the heart, or, at most, a case of a young woman hiding from domestic abuse. Either way, I might be able to do more than the police. "Okay.

I'll try to identify her. If she was adopted, I may get nowhere. If I find her, I mean it when I say that contacting you will be her decision." I found myself shaking my index finger, scolding Charlie like a delinquent student from my previous life.

He grinned at me in relief. "Fair enough."

Charlie supplied me with the genetic results he'd received, and I promised to contact him when I had information. After he left, I began researching Angel's genealogy, sustaining myself with a bowl of chocolates and a cup of black coffee.

* * *

Working backward in time from the cousins listed on the DNA report, I located three sets of Angel's great-great grandparents and a set of great-grandparents. Then I used obituaries, newspaper birth and marriage announcements, and death records to work forward in time, identifying people who could be Angel's parents. The name Angel had given Charlie belonged to a deceased relative, probably a maternal great-aunt.

The whole process took less time and fewer chocolates than I expected because the families involved were wealthy and socially-active in the twentieth century. Family marriages and births were well-documented in newspaper society columns, including the births of the people most likely to be Angel's parents, a pair of Texas-born scions of East Coast families. Birth records led me to their three daughters, all born in Houston. All I had to do was decide which daughter was Angel.

The oldest of the sisters, Valerie, had spilled her life story onto her social media pages. She went to high school in a ritzy area of Houston, graduated from a posh, East Coast liberal arts college, and married a lawyer in a grand society wedding. She posted frequently about the charities she supported and her children's pre-school activities.

The second sister, Gloria, was less vocal on social media. She had an Ivy League education, worked briefly in pharmaceuticals, but quit to become a high school biology teacher. Students gave her glowing reviews, suggesting she was an effective and inspiring teacher.

The two older sisters lived and worked in Houston, and their social media posts showed they hadn't spent any time in Dallas recently.

That left the youngest sister, a twenty-two-year-old named Angelia Morris, whose social media consisted of fashion, food, and concerts. I found posts confirming that she was looking for information on attending graduate schools. Photos showed her with six different young men in the past year. The men gazed at her with adoration while she gazed at the camera. "Love 'em and leave 'em" appeared to be her style, which might also explain why she was watching her back. Maybe one of the men she'd enthralled didn't want the relationship to end. I was reasonably certain that I'd found the right person and that she'd ghosted him without compunction.

Nothing indicated why the young woman might be using her great-aunt's name as an alias other than that it was a handy fake name to give a gullible man. I did notice that the only other place I'd seen the name "Angelia" was in a Richard Marx song title, and that both of Angel's sisters—Valerie and Gloria—bore names that were song titles in the 1980s.

Once I had Angel's real name and birth date, I ran another background check. Angelia Morris had no arrests, no bankruptcies, no loans, and no employment history. She was a college student whose parents could afford to buy her a car and pay for her education.

I sent her direct messages via social media explaining who I was, assuring her of her right to privacy, and asking her to contact me. Then, I called it a day, looking forward to a Friday evening with 1980s songs stuck in my head.

By Saturday afternoon, I hadn't received a response from Angel. I sent another set of messages, again assuring her that I only needed to verify her well-being. By the end of the day, she still hadn't responded.

Sunday mid-morning, I packed a few essentials, collected my laptop, and set out for Houston to seek her at her parents' house, singing to a playlist of 1980s music as I drove.

* * *

Four hours later, I pulled onto the pine-tree-lined street where Angel's parents lived. The road was blocked by a fire engine. A car in the driveway of Angelia's parents' two-story, red brick house had burned to a smoking shell but the house beyond it was undamaged. I parked by the curb and stepped out of my car to get a better view. The stench of burning tires filled the humid air.

A car screeched around the corner onto the street and parked crookedly behind mine. The driver, a twenty-something woman in gray slacks and a seafoam blouse, rushed from the car toward the house. It took me a second to recognize one of Angel's sisters. While all three sisters had dark hair and large eyes, this one was Gloria, the teacher. She looked panicked as she raced past me. Ignoring the yellow police tape, she bolted toward the front of the house. As a police officer yelled at her to stop, Gloria ran into the house, barely checking her pace at the door.

I heard another a car pull around the corner, but didn't turn to look. Then, the car parked behind mine, exploded, knocking the breath out of me as it blasted me off my feet. Dazed, I rolled to my back. Firefighters rushed to extinguish the flaming car. I let an EMT check me for a concussion. My head hurt, but I didn't have any other signs of a brain injury. The pain I felt was likely from the lump on the back of my head, inflicted when I hit the ground.

My own car was scorched and dented by flying debris, but functional. I was assessing the damage when a police officer approached and asked for identification. His demeanor changed the moment he found out that I was a private investigator. He signaled to someone else.

A moment later, a dour-faced Houston police officer approached. His dark eyes under heavy, drooping eyelids held irritation that seemed as if he was having a perpetually bad day. He stood with a notepad in his hand.

"Hello, Ms. Laster," he said, the frown on his face frozen place even as he spoke. "I'm Sgt. Raimundo. What's a private investigator from Dallas doing on a street in Houston when two cars erupt in flames?"

"Searching for a missing person," I said. The bump on my head throbbed when I spoke, and I winced. "A client hired me to verify someone's wellbeing. I arrived in the neighborhood, but the fire engines were blocking the road. I was waiting for them to leave so I could knock on the door. Then, boom. The car parked behind mine exploded."

"You didn't see anyone tampering with that car, did you?"

"I only saw the driver get out and run into a house. She crossed the yellow tape and got yelled at by an officer, but didn't stop."

He grunted and wrote something in his notepad. "Did you notice any other vehicles turn onto this street? Or drive past at the intersection?"

I remembered my impression of a car's presence. "I heard a car engine, but I didn't see it."

"Can you tell me if your case has anything to do with either Gloria Morris or Valerie Morris Stroop?"

"Not that I know of."

"Who is your missing person?"

"Angel DiRossi is the name I was given, but it's an alias for Angelia Morris."

His drooping eyelids almost opened. "An alias?" He thumbed through his notepad. "Angelia Morris is the younger sister of the ladies who lost their cars today. Why was she using an alias?"

"I don't know. I was hired to verify that she is safe. My client was afraid she was being threatened when she disappeared and stopped communicating."

He stared at me. "She disappeared? From where?"

"Dallas."

"I may need your client's name." He held his pen ready over his notepad.

"It won't help you. My client only knows Angelia's alias, not her real name or her address here. If he knew her real name, he wouldn't have hired me."

He rolled his eyes and said, "Fine. No one else in the family has volunteered any reason for why someone would blow up two of their cars. Perhaps I need to speak to Angelia Morris. Her family didn't mention that she was missing."

"Maybe she isn't. Maybe she ghosted my client to end their relationship because she didn't feel like talking to him anymore. I was going to ask her parents." I gestured toward the house.

"Not until after I've spoken to them. Stay here and don't interfere." He flipped his notepad closed and glared a warning at me before walking away.

I had to wait for the police and fire department to finish their work before I was allowed to speak to the Morris family.

As I rang the doorbell, I could see a woman peeking out a front window. The woman—middle-aged with a creamy complexion and carefully dyed and expensively styled dark hair—cracked open the door and asked, "Are you with the insurance?"

"No, ma'am. My name is Maya Laster. I'm a private detective. My client hired me to verify the safety and well-being of your daughter, Angelia. I was hoping to speak to her." I displayed my investigator's license.

"Just a minute," the woman said. She closed the door, leaving me standing on the porch.

I saw her walk by the window at the front of the house.

A moment later she returned with a man who yanked the door open and scrutinized me.

"I didn't mean to impose," I said, raising both hands to reassure them that I meant no harm. "I have a bit of a headache. Your daughter's car was parked behind mine, and the blast knocked me to the ground."

"You're the one," the man said. "We saw that someone was injured, but we didn't know who."

"Are you Mr. Morris?" I asked, noticing that they were too nervous to invite me into their house.

He nodded.

I introduced myself and explained why I had come.

Mrs. Morris said, "The police sergeant mentioned that a boyfriend of Angel's hired you to make sure she's safe. Why did he think she was in danger?" She grabbed her husband's arm, and I could hear the fear in her voice.

"She seemed nervous. When he asked her why she kept looking over her shoulder, she told him that she was trying to avoid an ex-boyfriend. Have you spoken to Angel recently?" I asked. "I only need to verify that she's safe and that she stopped communicating with my client of her own free will. My client will be disappointed if she decided to break up with him without saying anything, but he'll accept that as her choice."

Mrs. Morris said, "Angel went to stay with a friend in Dallas. She's visiting graduate schools to decide where she wants to go to school. She's supposed to let us know when she leaves Dallas, but we haven't heard from her. She isn't answering her phone."

"Do you know the name of the friend she was visiting?"

"She was visiting Ella Hernandez, but I just spoke to Ella. Ella said Angel left two days ago." Worry etched deep lines around her mouth and across her forehead.

"Did you report her as missing to the police?"

"Yes," said Mrs. Morris.

"Good." I was relieved. If the police knew Angel was missing and that two cars had been destroyed in front of her family's house, they would do their utmost to track her. I decided to go back to Dallas and speak with her friend, Ella. Mrs. Morris gave me Ella's phone number. "If you hear from Angel, please ask her to call me. I only want to speak to her." I handed Mrs. Morris my business card. "Do you have any idea why someone would destroy your daughters' cars?"

"No! We have no idea!" Tears came into Mrs. Morris's eyes. "I'm so worried. We don't know why this is happening."

I glanced at Mr. Morris. He was pale, and obviously distressed, but silent. "And you, sir? Can you think of any reason someone might want to threaten your family?"

He cleared his throat before he spoke. "No. We already went through this with the police. We aren't going over it again with a stranger. We will give Angel your card when we see her." He retreated a step, taking his wife with him.

Taking my dismissal with good grace, I said goodbye, and left.

The drive back to Dallas took longer than usual. A headache forced me to stop and rest. Night was falling by the time I reached the city limits, so I decided to visit Ella Hernandez in the morning.

* * *

Monday morning, I sat with Ella in her North Dallas apartment and listened as she said, "Angel starts these intense relationships where she knows the guy is way more invested than she is. She claims she's looking for 'Mr. Right,' but it looks more like she's playing to me. She walks away from relationships with no explanation when she gets bored, leaving the guy confused by her sudden change of heart. I told her she needed to consider other people's feelings, but she ignored me. She's used to getting everything she wants. She's spoiled." Ella brushed her long black bangs away from her forehead, revealing eyebrows bunched in frustration and worry. "She can be so thoughtless."

I was seated on a futon across from Ella, having arrived to see her as police were leaving. She sat on the front edge of a second-hand, straight-backed chair, eager to impart information or help in any way she could. Her apartment appeared to have been furnished from thrift stores on a frugal student's budget. Unlike her friend Angel, Ella appeared to be neither spoiled, nor thoughtless. I asked, "Did one of her dating games backfire?"

"She dated a possessive guy named Adrik in Houston. He's wealthy, and I wouldn't be surprised if he's involved in something criminal. He has that vibe, kind of dangerous. Initially, he liked Angel because of her spirit, but the more they dated, the more he tried to control her. She ghosted him three weeks ago. Then he claimed she took something of his. He started sending her threatening messages about what would happen to her and her family if he didn't get it back."

"Did he threaten her sisters?"

"Yeah, but Angel didn't take him seriously."

"Both of her sisters' cars were burned in front of their parents' house yesterday. Didn't the police tell you?"

Ella bounced from her seat like a tightly wound spring. "Oh no! They only said Angel was missing. Do you think Adrik is involved? Do you think he kidnapped Angel?"

"She may be hiding from him. If he had kidnapped her, he wouldn't bother to destroy her sisters' cars in an effort to threaten her."

"I hope you're right." Ella interlaced her hands, gripping them together like she was praying a desperate prayer.

I asked, "Have you tried calling or texting her?"

"It wouldn't do any good. She shattered the screen on her phone when she was leaving here. She dropped it down the stairs to the parking lot, and it landed on concrete. She needs to get it fixed or get a new phone. She's hoping her dad will buy her the latest model."

That explained why she hadn't called her parents. "Do you know Adrik's last name?"

"Angel said his name meant he was a Venetian. I was trying to remember it. Let me think." She frowned at the ceiling and tapped her foot.

"Veneziano?" I asked.

"That's sound right," she said, staring at me. "How did you know?"

"I do a lot of family history research. Some Italian last names are based on the place the family originated. Did Angel regularly use aliases with the men she dated?"

"Sometimes. Not with Adrik though. He knew her real name and where she lived." Ella paced across her small living room, a vision of nervous energy.

"Can you think of any place Angel might go to hide from Adrik?"

"No."

"Can you think of any place she liked to go to escape, relax, or take a break?"

She stopped pacing and jerked around to face me. "She might go to her family's condo on South Padre Island. Angel loves the beach. She likes to go there when she has to make big decisions. She likes to walk in the sand and watch the sunrise. She says it helps her think."

"Did you tell the police about the condo?"

"I didn't think of it until now."

"Call and tell the police what you remembered. If Angel is at the condo, she may need police protection."

Ella pulled out her phone. While she called the detective, I called Angel's mother.

Angel's mother confirmed that the family owned a condo on South Padre Island. She seemed relieved when I asked if Angel might be there.

"I hadn't thought of that. I hope she's there," said Mrs. Morris.

I explained about Angel's shattered phone screen. Mrs. Morris said, "If her phone is broken, I can call the condo and ask if she checked in at the desk."

When Ella and I ended our calls, my mind began to spin with concern for Angel. "Can I see where Angel stayed while she was here? Do you have a guest room?"

Ella led me to a space that served as both an office and a guest room, featuring a desk workspace opposite a worn-at-the-edges, vintage, bronze-framed day bed. "Do you mind if I check the trash?" I pointed to a wastebasket under the desk.

Ella grabbed the wastebasket and handed it to me. We both looked inside. A number of crumpled papers were in the bottom.

"Are these yours?" I asked.

"No. Angel left Friday, so these must be hers."

I tipped the papers out onto the desk and began to uncrumple one. Ella grabbed another and began to do the same. We found restaurant receipts, a drug store receipt, and a torn envelope addressed to Angel and covered in doodles. The doodles were sunshine, waves, and a turtle. In one corner in neat cursive someone had written "*sea turtle 2 Tuesday*."

"Is this Angel's writing?" I asked, pointing to the words.

"Yes."

"Any ideas on what it might mean?"

"When she's at the condo, Angel loves to visit the sea turtles at the rescue center on South Padre Island. She might be going there at two o'clock tomorrow."

If her doodles were any indication, Angel was headed for the coast. I needed to leave as soon as possible since I was over five hundred miles from South Padre Island.

After leaving Ella, I retrieved my overnight bag from my house. Before setting out, I called Angel's mother and asked, "Did they find Angel at the condo?"

"No. The manager checked our unit. Someone broke the door and threw things everywhere—emptied drawers and cabinets and ripped open pillows. Why is this happening? Why hasn't Angel called?" she asked, sobbing between her words.

I couldn't guess why Angel hadn't borrowed a phone yet. "As to why this is happening, Ella told me that an ex-boyfriend of Angel's believes that Angel has something of his. He may be searching for it. He may have destroyed your other daughters' cars to intimidate Angel into giving the item back to him. I'm traveling to South Padre this afternoon to see if I can locate Angel. Will you tell me the address of the condo?"

She gave me the address.

"Can you think of anywhere Angel might go if the condo wasn't safe?"

"A hotel, I guess."

"Thank you for the information, Mrs. Morris."

"Please, if you find her, call me. Her father wants to drive to Padre to look for her, but I think we better wait here in case she comes home for help."

"You and your family need to stay safe. Stay in Houston. I'll call you if I find Angel." I ended the call, booked my favorite dog-sitter to look after my dog, and left for South Padre.

* * *

Monday night, I arrived at my hotel in South Padre. The breeze blowing off the Gulf of Mexico was steady, and it smelled like rain. Towering white and gray cumulus clouds filled the horizon over the water. I longed to walk in the sand and listen to the roar of the surf, but instead, I checked the hours of the Turtle Rescue. It was closed for the day and wouldn't reopen until ten the next morning. I dropped my things in my room and started canvassing hotels for Angel.

The clouds burst, dropping heavy rain while I spent the next several hours going to hotels, showing Angel's photo, and asking desk clerks if anyone had seen her. My last stop of the night was Angel's parents' condo, which the police had already searched, where no one admitted to seeing Angel. I returned to my hotel for the night, set my alarm, and slept.

I awoke in the pre-dawn grayness Tuesday morning. Remembering that Angel liked to watch the sunrise on the beach, I threw on shorts and a T-shirt, placed a headband around my short blonde hair to keep it from blowing in my face, and headed for the beach.

The storm from the night before had vanished. People were fishing in the twilight and walking or jogging on the sand. I joined the walkers making my way down the beach. As the sun rose over the Gulf in a glorious display of brilliant light, I scanned each woman I passed looking for Angel. I'd been walking for thirty minutes before I came upon a young woman in a Houston Astros baseball hat standing at the water's edge with her bare feet sunk into the wet sand. Her sandals were dangling from one hand. Aviator sunglasses covered half her face, so I couldn't immediately decide if she was Angel.

I stopped a few yards beyond her and looked back at her while pretending to examine a seashell. She wore pink yoga pants and a matching fitted tank top. I said, "Excuse me, but are you Angel Morris?"

The woman hastily pulled her feet from the wet sand and began to back away from me.

I raised both hands. "Wait. Angel, your parents are very worried about you. Your sisters' cars were destroyed on Sunday, and I think you know why that happened. We need to get you somewhere safe. If I can find you, the person you're hiding from can, too."

"Who are you?" she asked.

"Maya Laster. I'm a private detective. I was hired to find out if you were safe."

"Did my parents hire you?"

"No. Actually a young man named Charlie Dunne, who couldn't figure out why you stopped talking to him, hired me. I suggested that maybe you had simply grown tired of the relationship, but he insisted you would have the courtesy to tell him if that was the case. He knew you were watching your back. Then, he discovered you were using an alias. He was afraid you weren't contacting him because you were in trouble, maybe running from something. He hired me to find you."

"Charlie sent you to find me? Why?" She sounded puzzled.

"All he asked was that I verify your safety. Charlie took a DNA sample from a cup and asked me to identify you. He understands that I won't tell him where you are, or who you really are, and that contacting him would be entirely your decision."

She dropped her sandals and flung herself down in the sand, sitting with her elbows resting on her bent knees and her hands on top of her bowed head. "Adrik seemed more assertive and masculine, more like what I wanted, so I gave *him* my real name. Then he started treating me like property, and now I'm afraid of him. Charlie seemed too polite, a little wishy-washy, so I gave him an alias. Charlie sent you to make sure I was safe, and Adrik is threatening me. I'm such an idiot. Why did I give Adrik my real name instead of Charlie?"

"You're twenty-two-years old," I said, walking toward her. "You're still learning what to look for in a partner. Your friend Ella told me that you like to come here to think. Is that what you came here to think about, Adrik and Charlie?"

"Adrik and Charlie and grad school and what I want from my life. I just can't make up my mind. My parents want me to go to grad school. I'm not sure I want to go." She took off the aviator glasses revealing a purple bruise on her right cheekbone.

"What happened to your face?"

"Adrik or maybe one of his friends—I didn't stick around to see which—kicked in the door at my parent's condo. It's a second-floor unit. To escape, I climbed over the balcony and dropped to the ground. I banged my face on the fence around the patio below ours when I landed."

"Let's get off this beach. If someone is searching for you, the beach is too open and exposed. We can order room service at my hotel while you tell me what Adrik wants. And you can call your parents. They are worried about you."

* * *

Over fruit, yogurt, waffles, and coffee, I asked, "Did you take something from Adrik?"

"He wants his stupid thumb drive. He left it attached to my laptop. The thing is so tiny that I packed my laptop in my bag and didn't even notice it was there. I don't know why he's so bothered about it. It's just music he brought over one evening to play."

"If he wants it badly enough to torch your sisters' cars, there must be something other than music on the drive. Do you have the thumb drive with you? Were you intending to give it back to him today at two o'clock at the turtle rescue center?"

She stopped with a spoon of yogurt half-way to her mouth. "How did you know that?"

"You doodled on an envelope at Ella's. I found it in her trash."

"You went through the trash?" She looked at me as if she thought I might be a little crazy.

"I'm a detective. Of course, I went through the trash. Do you have the thumb drive with you?"

"Yes."

"Why didn't you give it to him before this?"

"I didn't think I had it. Then, I checked my laptop bag and found it. I offered to mail it to him, but he insisted I return it in person. I thought it was a ploy to make me see him again, so I said no. We texted back and forth about getting it back to him. I could tell he was angry, but I thought he wanted me, not the drive. I thought if I met him in public, it would be safer, so I arranged a meeting at the sea turtle rescue."

"And you couldn't have done that in Dallas?"

"I was scared. Some guys were following me. They almost forced me off the road when I was driving back to Ella's after the last time I saw Charlie. I decided to leave town early and come here instead of going home. He knows where I live, so I thought he or his friends might stop me on my way home. I wanted to hide, and I didn't think he'd find me here. I thought he'd have to wait to see me at the Turtle Rescue."

I sipped my black coffee. "Have you looked to see what's on the thumb drive?"

"Yes. A bunch of files. Mostly music. From the file names, nothing looks very important."

"Do you mind if I look at it?"

"Go ahead." She reached under her shirt into her Lycra sports top bra and extracted the drive.

"Nice hiding place," I said, accepting the drive as she dropped it in my hand.

She grinned at me, shedding her worry for a moment, making her look much younger than twenty-two. "I didn't want to get sand in it."

While Angel finished eating, I sat at the desk and inserted the thumb drive into my laptop. As she said, it contained a lot of music files. I opened a folder labeled "household" and found documents. Some were receipts. Others were invoices. All looked harmless enough. I tried another folder unhelpfully titled "work" and found files labeled with names taken from the military alphabet. Under "alpha" I found a series of scanned documents with the word "classified" stamped at the top. Next, I opened the file labeled "bravo" and found a document labeled "Top Secret." The documents themselves seemed to be discussing military installations in various parts of Europe. Angel was mixed up in something far more dangerous than I had expected. "Angel," I asked, "what does Adrik do for a living?"

"He said he delivers information to help people makes financial decisions. I asked if it had to do with stocks and bonds trading or something, but he laughed."

"Some of the documents I found on this drive are marked 'top secret' and 'classified.'"

Angel's eyes widened. "Does that mean he's some kind of spy?"

I rejected the idea almost instantly. The situation lacked the subtlety needed for espionage. "Destroying your sisters' cars to intimidate you doesn't seem like a spy move."

She said, "He travels a lot, all over the world. He said he was personally delivering private information."

"Maybe he's a courier."

After Angel finished her breakfast, I drove her and the thumb drive to the nearest police station.

* * *

When two o'clock rolled around, Angel and I found ourselves standing next to a massive water tank watching injured turtles swim. Some were missing flippers. Some had devices attached to their shells to help with buoyancy. All were permanent residents of the turtle rescue center because they would never recover well enough to be returned to the open ocean.

Angel was jittery, and I wasn't completely calm either. We were waiting for Adrik to appear to reclaim his lost thumb drive. My simple case to discover why a girl had ghosted a guy had turned into an international stolen documents incident that could still turn violent.

Finally, after fifteen minutes, I saw a dark-haired man in sunglasses wearing a sports jacket over a blue shirt coming toward us. His formal attire contrasted sharply with the beach-going vacationers walking through the turtle rescue facility. I nudged Angel. "Is that him?"

"Yes," she hissed under her breath.

As he got closer, I said, "Stop. Angel will give you the drive. Don't come any closer."

He scowled and lifted the edge of his jacket to reveal a holstered gun.

"Give it to me now."

I said, "Angel, toss him the drive."

Angel tossed the drive to Adrik who caught it with one hand. He examined it, shoved it in his pocket, and smirked at us. "Now, come with me." His hand went under his jacket toward the gun.

"Now," I said.

Angel and I ran behind the turtle tank as police and federal agents appeared from everywhere with weapons drawn and disarmed Adrik.

Angel leaned against the tank, breathing rapidly. "I can't believe this happened. I can't believe it."

I patted her arm. "It's okay. You're safe."

After a few hours spent giving statements to a variety of agents and officers, Angel called her parents again and reassured them she was safe.

I said, "I will report to Charlie that you are safe. Do you want me to tell him your real name?"

Angel looked at her feet. "He's a nice guy." She squirmed. "Can you imagine us together? Charlie and Angel? People would ask me if I'm Charlie's Angel."

"You could always go by your full names and be Angelia and Charles. That sounds less cliché."

She gritted her teeth. "Ugh. I never go by Angelia because people associate the name with the Richard Marx song. My sisters are named after songs too, but their names are more common."

"It's your choice, but I don't recommend being the girl who's always ghosting guys. It's better to end things properly. Leaving people hanging is pretty childish behavior."

"I was focused on avoiding Adrik, and then my phone broke, so I couldn't contact Charlie," she said, not meeting my eyes.

She sounded regretful, but I doubted she would contact Charlie when she got her phone fixed. If vanishing had been her usual modus operandi with men, then ghosting Charlie was probably part of her plan.

I left Angel at the police station and drove to my hotel to pack up to head back to Dallas. Before leaving, I called Charlie. I told him Angel was safe.

"What happened to her? Was she in danger?" he asked.

"It's a long story, but, yes, she was running from someone." I promised him a report and ended the call.

Then, I drove back to Dallas, during which time I had ample time to mull over my decision in taking the case. I'd violated my own rule against taking current cases, but at least I'd been smart about it. Federal agents and police were waiting in the wings. On the whole, the situation hadn't been that much worse than some of my cold case investigations that had gone awry. In truth, I could take current cases, even if I still preferred cold cases. Maybe, taking an occasional active case might not be a bad idea.

The Roosevelt Affair
Adam Meyer

Albany, NY — April 1932

I flattened my bob cut and smoothed my crepe skirt as I stepped outside my Lancaster Street office, startled by the sound of a car engine turning over up the street. A large rounded vehicle crept toward me like a safari animal, headlamps the size of salad plates glowing in the dark.

I locked and closed the door behind me, running my fingers across a small brass plate that said MURNANE AND ASSOCIATES INVESTIGATIONS. The sign was a lie. Jimmy Murnane hadn't crossed the threshold in months and there was no associate, only me, Rosie Perkins, the firm's owner. But that was a secret I held closely, and these days, not the only one I kept.

I started quickly up the street, the sound of the car growing louder with each step.

The long vehicle pulled up beside me. It looked like it had just rolled off the assembly line, its black metal doors and whitewall tires gleaming. A light glowed inside. The driver peered out the open window, wearing a chauffeur's hat and a uniform as tidy and flawless as the car itself.

"Excuse me, Mrs. Perkins?" the driver asked, raising his voice over the engine's rumble.

The sound of my last name surprised me. Most people came here looking for Jimmy Murnane, if they came at all.

"Mrs. Perkins?" the driver asked again.

"Miss Perkins," I said. "And you are?"

"I'm simply the messenger. It's my employer who'd like to speak with you."

I stopped walking, curiosity winning out over frustration. "And who's your employer?"

"I'll explain everything when you get in the car. But let's just say, he's eager to speak with you."

"And I'm eager to get to my next appointment. Good evening to you."

As I started walking again, the car kept pace with me, the smell of its exhaust fumes mixing with the perfume I'd applied before leaving the office.

"Are you going to follow me until I get where I'm going?" I asked, stopping halfway to the corner.

"Unless you get into the car to see my employer, then yes."

The driver got out, his shiny black shoes clopping on the brick street as he opened the car's rear door. His face was lit by the gas streetlamp nearby. He looked handsome, despite his slightly crooked nose.

I sighed. "Since you won't tell me your employer's name, at least tell me yours."

The driver wrinkled his brow, his crooked nose moving even more off-kilter. "Mine? I'm Patrick Cassidy."

Now it was my turn to be surprised. "You're a Cassidy? Then I think I can guess who you're working for."

The Cassidy family's desperate ancestors had fled Ireland for Albany during the potato famine and rose to prominence through some mix of ingenuity, luck and lawless behavior. Rumor had it family patriarch Declan Cassidy might've been involved in the shooting of Jack "Legs" Diamond, the city's most powerful gangster, and a man I'd once worked a case for.

The driver tilted his hat back, looking at me beneath its short brim. "I've no connection to that part of the family," he said, though his once-broken nose suggested the relation was closer than he wanted to admit. "I work for the governor."

"Governor Roosevelt?" I asked, caught off-guard.

"Has New York got more than one?" he asked, seeming to relish my confusion.

"Why would the Governor want to see me?"

"That's his business, not mine. I simply follow orders. And I was told to bring you to see Governor Roosevelt."

Albany was big enough to have a Pinkerton branch office and the Burns Agency—one of the big national investigative firms—had a local presence, too. What would FDR want from a small PI agency like mine? But if he was looking to hire me, a government check was guaranteed to clear, unlike with many of my smaller clients.

"All right," I said, sliding into the back seat.

Patrick headed east along Lancaster to Dove Street. More than a third of the storefronts had been boarded up, and the windows of the apartments above were mostly dark except for the warm glow of radios.

I ran my fingers along the buttery leather seats, a sense of unease turning in my belly. "How long have you worked for Governor Roosevelt?"

"I've been driving for him and the First Lady since they came to Albany."

"Do they know about your family connections?"

"As I said, that part of the family is only a distant relation." He gripped the wheel tightly, making a sharp turn onto Eagle Street, a wide road with massive elm trees on either side. "But to answer your question, yes, they know all about me. Thankfully, the Roosevelts don't judge people on the family they're born into or where they're from. They make up their own minds."

As the car glided on, the Executive Mansion rose in the distance, a soaring building made of red brick and stone, with a turret in front. In a city where most people lived in railroad flats, this was a palace, and for the last three years Governor Roosevelt had sat on its throne. I'd been near the Mansion many times, but never inside. Growing up, my friends and I would raid the grounds for apples, filling our bellies and burlap sacks, until city officers with nightsticks—most of whom I knew from my father's cops-only poker games—chased us away.

I leaned forward as Patrick parked in the circular drive. "What's the governor want to see me for?" I asked, trying to quiet the flutter of fear in my chest.

Patrick came around to open my door. "Excellent question, Miss Perkins. But as I said, that's one I can't answer." He nodded at the massive wooden doors leading into the mansion. "Go on. You'll do fine."

I almost said I'd changed my mind about coming here and asked him to drive me back to my office, but before I could speak my legs carried me up the broad stone steps. An older woman wearing a black maid's uniform met me at the front door.

"If you'll please follow me, Miss Perkins."

She led me past a grand staircase and down a hallway lined with massive oil paintings of former governors. Turning a corner, we stepped into what must've been someone's office. It was three times the size of mine and a lot nicer. Two red leather chairs faced a mahogany desk. A crystal vase full of tulips sat on a window ledge, beside a small collection of leather-bound books.

The maid gestured for me to take one of the chairs. As I did, I sensed movement behind me.

"Miss Perkins, thank you for coming."

Turning, I saw a small man with thinning silver hair slicked with pomade. He had a surprisingly youthful face and wore a tweed suit straining at the buttons. He held a manila envelope in one hand and started to put out the other for me to shake, then seemed to think better of it. Perhaps he'd forgotten he was dealing with a woman instead of a man.

"Mr. Cassidy said that the Governor wanted to see me," I said.

The man circled the desk, settling comfortably into a leather chair.

"Perhaps he misspoke. I wanted to discuss a business proposition with you." He parted his lips, showing a mouthful of square straight teeth, which suggested an upbringing more privileged than my own. "I'm Louis Howe and I handle the Governor's affairs. You might say I'm his right-hand man. I do whatever Governor Roosevelt needs."

He smiled, revealing his teeth again. I smiled back. I didn't tell him that in the Albany gangs, the word for a right-hand man was an enforcer.

"So what is it you want?" I asked, noting the manila envelope Louis had set on the desk.

"This is a sensitive matter. I'll need your assurances that what you learn will go no further than this room."

"Of course. The only person I'll share any of this with is my boss, Mr. Murnane. I'm sorry he couldn't be here."

"It's not him we want to hire." Louis flashed teeth as carefully sculpted as the crown molding overhead. "It's you. Besides, your relationship with Mr. Murnane is not as it seems."

"What are you suggesting?" I asked, feeling heat in my cheeks.

"Simple. Although Mr. Murnane is presented as the leader of your firm, he hasn't stepped foot in its offices in … what, three months?"

Almost four at this point, but I didn't correct him. Jimmy Murnane had taken time off for a medical leave related to injuries he suffered during the Great War, and though he was mostly recovered, he still hadn't come back to work. At least not yet.

"While you present yourself as an employee of Mr. Murnane, surely the opposite is true. He is your employee and you run the firm. But what would happen if your clients knew that Murnane and Associates is a woman-led firm? Times are tough enough as it is, I imagine, without adding any more obstacles."

"You've made your point," I said. "Now what do you need?"

He drew a series of photographs from the envelope, spreading them out like cards at a poker table. His expression was that of a man who had bluffed his way through the game and, after causing everyone else to fold, was finally showing his hand.

"We received these photos a few days ago along with a note demanding payment of a thousand dollars … unless we want them to be released to the newspapers."

I studied the half dozen photos. They showed images of Governor

Roosevelt captured through a window, standing with leg braces, a bit unsteady. A woman was beside him, helping to support him. She had a full face with high cheekbones and a brightness in her eyes. She looked nothing like the photos I'd seen of New York's first lady, Eleanor Roosevelt.

"Who's that?" I asked.

"Lucy Rutherfurd. She was Mrs. Roosevelt's social secretary many years ago. She and Governor Roosevelt have kept up a cordial relationship."

"Very cordial, from what I can see."

Louis glared at me. "Mrs. Rutherfurd remains a good friend of the family and a trusted advisor. They met to discuss strategy related to Mr. Roosevelt's possible candidacy for President."

I looked more closely at the images. Roosevelt wore a pained expression. I'd heard that he had physical limitations from his bout with polio and even used a wheelchair sometimes. But the photo badly undercut the image he'd cultivated of himself as healthy and vigorous, not to mention a dedicated family man.

"Who took these photos?" I asked.

"That's the question we are hoping you can answer."

"Where was the Governor when they were taken?"

"The Kenmore Hotel. This was last Thursday afternoon."

"Okay, and how were they taken?" I studied the photos a moment, answering for myself as I thought aloud. "Must've been a window facing the hotel on the far side of North Pearl Street. Maybe from one of those office buildings across the way?"

"That's what we assumed, yes. But perhaps you can tell us for sure. The bottom line is, I want to know who took these photos and I want you to get any other copies and the negatives." Louis tapped one of the photos. "You have until Friday evening."

I understood. The Executive Mansion was grand, but it was small time compared to the White House, and the Democratic convention was only two months away. Governor Roosevelt was assumed to be the frontrunner for the nomination. With President Hoover about as popular as tuberculosis, whoever faced him on Election Day had a good chance of winning.

If these photographs were made public, however, the speculation about a President Roosevelt would vanish overnight.

"And if whoever took these photos doesn't want to hand over the negatives?"

Louis slid the images back into the manila envelope, smiling thinly. "Then let me know where to find them. I can be very persuasive."

Standing, Louis tucked the envelope under his arm. In the door, the elderly maid had appeared again. She came over and whispered in his ear. He nodded, his lips puckering with distaste.

"Miss Perkins, before you go … the Governor would like to speak with you for a moment."

The maid whisked me down a long hallway and around a corner until we came into what looked almost like a hothouse, tall glass windows all around. A security man with a gun on his hip stood in the far corner, beside a tall potted plant and about as lively. The centerpiece of the room was an in-ground swimming pool, in the middle of which stood a tall man with a sweep of brown hair.

His hair was wet and gleaming, swooping down across his broad forehead. His eyes shimmered with vitality and curiosity. If he was indeed more limited in mobility than people knew, he showed no sign of it, wading toward me through the water, his strides purposeful and confident.

"Miss Perkins, I understand you're going to help us."

"I'm going to try."

"All we can ask, of course."

I'd been in rooms with powerful men before. Politicians sometimes and gangsters others, and occasionally both at once. Only rarely did they intimidate me. After all, powerful men never looked at a woman. But Roosevelt studied me with unexpected intensity.

"Governor…can I ask why you hired me for this job?"

"I asked Louis for a list of the best private investigators in the city, and your name was on it. That intrigued me." He began frog-marching across the pool again, moving with purpose. "In my experience, it's women who are the most adept at getting things done. Without Eleanor … who knows where I'd be right now?"

"You're being modest, sir."

"Not at all. Eleanor is the reason I'm here."

I nodded, taking in what he'd said as much as what he hadn't. The photos would ruin his career, but that wasn't all. They would be a personal embarrassment, both to him and to his wife. Did she know about the affair? Maybe, but knowledge was one thing, her husband's affair made public another.

"I'll do everything I can," I said.

"I know," he said, turning his back on me as he started across the pool again.

I went back out through the doorway I'd entered, the security man shifting his head slightly to track me. I followed the maid back down the long hallway with the oil paintings of the governors. The silhouette of a figure stood at the far end. Her profile was as distinct as in newsreel footage, but I felt my breath catch at the sight of her.

Eleanor Roosevelt moved toward me, heels echoing on the marble floor.

"You don't look like a private investigator," she said.

"Mrs. Roosevelt … I'm not sure what one ought to look like."

"Generally speaking, they look like men. Which you are most certainly not."

Eleanor's cheeks were red with rouge, her lips the color of fresh cherries. She was not a beautiful woman in most senses of the word, but she was regal and her intelligence shone in her eyes, making it hard to turn away.

"Frankie could be a great President someday," she said. "I understand you're going to help him out of this mess."

"I hope so, Mrs. Roosevelt."

She nodded slowly, as though her helmet of silver hair were heavy. "Do you have any idea who, could've done this to us?"

I considered the question, and the way she had framed it.

"I'll need to investigate further," I said. "But based on what I know…whoever took those photos had a good vantage to shoot from. And a powerful enough lens to capture what they saw."

"Meaning they knew that Frankie was going to be there."

I wasn't surprised at Eleanor's quick thinking. Most women I knew were smarter than the men they'd attached themselves to. But we'd all learned at an early age to hide our intelligence, or at least deflect it. Eleanor seemed to have learned a different lesson.

"Can you tell me who might've known your husband would be at the Kenmore Hotel that day?" I asked.

"His security team, his social secretary, his driver, Patrick, and of course Louis Howe."

She hadn't included herself in that list. Was that an oversight or an admission that her husband was sneaking around behind her back?

"I'll look into all of them," I said. "And see where that leads."

"You're good at your job."

It wasn't a question, and I didn't know how to reply.

"You're not married, are you?" she asked.

Most people posed the question as an accusation. But she seemed curious.

"I haven't met the right man, I suppose."

"You like being on your own," she said. "Doing as you please. You're not wrong, marriage can be a trap. But for women, independence has its own limitations, does it not?"

This time I wasn't sure if she was asking a question or not, and if she was, whether she had posed it to me or herself.

"Find out who's blackmailing my husband," she said, her voice steely. "And stop them."

I knew there was only one thing to say.

"Yes, ma'am. I will."

* * *

Later that night, I got back into the long fancy car that had brought me to the Executive Mansion. As Patrick Cassidy drove away, narrow brownstones on either side of the road, he said, "Heading home?"

"Of course," I said. "Where else?"

"You mentioned an appointment earlier."

I hesitated. "No, it's too late. Home is fine."

He didn't ask where I lived. He and the Roosevelt team had clearly done their research on me. When he pulled up in front of my rowhouse on Quail Street, I leaned forward.

"What do you think of Mrs. Roosevelt?" I asked.

Patrick blinked as if surprised.

"I've known a lot of rich people," he said. "My mother cleaned houses in Central Square, and I've driven for several families over the years. Most of them treat you well enough, but they don't ever really see you. Mrs. Roosevelt's not like that. She knows what it is to suffer, to deal with hardship. But she also knows that not everyone can fight, and she wants to fight for them."

No wonder I had felt some kinship with Eleanor. I opened the backdoor before Patrick could come around and get it for me.

"Did you drive Governor Roosevelt to the Kenmore last Thursday evening?" I asked, looking across the top of the car at him.

"Yes, I did."

"And did you tell anyone he was going to have an appointment there?"

He shook his head. "I had no idea he was going until I was told to take him. I'm just the driver, Miss Perkins."

Nodding, I said, "Good night, and thanks for the ride."

After a short and restless sleep, I spent the next day speaking to other members of President Roosevelt's staff, hoping to discover who might've shared his schedule on the day the photographs were taken. I questioned everyone from his maid to his security detail. They all swore they hadn't told anyone else about his movements.

Later that afternoon, I went to all the buildings which sat across North Pearl Street from the Kenmore Hotel. At the first two, I had no luck. The third was a ten-story office building. I talked to the manager's wife, Delores, who wore a brown dress with patches at the elbows and had a slightly uneven bob cut.

We sat in her small ground floor office. The metal desk was neat, the room's single window looking out on the sidewalk, where the line for food at St. Peter's stretched around the corner.

"I'm wondering if you have any openings on the sixth floor," I asked. I had presented myself to Delores as a small business owner looking for space to rent. There was a nugget of truth in the lie, which was usually the best kind.

"Yes, I believe we have some availability … I'll have to check with my husband, of course. Dennis is the manager, I'm just helping out here."

"Have you shown anyone that space on the sixth floor in the last couple of weeks?"

From the other room, the faint sound of coughing.

Dolores stiffened. "No, I don't think so. Besides, the views are much better on the eighth floor, and we have space available there too. At least we did … I can check with Dennis …."

"I'm really more interested in the sixth floor. You're sure you haven't shown it to anyone lately?"

"Positive."

"Maybe your husband has. Could I talk to him?"

Again, the faint sound of coughing from the other room.

"Not today, I'm afraid. He's a little under the weather."

More coughing. This wasn't the hacking bark of someone with a spring cold. It was the wet phlegmy rasp of someone straining to breathe.

"Your husband's sick, isn't he?" I asked. "Very sick."

The stricken look on Delores' face gave me my answer.

"He'll be better soon," she said defiantly. "He just caught a bug."

If he was that ill, Delores' husband had likely been sick for weeks, maybe months. She must've stepped into his role as manager and been covering for him. If his employer knew that Dennis was sick, he could've been fired, and the couple likely relied on his income—and maybe even free housing—to make ends meet.

I didn't want to strongarm this poor woman, but she'd been lying to me. And whatever she knew, I wanted to know too.

"Dolores, I'll be honest with you. And I hope you'll do the same."

I set my elbows on her husband's desk—*her* desk—and leaned in closer, the faint smell of death wafting off her clothes. I remembered it from my father's last days.

"I'm a private investigator and I'm working on a very important case. I know you let someone up to the sixth floor—someone with camera equipment, right?—and I want to know everything you can tell me about them." I fished a five-dollar bill from my purse and set it on the desk. "Maybe you could use this to buy something for your husband, to make him more comfortable while he's sick. Or for yourself."

Dolores swept the money into her palm, fist closed tightly around it.

"I promised I wouldn't tell, but … there was a man, a week ago Thursday. He said he wanted an office on the sixth floor, for the day. He paid me well for it. And yes, he had a camera and lots of bags."

"What was his name?"

"He didn't give a name. He said it was better if I didn't know."

"What did he look like?"

She thought. "He was about as tall as Dennis, maybe six feet. Stocky but not fat. Thick brown hair."

"What time did he leave?"

"I was just closing the office for Dennis so maybe … five, five-thirty."

Everything she had said fit with what I knew about Governor Roosevelt's visit with Lucy Rutherfurd.

"Did you talk to the man on his way out?" I asked.

From the other room, a fit of coughing. Dolores looked defeated. She must've heard this day and night, only instead of getting to where she didn't notice the sound, she seemed highly attuned to it.

"Briefly. When he left, I asked him if he got what he needed up there … and he said that he most certainly had."

* * *

Around eight that evening, long after it was proper to call on most civilized people, I went through the front door of the unmarked storefront. Shadows fell across empty shelves and countertops. The air smelled musty with an undercurrent of cheap perfume. From the rear of the store, I heard a young woman giggling.

"Florence?" I called out. "It's me."

"Back here, honey."

More laughter. The smell of cheap perfume grew stronger and so did the scent of gin. The tableau at the rear of the store was artfully designed: a long plush sofa with curved wooden arms, a backdrop draped in silk, a silver lamp. A pretty young woman stood in front of the tableau, wearing only a corset, her hands pushing her breasts upward as she looked longingly into the wooden box of the camera. Florence Silva peered through the lens at her.

"Beautiful."

The woman giggled again. "I feel ridiculous."

"But you look great."

A burst of light as Florence clicked the flash and took the picture. The young woman dropped her hands from her corset and looked over, sizing me up much as Eleanor Roosevelt had done. "You next?"

Before I could answer, Florence shook her head. "Rosie's just an old friend."

"Anyway, I doubt I'd look as good on camera as you do," I said. That was true. Of course, I'd never pose in front of a camera in my underwear for men's titillation. But then, we all did what we had to do for money.

"Why don't you take a little break?" Florence said, backing away from the camera. "And put a little powder on your …" She gestured at her chest. "… so you're not so shiny."

The young woman flounced off, blond hair swaying behind her.

"One of Maddie's?" I asked. Maddie Griffin ran the top brothel in Albany and had always looked after me when my father came to see her girls, and also sometimes when he had to work an overnight shift. As a young girl growing up without a mother, I was grateful for her presence.

"Of course," Florence said. "Where else am I going to find girls willing to pose in their birthday suits for five dollars?"

"Easiest five dollars I ever made!" the young woman called from across the room.

"So what brings you here?" Florence asked, flopping down on the plush sofa. She looked tired. For the last decade, she had run her own photography studio, taking portraits of newlyweds and families. But business had dried up since the market crash, and like so many others in this city, she'd had to find some way to adapt. Taking racy photos she could sell to men at the VFW or the American Legion had turned out to be quite lucrative.

"Flo, I'm looking for information."

Florence kicked her legs out on the sofa. "What about?"

"I have a client who's being blackmailed. With suggestive photos."

Florence sat up straighter. "Who?"

"I can't say. But I'm wondering who would have a camera that could shoot someone through a window from across the street."

"You'd need a powerful lens … so not an amateur photographer, that's for sure." Florence leaned forward, face screwed up in thought. "Maybe a shooter at one of the papers?"

"You know a likely candidate? Maybe someone in your line of work."

"I've got the market cornered but …" She put a finger to her chin. "Mmm, you remember Floyd O'Brien? Worked as a stringer for the *Times-Union*, the *Knickerbocker Press*, a couple others. He got caught taking pictures of girls in the locker room at the teacher's college a couple years back. Not sure this is his style, but then again I wouldn't put it past him."

"You know where I can find him?"

"Far as I know he still lives with his mom in Ideal Heights." She looked at me more closely, her eye as powerful as any lens. "Rosie, how're you doing?"

"I'm all right. Business is okay. Slow but steady."

Florence patted the sofa beside her and I sat. An only child, I'd never had an older sibling. Florence liked to play at it, especially when she disapproved of my choices or there was advice to be given.

"That's not what I'm asking. How are *you*?"

I didn't know how to answer. With my father gone, I had no other close relatives. Unlike most women my age, I wasn't married and had no children. My life *was* my business, for the most part.

"I can pay the bills, I'm healthy. What else does a woman need?"

"A man, maybe."

I shifted on the sofa, trying to get comfortable.

"I'm back!" The blonde had returned, her cleavage freshly-powdered, her bright eyes gleaming. The thought of being in front of the camera seemed to excite her.

"You'll find someone," Florence said, patting my knee. "It's just a matter of time."

* * *

Ideal Heights was a neighborhood full of modest single-family houses, most thrown up cheaply toward the end of the Great War and meant for returning veterans and their brides. In the last few years, those homes had filled, bursting to the seams, as their residents raised children—many now teenagers—and their elderly parents moved in, too.

I found the address I'd gotten from the White Pages halfway up Rose Street. As I approached, a young woman in the yard next door was hanging out sheets on a clothesline. She was maybe fifteen or sixteen, humming to herself as she pinned the corners of each piece of fabric. What did she want from life someday? I wondered. Did she dream of being a doctor, a lawyer, even a police officer, or did she just want to live in a house like this and be someone's wife?

The girl smiled as I passed, though her smile slipped a little as I went to the O'Briens front door.

I knocked on the screen, the scent of boiling cabbage and burnt meat wafting toward me. Something rustled at a window above but no one came to the door. I knocked again.

"Hello?" I called out.

A woman ambled to the door, wiping her hands on an apron splashed with grease and brown sauce. "Yes?"

"My name's Rosie Perkins. I'm looking for Floyd O'Brien."

"Is Floyd in some kind of trouble?"

"No, ma'am." Meaning: At least not yet. "I just want to talk to him."

"Floyd's a good boy," she said, glancing behind her at a dark shadow in the hallway.

"I have some questions, that's all."

"What kind of questions?" a man's voice said.

He moved in behind his mother, looming over her. He was easily six feet if not taller, and his eyes blinked against the sunlight, as though he'd been working in his darkroom when I got here. His hair was as dark as shoe polish.

"Maybe we could talk in private," I said, glancing at his mother.

He pushed the screen door open. His mother stepped aside to allow me in, but looked at me warily.

"Our supper's going to be ready soon," she said. "I don't want it to get cold."

"I'll make this as quick as I can."

Floyd led me through the front room and into the kitchen, where the smell of cabbage nearly overpowered me, and back to a sun room. With the houses so close together and the sun on its way down, only faint traces of light cut through the windows. I sat on a wicker chair with a hole. Floyd was across from me, watchful and nervous.

"What do you want?" he asked.

Direct. In some ways, that made my job easier.

"You got a lot of camera equipment, Floyd?" I asked.

"I got a few cameras, lenses, a darkroom. I do stringer work for a bunch of the papers."

"Has your work ever brought you to the Kenmore Hotel?"

He frowned as if the question was a stumper. "No, I don't think so. No. Definitely not."

"You sure?"

"Why wouldn't I be? I know where I've been and where I haven't."

Nodding, I said, "Sure, just like I know you've been to the girl's locker room at the teacher's college. Great place to take photos, right?"

His face reddened. "That was a long time ago. I'd never do anything like that again."

"Even if someone paid you for it?"

This was a hunch, not a certainty. But the more I thought about it, the more I wondered if whoever had taken those photos had been put up to it by someone.

"No one's paid me anything," he said, his voice steely.

"Not even to take photographs at the Kenmore Hotel?" I asked.

"Didn't I just say the answer was no?"

From the other room, a voice called out. "Floyd, you want a snack before dinner?"

"No Ma! Leave us alone." Floyd folded his arms across his chest, looking like a stubborn twelve-year-old. "I told you, I got nothing to do with what you're asking about."

"Well, Floyd, I don't believe you." I got up, looking over as the fading lit reflected off the windows of the house next door. "Because you're acting like a man with something to hide."

"I think you better go."

As the light shifted, I saw the young woman who'd been hanging sheets earlier setting out dishes on the dining room table. Then I looked up at the second-floor window, where lace curtains fluttered in the breeze. I decided to take a flyer, as my father used to say when he took a gamble while questioning a suspect.

"What would your mother say if she knew about the photos you've been taking of that girl next door?" I asked.

Floyd's mouth hung open. "What're you … I never …"

"We could go into your darkroom right now and take a look at the pictures, if you want. I'm sure your Ma would be quite shocked."

"That's … how do you …"

I leaned in toward Floyd, hands on my knees. "One more time— what do you know about the pictures taken from the Kenmore Hotel?"

"A guy I know from the *Times-Union*, a photographer, came to me." He rubbed his palms on his slacks as if to dry the sweat from them. "He didn't say nothing about the Kenmore. He said he had to take a picture from about fifty feet away, needed the right lens. Wanted to make sure he didn't miss the shot."

"Why didn't he have his own equipment?"

"Most of the stuff he used belonged to the paper. And since he'd gotten canned recently … I rented him a lens."

"What's his name?"

Floyd clenched his fists. "I shouldn't tell you that."

"Lots of things you shouldn't do, Floyd." I nodded at the window, where the young woman had begun setting out silverware. "Hasn't stopped you before."

"Kurt. Kurt Fischer."

From the other room, Floyd's mother called out. "Supper's ready!"

Floyd leaned forward, looking like he wanted to stand but not moving.

"Go on, Floyd," I said. "Wouldn't want your supper to get cold."

* * *

It was nearly dark by the time I got to Kurt Fischer's house. I knocked on the door several times and got no answer, though I heard the faint sound of a baby crying from within. Finally, a harried-looking woman about my age answered. She had an infant in her arms and another child, maybe three or four, clung to her worn skirt, looking up with heavy-lidded eyes.

"I'm sorry, we can't afford to buy anything right now," the woman said.

"Mrs. Fischer?" She looked surprised that I knew her name. "I'm not a salesman. I'm a private investigator. I'm here to see your husband."

Her eyes narrowed. "A private investigator? To see Kurt?"

"I have some questions, that's all."

The infant started squawling again. Tears shimmered in the woman's eyes. From deeper in the house, I heard the sound of a little boy calling, "Mommy!"

"He's in the yard. You might as well just go around back."

I went through a side yard cluttered with garden tools, a weathered rocking horse lying on its side in the path. When I came around back, I saw the outline of a man standing by the picket fence, the tip of a cigar glowing in the dark. He must've heard me coming because he turned, his face cast with a faint red glow.

"Who're you?" he asked.

I told him who I was and why I had come.

"You used to work at the *Times-Union*," I said. "You're a photographer."

"Yeah, that's right. But circulation's down and they fired almost a quarter of the staff. Now I'm looking for work. You ever need a shooter for your business, you let me know. I take great photos."

"I know. I've seen your work. The photos you took at the Kenmore Hotel."

His shoulders slumped a little. Clearly he knew why I had come.

"What do you want?" he asked.

"I want to know who tipped you off about the Governor being there."

He blew out a long puff of smoke. "It'll cost you. Twenty dollars."

"I'll give you ten."

He didn't hesitate. "Deal."

I pulled a ten from my purse. Kurt stuck the cigar in his mouth and took the bill, folded it in half, tucked it into his front pocket.

"I used to make this much for a day's work," he said.

"And today all you've got to do is talk. Sounds like a good deal. Now tell me about the photos."

"Wasn't my idea."

"Whose was it?"

He hesitated and took a short puff on the cigar. "I'm not sure. Got a note under my door one day. Said they had a business opportunity for me, all I had to do was meet them in the lobby of Union Station at seven that night. At first, I thought it sounded crazy … and then I figured, what've I got to lose?"

"You met someone there. Who?"

"Nobody. I got a call." He tapped ash off the cigar and jammed it between his teeth. "I'm waiting there at seven when this payphone in the lobby starts to ring. At first I just look at it, then I pick up. Guy tells me he needs someone to take pictures through the window of room 61s of the Kenmore the next afternoon, he'll pay two hundred bucks."

"So you borrowed a zoom lens from Floyd O'Brien?"

"Sure, I've got my own gear but not that kind of lens. I figured he'd have it from his … extracurricular activities."

Anger welled up inside me as I thought of Floyd secretly taking photos of the girl next door. But I pushed it down, focusing.

"And that Thursday, you used an empty office across from the Kenmore to get the photos." It wasn't a question.

"Yeah, I knew they had a lot of space for rent up there. Figured it was a good spot to get the shots I needed." He let out a slow stream of smoke. "Didn't figure I'd get pictures of the Governor and some broad."

"What'd you do with them?"

"What the guy on the phone told me to do—come back to Union Station at seven that night. I get there, same phone rings, he tells me to print the photos and leave them and the negatives at a pool hall called the Golden Cue. You know it?"

I'd gone there a few times as a kid, in search of my father. Back then, the pool hustlers and gamblers had thought I was cute. But as a grown woman, I wasn't welcome, and I hadn't been there in almost twenty years.

"Who'd you leave everything with?" I asked.

"This guy Freddie tells me he'll pass the stuff along, gives me an envelope with cash. Two hundred bucks, as promised. That's it." He stubbed out the tip of his remaining cigar. "Can't tell you any more than that."

I looked into the dark, trying to think of more questions. I had a thousand but probably none Kurt could answer.

"What'd they do with the photos?" he asked. "Blackmail or something?"

"Something like that."

"Sorry to hear. I like the governor … but I got three kids. Somebody's got to feed them."

I started to cross the yard and looked back. "Your wife."

"Huh?"

"Your wife's the one feeding them, changing their diapers, putting them to bed, while you're out here smoking a cigar and feeling sorry for yourself. Yes, times are tough and you lost your job, but it's no excuse to be a lousy father."

I couldn't see his face in the dark, but he took a step toward me. Anger wafted on the night air along with the smell of cigars, which reminded me of my own father.

"Have a good night," I said, and marched back to the street.

* * *

The next afternoon, I headed out to the Golden Cue on Lark Street. As I stepped inside, the scents of cigarette smoke and moonshine hit me like a wave. I looked through the cloudy air at the men leaning over pool tables with worn felt, while others watched, nursing glasses of brown liquid. Everyone studied me but I didn't pay any attention, looking around for a friendly face, someone to ask about a player named Freddie.

"What're you doing here, lady?"

A guy with slicked-back hair and ketchup stains on a rumpled T-shirt looked at me. Anger filled his eyes, building from a low simmer to a boil. He must've seen his wife or girlfriend in me, the way I'd seen my father in Kurt.

"I'm looking for Freddie," I said.

"That your sugar daddy?"

"Leave her alone," another player said. "You want Freddie? There he is."

The other man nodded at a table in the corner, where a heavyset fellow wearing a gray suit leaned across the table, angling his stick at the cue ball. He was trying to get the seven in the corner pocket but his aim looked slightly off. He turned to me.

"Who're you?" Freddie asked.

"My name's Rosie Perkins. I'm a private eye."

"Perkins? The cop's daughter."

I nodded and looked closely at him. His profile was familiar, though I couldn't place it.

"You did a handoff here," I said. "Some photos and negatives for cash."

"I do a lot of transactions. But I'm not in the picture business. Besides, a pretty girl like you shouldn't be asking questions about stuff like that."

"So you do know what I'm talking about."

Ignoring me, he focused on the shot he'd been about to take earlier. The balls clinked and the seven rolled toward the corner pocket but bounced off the bumper and rolled away from the hole.

"Looks like you should've gone a touch more to the left," I said.

"Or maybe you're just bad luck, lady."

"I asked you a question. You still haven't told me the truth."

Freddie looked up from the table, fire in his eyes. Suddenly, I knew why he looked so familiar.

"You better watch what you say. You know who I am?"

"I do now," I said under my breath as I turned to go.

* * *

The next day, back in his office at the Executive Mansion, I stood up as Louis Howe entered. Unlike the first time I'd met Governor Roosevelt's fixer, he put his hand out for me to shake. I took it. His grip was firm and so was mine.

"I read your report," he said. "Excellent work." He held up an envelope. "We just got this a little while ago—a note from the blackmailer and all the photos and negatives."

After consulting with Louis, I had gone back to the Golden Cue and left a note with Freddie to pass along. It said that the blackmailer would get half the money he'd asked for, one thousand dollars, in return for any printed photos of Governor Roosevelt and Lucy Rutherfurd, as well as all the negatives. In return, I'd added: DO AS I SAY AND YOUR IDENTITY WILL REMAIN A SECRET—OTHERWISE, I'LL TELL HER EVERYTHING.

I hadn't shared that last part with Louis. But it was still case closed, more or less.

"Of course, we still don't know who took the photos." Louis seemed to sense that I'd kept some details to myself and was fishing for more. "That leaves us with a loose end."

"All these years in politics, you must be used to those."

"I like my job better without them."

"I promise you, whoever took those photos won't share them. Ever."

Louis knitted his eyebrows together, studying me. "You sound certain."

"I am. You paid the blackmailer well, and I'm sure they know the consequences of double-crossing you and a potential future president would be considerable."

Louis smoothed out his suit jacket. "Good point."

One thing I'd learned early in life: you could never go wrong playing to a man's ego.

"In any case, we appreciate your hard work on this matter." Louis reached into his jacket and pulled out another envelope, this one letter-sized. "For you."

I counted the hundred-dollar bills inside. "This is a lot of money."

"Governor Roosevelt insisted."

"I'd like to thank him."

Louis shook his head. "He's up in New York on the campaign trail.

Eleanor will be joining him later today."

A faint tap at the door. Clearly a woman. A man's knock was always more firm.

"Yes?" Louis asked, eyes widening in surprise as the door opened a crack. "Mrs. Roosevelt … I thought you were getting ready for your train ride."

"I wanted to speak to Rosie first."

Louis waited a moment, then realized Eleanor meant for us to have privacy. He closed the heavy door of his office behind him. She sat in the chair next to mine, our knees nearly touchings

"I understand the matter is settled," she said. "Only we don't know who took the photos."

"No. Although for a moment, I thought you might've played a part in it."

"Me? I would never stand in the way of Frankie's ascent," she said, frowning. "I told you, he could be a great President someday."

I saw no hint of deception in her gaze. That meant nothing, but there was something beneath it that suggested she was telling the truth. At first I thought it was confusion. Then I realized it was something I'd seen in the mirror. Ambition.

"You'll never get to the White House without him," I said.

Eleanor smiled thinly, flecks of cherry-red on her teeth. "Look at what Edith was able to do while Teddy was in the Oval Office."

Edith Kermit Roosevelt had been Theodore Roosevelt's first lady. Rumors had swirled that she had was a close confidant during his time as President and had wielded considerable power over his decision-making.

"It's worth it to you, putting up with your husband's … indiscretions, for that kind of influence?" I asked.

"I'm surprised you have to ask," she said. "You know what it's like being a woman in this world, and how it can be necessary to shield ourselves behind the ornament of a man."

I felt a wave of rising anger but I didn't contradict her. She was right, after all.

"Thank you for everything," Eleanor said, smoothing her skirt as she stood. "I've enjoyed our talks, Rosie. Perhaps you could come back for tea sometime, a personal visit instead of business."

"That would be lovely."

I smiled. Eleanor and I both knew that seeing me would only be a reminder of her husband's infidelity, and as expected, I never saw her again—only on the newsreels or in the paper.

As I came out the front door, the long black car was waiting. Patrick Cassidy stood by the front fender, using a rag to rub away a smudge I couldn't see. He tucked the rag in his pocket as soon as he spotted me. "Miss Perkins. I'm afraid I can't offer you a ride today. I'm taking Mrs. Roosevelt to the train station."

"That's all right. It's a lovely day and I can walk."

He nodded, looking uneasy.

"By the way, I'm glad to see you got my message," I said.

"Your message, ma'am?"

"The one I left with your cousin, Freddie. At the Golden Cue."

Patrick's face was blank. But he nervously adjusted his chauffeur's cap, sliding it this way and that. "I've no idea what you mean."

"You must really care about her," I said. "Eleanor, I mean. I assume that's why you tried to expose her husband's affair."

Patrick frowned, turning so that his slightly crooked nose was aimed at the big house behind us. "She's an extraordinary woman. In another world, she might be the one running for president. Instead … he takes her for granted and she doesn't seem to mind."

"Or maybe she minds and doesn't have a choice."

"Everyone has choices."

That was the kind of foolish statement most men believed and most women knew better than to argue.

"You've made different choices than Freddie," I said. "But you're not above using your family connections when it suits you."

He flicked at the car's shining black surface as if to clear a speck of dirt. "I thought it was for a good cause."

"Did it ever occur to you that he loves her?" I asked.

"Eleanor? I suppose she does. Doesn't make it any better, though."

I'd meant Lucy Rutherfurd. I was asking whether she was really such a bad person for sleeping with a married man. But maybe that was the wrong question.

Patrick adjusted his chauffeur's cap as he turned to the house again. "You won't tell them, will you?"

"No. As long as you never try anything like this again."

He put a hand over his heart, turning so that his once-broken nose was tilted to the sky. "I promise."

With the afternoon sun bleeding through the clouds, I made my down Eagle Street to Madison Avenue. Instead of stopping at my office, I headed up Willet Street past Washington Park and toward Arbor Hill. I followed the same path I would've taken the other night, if only Patrick Cassidy had not brought me to the Executive Mansion instead.

I climbed up the back steps to the small apartment behind the brick house, the one that the man I was seeing had rented a few months ago. He must've told his wife he was using it as an office or a place to get some quiet from their young son.

My so-called employer, Jimmy Murnane, was waiting for me. He limped toward me on the leg that had taken shrapnel during the Great War and embraced me, starting to kiss me. But he must've sensed my resistance, because he pulled back.

"What's wrong?"

"It's over," I said.

"Why?" he asked, puzzled. "You and I are consenting adults, and Miriam has no idea what's going on."

I told Jimmy that didn't matter. I told him a lot of things. He listened and he argued but I wouldn't be swayed. Whatever he and I had had these last few months, it was done. Maybe Patrick Cassidy was right. People always had choices to make, and mine was whether or not to be on my own again. I didn't want to ruin Jimmy's family or pretend that what we were doing had no consequence. I told him goodbye.

"Okay, fine, but what's the hurry?" he asked, patting the bed beside him.

The mattress creaked beneath me. I started to tell myself a story— what would it hurt anyone?—when I thought of Eleanor. Not the hurt she'd shown but her love for her husband.

"I can't. Not anymore."

I went back to the street, walking quickly, fighting off tears.

On the way home, I stopped at a payphone and called the 6th precinct on Central Avenue, the one where my father used to work. I reported to the dispatcher that I'd seen Floyd O'Brien taking secret photos of his neighbor. When the dispatcher asked my name, I told him simply to check it out and hung up. I thought again of that teenage girl, hanging her family's laundry and setting out their silverware, and the dreams she might harbor for her future. Would they ever come true?

I wiped away my tears, praying they might.

The Usual Unusual Suspects

Judge **Debra H. Goldstein**'s writing credits include seven novels and more than sixty short stories which have been published in journals, periodicals, and anthologies including *Alfred Hitchcock Mystery Magazine* and *Black Cat Magazine*. Her collection of award winning or finalist stories, *With Our Bellies Full and the Fire Dying*, was recently published by White City Press (February 2025), and her *Who Shot J.R.?* appears in *Sleuths Just Wanna Have Fun* (Down & Out April 2025). To find out more, go to https://www.DebraHGoldstein.com

John B. Elliott has worked as a typesetter, pressman, bartender, social worker, biologist and teacher. He has a passion for the natural world, especially deserts and mountains; has had play productions, notably one about Federico Garcia Lorca, and published fiction in, or upcoming in, *Calliope, Sonoran Horror, Open Ceilings, Lifespan Anthologies Loss and Older, and Crimeucopia*, as well as poetry in *The Comstock Review, Southwestern American Literature, Poetry Quarterly, Borderlands: Texas Poetry Review, Tanka Journal, The Fourth River*, and three anthologies.

Steve Liskow is a former English teacher who worked in theater as an actor, director, designer, technician, musician, and occasional producer. He has published 16 novels and 70 short stories in *Alfred Hitchcock's Mystery Magazine, Black Cat Weekly, Tough*, and several anthologies. This is his first publication for Murderous Ink. Steve can be found at www.steveliskow.com

Sandra J. Cady is a former Detroit police officer and past owner of a licensed private investigative agency. A member of The Short Mystery Fiction Society and Sisters in Crime, she has a bachelor's degree in criminal justice, and a master's degree in hospital administration.

Her detective novel, *A Game of Luck*, is due out at the end of April, 2026 — and her PI novel, *The Return of Bonnie Rutkowski, P.I.*, is under consideration.

Her non-fiction has been published in several trade publications, and her short blurb on what the song, *Philadelphia Freedom*, means to me is in the introduction to the mystery anthology, *Better Off Dead, Volume 1* (Down & Out August 2025.) Sandra can be found at http://www.sandrajcady.com

Debra Bliss Saenger's writing and publishing hats include print and digital editor, marketing professional, English teacher, and public television director. Seen in numerous literary and mystery fiction anthologies and publications, she delved into writing fiction and poetry as a Sisters in Crime and Short Mystery Fiction Society member. She and her family live in Northern Virginia with a fetching rescue dog. Find her at www.dblisssaenger.com.

Kathleen Marple Kalb describes herself as an Author/Anchor/Mom… but not necessarily in that order. An award-winning weekend anchor at New York's 1010 WINS Radio, she writes short stories and novels including the Old Stuff, and (as Nikki Knight) Vermont Radio Mysteries. Her stories have been in Crimeucopias, *Alfred Hitchcock's Mystery Magazine*, other major publications, and short-listed for Derringer and Black Orchid Novella Awards. She is a member of the National Board of Sisters in Crime and a former VP of the Short Mystery Fiction Society. She, her husband, and son live in a Connecticut house owned by their cat.

Wil A. Emerson has been on the writing path for approximately 15 years. While not fresh out of college to write the Best Seller, she spent her early years as a Registered Nurse. Now on the fringe of being overlooked due to the inconvenient late start, she's successfully published in anthologies and has one novel under her belt. *Taking Rosie's Arm*, a Five Star, Thorndike publication, recounts the story of an elderly woman who befriends a troubled, but determined young girl. Writer, artist, traveler, cook: soup's on.

Wil's recent work is mainly mystery and women's fiction, and she has appeared in the following *Crimeucopia* anthologies: *Careless Love*, with her piece, *The Driver* — followed by the 'second installment' *The Road to Reconciliation* in *Crank It Up!*, and *Cracker Jacks and Granny Cases* in *Great Googly Moo!*

Also a struggling artist, her art can be viewed on her website. *www.wilemerson.com*

Karen Odden earned her PhD in English at NYU in 2001, writing her dissertation on the medical, legal, and fictional literature written about Victorian railway disasters, tracing textual connections among 1800s "railway spine" injuries, WWI "shell shock," and present-day PTSD. She subsequently taught at UW-Milwaukee, wrote introductions for Victorian novels in the Barnes & Noble Classics Series, and edited for the academic journal *Victorian Literature and Culture* (Cambridge UP). She has been nominated for the Lefty, Agatha, Anthony, and Shamus awards for her novels and short fiction. Her forthcoming mystery, *An Artful Dodge* (Soho Crime, June 2026), features Kit Jimeson, as this volume's story does, but the novel is set earlier, when Kit was still a thief. Karen serves on the national board of Sisters in Crime. Originally from New York, she now lives in Arizona with her family. Connect with her at www.karenodden.com.

John W. Salvage has published a variety of short stories, including *The Hunger Shrine* in the anthology *Beautiful Darkness Vol 1* (Dragon Soul Press Oct 2023), and *Mercy*, which appears in the anthology *SNAFU: Dead or Alive* — part of the long running Cohesion Press SNAFU series.

Michael J. Ciaraldi is a retired computer scientist, roboticist, and playwright. His work has been published in Alfred Hitchcock's Mystery Magazine, in Androids & Dragons, and elsewhere. Summer Cum

Laude's first adventure, *Film Blank*, was published in 2024 in *Crimeucopia: Great Googly Moo!* Mike lives in Shrewsbury, MA USA with his wife and Daisy, a chihuahua. Find out more at www.ciaraldi.com.

A fan of all things fantastical and frightening, **Shannon Lawrence** writes primarily horror and fantasy. *The Killing Tree & Other Afflictions* is the newest of her seven books. You can also find her as a co-host of the podcast *Mysteries, Monsters, & Mayhem* and a columnist for *Rocky Mountain Reader*. When she's not writing, she's hiking through the wilds of Colorado and photographing her magnificent surroundings, where, coincidentally, there's always a place to hide a body or birth a monster. Find her at www.thewarriormuse.com.

Elle Higgins, Ph.D., has taught writing and literature on the college and community levels. Her published work consists of personal essays, as well as essays in pedagogy and literary criticism. A transplant to New York's Capital District, Elle is a member of the Short Mystery Fiction Society and Sisters in Crime, founding the Mavens of Mayhem, Upper Hudson Chapter in 2007. On the side, she's worked on fiction projects, including flash pieces, short stories, and 3 novel-length manuscripts. Her series character, Emma Grant, makes her next appearance in *The Burmese Kitten*, the debut novel set in Albany, NY, and coming out early in 2026. Learn more at https://ellenhiggins.com/writings-by-ellen/.

Bonnar Spring is a Derringer award-winning author whose work has appeared in many anthologies. She made the switch to short fiction from international thrillers to satisfy her urge to write morally ambiguous characters. She lives in a tiny house perched at the edge of a New Hampshire salt marsh and, when not concocting nefarious plots, she hosts *Crime Wave*, the top-rated podcast from Authors on the Air. (https://bonnarspring.com/index.php/category/crimewave/)

N.M. Cedeño writes short fiction that has appeared in multiple anthologies, including the Crimeucopia series: *Say What Now?*, *One More Thing to Worry About,* and *Chicka-Chicka Boomba!* Her work has also appeared in magazines and e-zines, including *Analog: Science Fiction and Fact, After Dinner Conversation, Black Cat Weekly*, and *Black Cat Mystery Magazine.* Her story entitled *A Reasonable Expectation of Privacy* placed third for Best Short Story in the 2013 Analog Readers Poll. Her story *Predators and Prey* was listed among the Other Distinguished Mystery and Suspense Stories of 2024 in Best American Mystery and Suspense 2025. She is a member of Sisters in Crime and its Heart of Texas Chapter and the Short Mystery Fiction Society. For more information go to www.nmcedeno.com.

Adam Meyer Is a Derringer Award winning and Shamus Award nominated writer whose work has appeared in *Best American Mystery and Suspense Stories 2023*, along with *Mickey Finn, Janie's Got a Gun, Lunatic Fringe, Crimeucopia: Tales from the Back Porch* (The Lifeguard), and many other anthologies.

As a screenwriter, he has written more than 200 hours of television, including the Emmy-Award winning PBS series *Made With Love.*

Adam is also co-editor (with Alan Orloff) of the anthologies *In Too Deep* (Down & Out March 2025) and *Hollywood Kills* (Level Short Sept 2025).

Small town, big city, watercooler or the back of that 1950s beat-up
Chevy Bel Air with the leather back seat that your parents told you
never to get familiar with. It doesn't matter where you hear it, gossip
is 100% pure ear addiction – and knowledge is, after all, power when
all's said and done.

So why don't you settle down, get yourself comfy, and pour yourself
a drink – long and tall, or just short and nasty, the choice is yours –
and let these 16 story tellers spin their tales as only they know how.

Paperback Edition ISBN: 9781909498365
eBook Edition ISBN: 9781909498372

CRIMEUCOPIA

Chicka-Chicka Boomba!

FEATURING:
Nina Mansfield
Vera Brook
donalee Moulton
Jill Hand
Stormy White
N. M. Cedeño
Maroula Blades
Mary Jo Rabe
Denise Johnson
Christina Hoag
Marie Anderson
Heather C.Morris
Wendy Harrison
Ruth Morgan
Diane Arrelle
Issy Jinarmo
Lyn Fraser
Kimberly Scott
and
Carol Goodman
Kaufman

It would be hard to pinpoint exactly when Crimeucopia moved from being a 'scratch project title' and became a masthead—but it seemed to match our idea of presenting as wide a spectrum of Crime fiction genres as we could.

From there it was probably *Fate* which brought together the Aly Fell base artwork, and the 16 contributors who went on to become the initial Countesses of Crime, and appeared in Crimeucopia—The Lady Thrillers.

4 years down the proverbial publishing line, we felt it was time to celebrate the anniversary with another all-women anthology—and let these 19 Countesses of Crime tell it like it is, was, or could have been....

Because, in the eclectic, off-centred spirit of our Murderous Ink Press motto: You never know what you like until you read it.

Paperback Edition ISBN: 9781909498662 — eBook Edition ISBN: 9781909498679

This is the first of several 'Free 4 All' collections that was supposed to be themeless. However, with the number of submissions that came in, it seems that this could be called an *Angels & Devils* collection, mixing PI & Police alongside tales from the Devil's dining table. Mind you, that's not to say that all the PIs & Police are on the side of the Angels....

Also this time around has not only seen a move to a larger paperback format size, but also in regard to the length of the fiction as well. Followers of the somewhat bent and twisted Crimeucopia path will know that although we don't deal with Flash fiction as a rule, it is a rule that we have sometimes broken. And let's face it, if you cannot break your own rules now and again, whose rules can you break?

Oh, wait, isn't breaking the rules the foundation of the crime fiction genre?

Oh dear....

Paperback ISBN: 9781909498426 eBook ISBN: 9781909498433

To misquote the Pointed Man (from Harry Nilsson's *The Point*): "A theme in every direction, is the same as, well, no theme at all." Which just about sums up Crimeucopia—You Ain't Read Nothin' Yet. So, opening the Scrabble bag of this anthology's short fiction, you'll find—

Jon Matthew Farber, Steven James Foreman, Peter W. J. Hayes, John B. Elliott, Merrilee Robson, Philip Pak, Tucker Struyk, Maurice Givens, Carol Willis, Veronica Gardner, Mary Jo Robertiello, Ariel Dodson, Allison Whittenberg, Devin James Leonard, David Bart, H.E. Vogl, Karen Bayly, Marula Blades and Michael Canfield —all of whom give you a spread from cosy through to hard edged Noir and grindhouse. So, as everything gently fades to black, we hope you'll find something that you immediately like, as well as something that takes you from your regular comfort zone—and slips you, gently or otherwise, into a completely new one.

Because, in the investigative spirit of our *Murderous Ink Press* motto:
You never know what you like until you turn over the page and read it.
Paperback Edition ISBN: 9781909498723
eBook Edition ISBN: 9781909498730

Crikey, Mellors, It's The Filth!

Yes, the Cosy Nostra have been at it again – though with an eye for what we hope will show just how wide the Crime sub-genre can enjoyably be.

Knocking back the sherry, claret and cocktails (amongst other things) are:

Richard Zaric, Daniel Marshall Wood, S. B. Watson, Ron Bruguiere, Aimee Kluck, Alexander Frew, Roly Andrews, Marian McMahon Stanley, Gerald Elias, Gregory Meece, Neil K. Henderson, AP Warren, Michele Bazan Reed, Bonnar Spring, Carol Goodman Kaufman, Kathleen Marple Kalb, John M. Floyd, and *Dave Dempster*

who are happy to take us from the sublime to the surreal, and back again — and all behind the backs of any number of butlers, batmen, or valet de chambres — even the ever omnipresent MIP Towers butler, Mellors....

Numquam scis quid tibi placeat donec id legeris.

The butler nodded his head. *Indeed, you certainly don't*, he thought...

Paperback ISBN: 9781909498709 — eBook ISBN: 9781909498716